IN THE STATE
OF EXCITEMENT

PAUL J. LAVERTY

First published in 2022 by Roadhouse Media
Copyright © Paul J. Laverty
ISBN: 978-0-6485187-4-7

Cover art by Donna Sadler
Enquiries should be made to the author at
mrpauljlaverty@gmail.com

A catalogue record for this book is available from the National Library of Australia

For my parents who brought us here x

And to the many who have inspired these stories.

Also thanks to Donna Sadler for the cover art.
And Anna Laverty, Maria Alessandrino, Ged Webster and
Shannon Hick for reading early drafts.

And to Night Parrot Press, Underground Writers,
Thoughtful Dog and *Tulpa* for publishing earlier versions
of these stories.

www.pauljlaverty.com
www.twitter.com/pauljlaverty
www.instagram.com/mrpauljlaverty

*I wish to acknowledge the traditional custodians of the
land, the Whadjuk people, on which these stories are set.
I respect their culture and the continuing contribution they
make to the life of this city and this region.*

**In the State of Excitement soundtrack by
Anna Laverty is out now on Spotify and all
good platforms.**

CONTENTS

PERTH

He was twenty minutes late. She took a sip of her virgin appletini wishing she still drank. The revolving restaurant showed her the Perth city skyline in all its glory as the sun dipped invitingly beneath the clouds. And yet, she longed to be on her comfy blue velvet settee, the one she'd treated herself to from Early Settler when she turned forty. In front of the television, watching nothing in particular.

When he arrived, he didn't say he was sorry. He complained about work and traffic and the long wait for the elevator, but mainly work. He didn't say he was sorry, and he didn't kiss her or wish her a happy anniversary. From the peel of perspiration reflecting off his balding head, and the way he went straight for the bourbon without first ordering a beer, she could tell he'd been drinking. Probably with *her*.

As he talked — and as they sat between the sunset and the bar, slowly spinning through the bright autumn sky — she looked out and thought of how much their city had changed since they'd gone on their first date at this very table a lifetime ago. How the street lights down below, now illuminating seemingly row by row, appeared to stretch forever. And how she didn't care anywhere near as much as she did when the affair first began, and wondered if he would ever notice that she even knew.

He drank some more and talked a lot more about how he'd have to be in Sydney next month for work. He talked of their dog and how her back legs had started giving out, and how much he would miss the old girl when the inevitable goodbye came. He talked of a client who'd got him box seats for some big game this Sunday at Optus Stadium.

He didn't talk about the children. Their son in Melbourne acting on stage, their daughter in London studying medicine, who had pooled together the little money they had to send them here for their thirtieth wedding anniversary. He didn't ask how she was, or about her upcoming long-service leave, her third lot, and how she'd like to spend it. He ate more of the chargrilled beef and drank a lot more bourbon and did what he did best — lying, boasting and talking about himself.

Maybe she was bored. Maybe it was all that sugar from the colourful beverage giving her an unnatural high, or maybe she was a little dizzy from the altitude. But she did something she'd never done before. She asked about *her*.

She asked about Angela.

He bristled. He wiped away the gravy and bourbon from around his thick lips and told her to grow up. They worked together, their relationship was business.

He shot back at her boss and how he'd never questioned anything about their relationship. Though she knew that if he'd bothered to turn up to any of her work functions, he would know that for the past two decades her boss, Jeremy, had been in a clandestine and troublesome homosexual relationship with a prominent City of Perth councillor.

Other diners glanced their way. Needing air, she lifted her handbag, excused herself and walked to the bathroom. It was here that she cried. She'd had such high hopes for life. In secondary school, she'd dreamt of being a sculptor, of seeing the world and all the treasures it held. Instead, she married at twenty and became the accounts manager of a mid-sized drilling firm and lived in a nondescript suburb, too far from the city, not close enough to the beach. At least she had her kids, both her pride and joy. But now, scattered across land and sea with their own vocations and their own partners and problems, and with her beloved sheepdog nearing its end, she wept as she realised she was left with nothing much at all.

When she could weep no more, she blew her nose and washed up. She touched up her mascara, then her lipstick, and went back out to face *him* and the next thirty years.

Only, a strange thing happened. He wasn't there. His jacket, his keys, his wallet were gone. A young waiter, perhaps by day an actor like her son, or a medical student like her daughter, was wiping down the table. At first, she felt a fleeting, giddy surge of exhilaration.

So much so, she had to steady herself on a bar stool. That was until she felt the eyes of the other diners upon her. It was then that the fury struck. *This*, after everything they'd been through, after all the shit he'd put her through. She'd stuck by him through bankruptcy, a cancer scare, adultery, and now this. The first time she tries to stand up for herself in three decades, he pulls the pin. She never even received a card or flowers, never mind an anniversary gift.

As nonchalantly as her snug red silk dress would allow, she sat on a stool facing the bar. A piano man had taken to the keys and gently played 'When I Fall in Love'. She thought of ringing him, but knew that would be completely caving in. She thought about calling her son and asking how to get one of those taxis home, the cheap ones he always talks about, only she feared he'd ask her how the night was going and she'd be too upset to lie.

'Can I get you a drink, madam?' the barman asked, his Italian accent strong, but his English good.

'I don't really drink,' she blushed. 'I haven't since I had children.'

'Look outside at the lights. It is a beautiful night. Life is too short. What was it you used to enjoy?'

Her mind wandered back. A long way back. Via the mirrors positioned behind the vast array of spirits, she could see the city, now in darkness and, indeed, wondrously magnified by the lights.

'Gin and tonic.'

He smiled, his dark eyes igniting. 'That is my special-ity. I make you the finest G&T there is.'

And he did. A quieter night than usual, he polished the glassware and told her his name was Marco. He was from Sardinia and had been here five years since he di-vorced his childhood sweetheart. He was a painter, yet couldn't quite make ends meet, so he worked the bar four nights a week. For the money, of course, but also for the view. How he loved this city's skyline. One glance out was all he needed to handle all that the world threw at him.

And then a stranger thing happened. When the sec-ond gin arrived, he asked her about herself. She couldn't remember the last time anyone had truly been interested in her, let alone another man, a younger man, and one so handsome. Sure, she still held on to the pleasant remains of her once youthful looks, kept her hair, skin and curves well-maintained. But it had certainly been a while.

She told him how she married too soon to the only man she had ever slept with. She'd abandoned her hopes and dreams and spent her best years pleasing his ev-ery whim. Nothing had worked out how she planned. Despite their now comfortable circumstances, she had never seen Europe.

'That is sad,' Marco said. 'Nevertheless, sometimes that is life.'

'It's been my life, anyway,'

He held her look. 'I finish soon. I know a place that serves better G&Ts than here. It is never too late to start living how you want to live.'

She thought of this. She'd never been with another man before. It excited her, made her skin prickle. And yet, the idea of a taxi alone afterwards scared her. The thought of telling their family and friends, of breaking up the home, getting her own place, sharing the dog and telling the children terrified her.

And it also excited her.

She reached for her handbag. She felt her phone vibrate. Eleven missed calls. Her eyes caught the mirror. In the reflection, among the city lights drifting slightly and silently by, she saw that balding, perspiring head. The undone tie, the empty glasses. She threw back her stool and turned.

'Alan,' she said.

'Julia,' he gasped.

'The room ... it spins.'

'I thought ...'

She stood by the table, their untouched sticky date puddings before them. This had always been their favourite dessert, one of the few things they still agreed upon. Alan had been drinking, but he'd also been crying.

'I've been a bastard.' He broke down. In all their years, the two births, a miscarriage and the passing of both his parents, she'd never seen him cry. 'I thought you'd gone,' he sobbed. 'Gone for good.'

'I thought the same,' she replied, plainly.

Alan looked old. He looked tired. And despite his relative success in real estate, his family, and his modest wealth, he looked beaten. Alan rose, he came over and held her. She couldn't place the last time he'd held her.

'I'm taking holidays. I'm calling her and telling her. I'm cancelling the trip. We're going to Bali, staying where we honeymooned.' He wobbled, grasping at the table. 'No, better. London, Paris, Rome, the lot, like we always said we would.'

Over his shoulder, she looked out at the city, *her* city, and noticed the lights and how they'd spread over the years. How much the landscape had changed. However, the large buildings, the overbearing river, the rolling hills in the distance and the sky above seemed so familiar, seemed the same.

'I have to go to the bathroom.'

As she walked across the floor, sensing the eyes of the remaining diners, she passed the barman who was studying her as he removed his apron. She didn't stop. Feeling the room revolve for the first time that evening, she headed for the restrooms and the safety of the stall. She locked the door, positioned herself on the seat, and imagined how the city lights would look when she returned.

ARMADALE

Clifton didn't know why his Tinder profile had got him zero matches in the two months he'd had it, but he knew who to ask.

'You have it listed here that you have a Health Care Card?' his sister Ruby told him on speakerphone as she checked out his profile.

'Indeed, I have.'

'You don't mention that you're on welfare on a fucking dating app, Cliff.'

'It's being honest. It's who I am, it's part of the package. It's a selling point.'

'How is being povo a selling point?'

'How's it povo? Instead of taking her to the movies twice a month, a fella like me can take her three times, maybe four. If she needs a script from the docs, I can get it for her for, like, six bucks. And the bus, we can travel up and down wherever we want for bugger all.'

'These aren't selling points,' Ruby cut in. 'Things you like, what you're like, where you live, what you drive, where you holiday, what's your job. That's what they

8

want to know.' She paused. 'Actually, maybe you should leave this part blank.'

'And if she plays it right,' Clifton went on, 'I could get us a subsidised home somewhere.'

A child screamed in the background. Ruby groaned. 'You can't do that.'

'I can do what I bloody well like.'

'Listen, you asked me if there was a reason why you're getting sweet fuck all out of this thing, and I'm telling you why. Because you're forty-whatever and your whole deal smells bum.'

Clifton hung up before he said something he might regret. He was angrier at himself for asking someone for advice, someone who had two failed marriages and four kids to three different dads.

He scrolled back through his contacts. He'd call his brother Gary. He was in Hakea Prison and would appreciate it. He was there because of an aggravated assault on his partner, but he did meet her on Tinder, so at least he knew what he was talking about.

MAYLANDS

The mining boom had been particularly good to Julian Pascali. After graduating as a geologist, he accepted a post down in Boddington on a small gold site. With his wife Leah and their two young children, they settled on the outskirts of Dwellingup near her parents, where they led a comfortable life.

Then, in 2006, things went haywire for the family. The price of iron-ore rocketed due to China's rapacious demand, and Australia couldn't get it out of the ground quick enough. With his skills highly sought-after, and an offer that would triple his wages, it made sense for Julian to make the most of the good times and accept a fly-in fly-out position up in the Pilbara. Three weeks onsite, one week at home. Julian and his wife vowed it wouldn't be forever, just until they set themselves up financially.

It made sense at this point to move back to Perth, something they'd been planning for a while. They chose Maylands due to its proximity to the airport, the city, and good schools, along with the Swan River for weekend activities with their kids. Maylands also held special significance for Julian, as it was the first suburb he moved to when he left home.

One of Perth's rising postcodes, the Pascalis bought a 1930s three-bedder, adding an extra floor to give them another family area, and kitted the garden out with a pool. It cost three times as much as their Dwellingup home had but with the sacrifices he was making, Julian felt it was worth it.

And initially it was. The extra pay offered them luxuries they'd never dreamed of. Reverse cycle air-con throughout. Cinema TV for the cinema room. Two brand new Jeep Cherokees. And on his off weeks, when the kids were on holidays, the family would fly to Bali, or further afield to Fiji, Hawaii and even Europe, thinking little of it.

But after a decade of this, the crash hit and mining companies began culling their workforce. With exploration pared right back, geologists, even good ones like Julian, were the first to go.

Julian didn't mind too much. He'd never been out of work before and was sure, in the land of milk and honey, that it wouldn't be long before something cropped up. Anyway, he was looking forward to the change of pace. The novelty of the big wages and life away had worn him out. The twelve hour-plus days in the relentless heat and dirt had left him exhausted. He missed his wife and missed much of their kids growing up. And he'd had limited time to enjoy the home, which his generous salary funded.

Julian was also looking forward to rediscovering the Maylands he knew from his teenage years. He'd lived there back in the late-nineties and drummed in numerous bands, the biggest of which, The Narrows, played around Perth at a time when Ammonia, Jebediah and Eskimo Joe were rocking local venues, and future heavyweights like The Sleepy Jackson, The Panics and Birds of Tokyo were preparing to take flight. Julian's band played hundreds of shows and support slots, the most famous of which saw them supporting big international names such as The Strokes, Pulp and Johnny Marr. They even made it across the Nullarbor for a tour. They self-released an album which garnered impressive reviews in the street press and were about to relocate to Melbourne when Julian pulled the pin. He'd met Leah at The Hydey one Friday night following a headline show, and a few months later she fell pregnant and was keeping the baby. After some thought, Julian decided to do the right thing and leave the band and stay in Perth. He recommenced the geology course he'd ditched after one semester at Curtin and sold his prized midnight blue Tama kit and reconditioned Combi to support his new family.

Back in Maylands two decades on, Julian hadn't thought about his old life in a long time. He'd heard from the bassist that the band had replaced him soon after, but were quickly swallowed up by the size of the Melbourne scene. But Julian was too busy with work and family to dwell upon what might have been.

That was until his redundancy began. Usually, he would dread that first Monday morning after his always too-brief week off. Kissing his sleeping wife and kids goodbye, followed by that five a.m. ride to the airport to leave life behind for another while. Out of habit, he still woke early, and with the first light flickering, he brewed a pot of coffee and took it out to the porch to watch the sun rise over the city. Only, he wasn't alone out there. He smelled pot in the air and heard the distinct sounds of The Triffids' 'Wide Open Road' plucked on an acoustic guitar coming from the paint-stripped weatherboard home across the street. It was a student house not unlike the one his band had inhabited nearer the Midland Line. He manoeuvred his head around the hedge by his fence to see. A male, not much older than his son, was playing. A red-haired girl in a singlet with a Sailor Jerry tattoo on her left arm was lying across his lap smoking, while the other two long-haired, bearded males lounged across, drinking cans of Export while sharing a joint. Julian hadn't seen such a scene in a long time. This didn't happen in Dwellingup or up north. It sent a buzz up his spine that this was happening in his suburb, on his street. It took him back to a good place.

Now that Julian was at home every day, he realised the young people were always out on their porch jamming and more often than not smoking and drinking. He worked out that they were in a band, a psych-rock outfit reminiscent of early Slowdive or Spacemen 3, and they'd practice along to a drum machine. The boys would endlessly jam, and the girl would come home from her job at the nearby Swallow Bar and add her vocals.

Julian found more and more excuses to go out to his front garden. Mowing the lawn, trimming the hedges, painting the fence, cleaning the gutters. His favourite thing to do was nurse a beer in the afternoon sun and listen to the young folks play and talk about bands while they goofed around and played records. Everything from hip-hop to metal, with lots of psychedelic stuff in between, most of which he didn't know. He could tell it was new, and he knew that he liked it.

Julian's wife grew concerned. It had been three months since he'd been laid off, and the bills were piling up. It wasn't that he wasn't looking for work. He was, kind of, but there were just so few positions cropping up in his field that whenever something did, there'd be hundreds of geologists ready to fill it. If he was honest, though, the thought of going away again up north and working those long hours in that dirt and that heat gave him the fear. He didn't want to leave his family or his home. Above all, he didn't want to leave the young people in the house across who he observed from the anonymity of his front deck night and day.

Leah became worried about a perceived change in her husband and the money he was spending on their credit cards without consulting her. There was the new turntable with the multiple imported vinyl he insisted he had to buy along with it. He'd also purchased a new drum kit and soundproofed the cinema room upstairs, which handily provided an alternative view of the house across the road via the skylight.

Eventually, after a lazy autumn day of sinking beers, listening to Brian Jonestown Massacre and drumming along — and with Leah and the kids down south with the in-laws — Julian, fuelled with Dutch courage, took the plunge. He went across the road and made contact with his neighbours.

'What's happening?' he said.

The kid with mutton-chop sideburns put down the acoustic. 'Hey, sorry, man. We'll keep it down.'

'No, no, it's just, well ...' The group looked at him, obviously wondering where this was going. Julian felt self-conscious about the salt and pepper patches in his hair and the Bintang singlet he wore when he was working in the garden, which did his beer gut no favours. 'I used to play in bands myself and, um ...' More blank looks followed as Julian realised he had nothing worthwhile to say to these young people. He glanced over his shoulder. 'I live across the street.'

'Cool,' the other guy said, changing the record on the player. 'You want a beer, neighbourino?'

'Hey, you're the dude with the drum kit,' the girl called over as she poured wine from a goon box.

A week later when Leah returned with their children and saw her husband, she feared the worst. That Julian had met someone else. He'd spent more money on their cards. This time on an angular haircut and black tint from a city barbers, a wardrobe full of band shirts, new skinny jeans and a pair of cherry red Doc Martens. With Julian now heading out every day and night and coming home smelling of beer and weed, she confronted him about having an affair.

'No, babe, no way,' he told her. 'Something good has happened. Great, even.'

'What is it?'

'I've rediscovered the real me.'

'You have?'

'I've joined a band.'

It turned out that the kids' use of a drum machine was a mere stop-gap until they found a real drummer and, after a brief rehearsal, Julian was in The Fight-Flight Response and playing In the Pines next month. Easy as that.

While Leah was happy to see her husband invigorated again, she wasn't overly pleased about the new development in this stage of their lives. With their own kids about to move out of home, she imagined this would be the phase when they would grow old gracefully and spend more time together. It was also urgent that Julian search for a job, not be jamming across the street and getting loaded in student bars. He had become distant with her, always tipsy or high or hungover and sleeping late like back when they met. Or, he was just never there. The final straw came when he used their last $500 in savings to contribute towards a new recording.

With the mortgage, electricity, water, car, everything in arrears — despite how she'd taken a weekend job as a waitress in a local Italian restaurant to tide them over — Leah, along with their finances, had reached a tipping point. The Jeeps were sold, the house put on the market. Leah spoke with her parents in Dwellingup and arranged for her and Julian to stay with them for as long as they needed to get back on their feet. Despite the recent change in her husband, she believed this would spur him into action and they would rebuild their lives and come back stronger.

'That's great, babe,' Julian told her as they waved goodbye to the same agent they'd purchased their home from over a decade earlier, after they'd signed the papers to sell for a eighty-grand less than which they'd bought it. 'I think you should do it.'

Leah dropped his hand which she'd been holding. 'You mean move? You mean *you* as in *me* and not *us*?'

'Of course.' He lit a rollie, something which infuriated her further as sometime in between not earning and them facing financial ruin, he'd decided he could afford to take up his old habit.

'What about you?' she nearly screamed. 'What about *us*?'

'The band's got a three-week tour booked to support the single. It's got killer reviews. *X-Press* and even *Pitchfork* are all over it.'

'You can't go away for three weeks!'

'Why not? I used to do it all the time.'

For this, she had no answer. She was too angry anyway to reason with him.

And so, he went. Whereas before when he worked up north, he would Skype or call every day, Leah never heard from him apart from the occasional text. He was a bit better with their children, communicating via Snapchat. It was through their 18-year-old daughter that she tracked his movements.

Leah shirt-fronted him when the tour ended, and he finally arrived in Dwellingup. 'What the fuck is going on with you, Julian? You're a forty-two-year-old husband and a father-of-two with responsibilities.'

The house sale had seen them just about break-even when all their debts were paid. She'd assumed Julian would now come down south with the band thing and the mid-life crisis out of his system, and he would find a job in the area or back up north as the economy was picking up. But she knew as soon as she said this that she'd might as well be talking to herself.

'I'm going to rent the spare room in the band house,' he told her. 'I'll spend three weeks in Maylands and a week down here.'

'But why?!'

'I've got a few shifts behind the bar in The Swallow to help pay for it.'

'What about you getting a real job? What about us getting our own place?'

'We did that. We did that for nearly twenty years and it didn't really work out.'

'You're old, and you're hanging out with a bunch of children.'

'Yes,' Julian put his arms around her and smiled. 'And I've never been happier.'

And Leah, who'd never harboured any lofty aspirations of her own, and was never particularly happy even when they had the house and the money and the lifestyle in Maylands, couldn't really argue. So, still loving Julian as much as the day they met, she gradually accepted it.

And with their own kids now self-sufficient in their own student houses near Maylands, she went along with it.

Though the three weeks apart were tough, the week they had together was bliss. A type of love and happiness they'd never experienced before grew between them as they reverted back to being teenagers. They swam naked in the river under the moonlight and made love on the banks. They drank boxed wine and danced to Iggy Pop and the Yeah Yeah Yeahs and got high and fell for each other all over again. They had nothing. No house, no cars, no cinema room, no holidays, no anything, and yet Julian's reawakening was rubbing off on her.

Much of this stemmed from the band sounding better than ever. They were booked to play Laneway. There was also big label interest with their new US-based management company telling them to move to Melbourne immediately. The rest of the band had been planning on doing so for a while, which gave Julian a fresh dilemma.

That is, until Leah missed her period and discovered she was pregnant with twins. Then everything took care of itself, as these things tend to do.

COTTESLOE

Judy climbed down from the Land Rover, her heels carefully feeling their way to the pavement so they wouldn't impact her new hip. She closed the door and waved to Imran. He had offered to help her out of the vehicle, or even bring the smaller Lexus instead, but she thought this was good for her. The specialist claimed she now had the hips of a twenty-five-year-old. It was time for her to start living like one.

As she walked up the steps of the beachside restaurant, she was conscious of being fashionably late. This was a first for her, and she liked it. No more getting here fifteen minutes early and having her heart broken because her children didn't have the decency to get here at something approaching on-time.

The waiter, a younger man with a Celtic accent who she hadn't seen before, directed her to the table they always booked. The one dead centre overlooking the Indian Ocean. Her eldest son, Roger, and her daughter, Tara, were waiting. There was no sign of David. She could tell by their sour expressions that they'd already started quarrelling.

'And where have you been, Mum?' Tara asked, putting down her phone.

'We were worried,' Roger added, sipping his coffee and looking anything but.

'I'm only ten minutes late.' Judy sat down as carefully as she could so as not to aggravate the new hardware.

'You're never late,' Tara said.

'Is everything alright?' Roger asked.

'Perfectly fine. I just had a lazy morning. Spa, facial, the works.'

'Why?' Tara asked.

'Is everything alright?' Roger asked again, slurping down the last of his beverage.

'It's Mother's Day,' Judy said.

'But *we* didn't get you that,' Roger said.

The children had so far given her nothing. They never did. They checked their phones and seemed extra keen for their brother to arrive, yet couldn't get hold of him. They all ordered coffees, a second for Roger, along with more sparkling water. This was the first time Judy had seen any of her children since Christmas. Roger was preoccupied with the Bali development he'd invested in, and Tara was in and out of New York planning her own conceptual art exhibition.

'The new hip not bothering you, is it?' Roger asked.

'You look so tired,' Tara said.

If anyone apart from her children had said this, she would have been insulted. But Judy had been insulted and let down and embarrassed and ashamed of her children so often over the years that she was virtually bullet-proof in this department. She'd been to the beauticians that morning. She was wearing a yellow Kookai strap dress and matching heels she'd purchased from King Street the day before, the first items she'd treated herself to since Graham's passing. Her hair was freshly cut and coloured. She was seventy-three and hadn't felt this alive in years. However, she wasn't offended as these were her children and she knew them well. Instead, she marvelled at how they always found new ways of making her feel less-than-brilliant, even on this, her supposed special day.

Judy could have told them they didn't look so shit-hot themselves, though that wasn't her style. Roger was wearing a blazer over a crisp white button-up shirt, yet she noticed he hadn't shaved and that it had been months since his last haircut. Tara had her hair dyed black with a neat plait peeking out from a purple beret, but looked painfully thin. Wasn't she supposed to be trying for a baby? Something this gaunt couldn't pass wind, never mind push out new life.

Judy asked Roger about the Bali development, the one he'd been working on for a decade. The one which Graham told him not to go near.

'Great, great, really great.' He heaped another sugar into his coffee. 'The slab's down and the first brick should be laid sometime next week.'

'Didn't the brickwork start just after dad passed?' Tara received a cool sideways glance from her older brother.

'Things take time out there. It's different out there. The other investors pulling the plug hasn't helped either, plus the whole global situation and whatnot, but we're getting there.' His old bashed BlackBerry made a noise, and he jumped up and looked at who it was, his expression switching from fear to annoyance, his flushed cheeks turning redder. 'I'll leave that.' He put the phone face down.

'And what about you, Tara?' Judy asked. 'How is the Big Apple?'

Tara took a long draw on her sparkling water and steadied herself. Judy knew she was smoking pot again. 'Wonderful. Just … just, y'know, wonderful. The gallery really seems to like my new stuff, y'know. I mean, we haven't sold anything yet, but we're on the verge, and my profile is really, really … evolving. There's a buzz, y'know.'

Judy didn't really *know*. All she thought of was how her daughter's transatlantic drawl had deepened and how she seemed even more affected by that bullshit scene than usual.

Roger snorted and turned away. 'Odd how you can still justify spending half a year there and rent a bloody Manhattan apartment. All on a *buzz* or a *profile*.'

Tara's back arched. 'I live in Brooklyn, and I wouldn't expect a builder to understand modern art.'

'I'm a CEO, not a builder.'

'Maybe that's your problem.'

'Um, where is Antonio?' Judy asked after Tara's husband, desperate to avoid a situation. She knew a situation was bound to occur between the siblings, same as it always did. She just didn't want it blowing up quite so early. Their talk had already attracted looks from the other mothers here with their normal families. She'd been coming to this restaurant since it was an ice cream parlour and she'd been a young woman dating Graham. In the past two decades, it had been the venue of the Holmes's Mother's Day celebrations and, though the music had become progressively trashier, and the clientele poorer looking in their shorts and thongs with the odd singlet thrown into the mix, she didn't want to be remembered here for all the wrong reasons for yet another year. 'Why can't Antonio be here?'

Tara rolled her eyes. 'You're not Antonio's mother.'

'You know what I mean.'

'He's still in the States. He's needed with the business.'

'And the baby plans?'

'There's a bit of a hurdle now, it's ... it's still happening though.' She nervously adjusted a stray lock of hair under the beret, keen to change the subject. 'David is meant to be bringing your present.'

'It's his turn,' Roger added.

'He's probably drunk,' Tara continued.

'Or lost.'

'Or in someone else's bed.'

'Or in a jail cell'

'David is —'

'Here!' Judy cut Tara off, spotting her other son at the entrance. She hurried to greet him, pleased not to feel anything in her hip. Happier still that he made it, however late, and that her children could all be together and the other two would stop bad-mouthing him. However, his appearance was a cause for concern. David had a full beard and wore a Caltex polo shirt. When he hugged her, he smelled of sweat and oil, with an underlying hint of red wine.

'Sorry, Mum. Car trouble. Happy Mother's Day.' He handed her a card in a white envelope covered in oily fingerprints, along with a bunch of withered daffodils, and shamelessly sat down. 'They're from the servo.'

'No shit,' Tara smirked.

'And why are you dressed like you work in one?' Roger asked.

'Waiter. Beer, please. Something cold and local,' David called to the young man clearing up the table opposite. 'That's because, Roger lovey, I do work in one.'

'Fuck me,' Tara let out a mortified laugh. She was thankful that the chances of anyone meaningful from the art world seeing her in Cottesloe were about zero. David fished out a half-packet of crushed Samboys from his shirt pocket. 'Mind?' he half-asked, forcing his dirty fingers into the foil and gobbling the remains. 'I'm starved.'

Roger tried to contain his anger. 'Why in God's name does a Holmes work there?'

'What the fuck's his problem?' David asked a little louder than he realised, the red wine he had after his shift making him a tad more animated than he'd planned. 'The rent doesn't pay itself. Or the child support.' His beer arrived, and he threw down a mouthful and winced. 'Flowery shit,' he muttered, examining the label of the boutique IPA from down south.

Judy frowned. She knew what happened when the family drank together. This was why they'd changed the Mother's Day lunch to brunch a few years ago.

'You could have got changed,' Tara told him. 'It's Mum's big day.'

'Oh, I don't mind.' Judy squeezed her younger son's wrist.

'You heard. She doesn't mind. I just finished the night shift.'

'It's eleven a.m.' Tara wasn't letting it go.

'Like I said, had a bit of car trouble.' David didn't let on that this involved his old Barina being unable to accommodate his bulk for an adequate kip to shake off the half-cask he'd consumed at the end of his shift.

'Anyway,' Judy took over, 'we're all here now.'

The waiter returned, and they asked for more time to order. Judy peered out the window at the beach below. There were kids learning to surf, fathers building sandcastles with their toddlers, older boys and girls flying kites. It reminded Judy of her family growing up, until she remembered that none of this ever happened. Graham was rarely around, always working. Each weekend Roger would be off playing cricket. David would be out and up to no good. Tara whining or crying or both in the bedroom she rarely left.

'How are the children, David?' she asked.

'I see them when I can. Tully's in Broome. Sienna's in Adelaide. Tristan's just past Mandurah.'

'So not at all then,' Roger mumbled, sending a text on his BlackBerry.

David let it slide. 'Almost forgot. Waan's expecting. Happy Mother's Day.' He took his mother's hand. 'You're going to be a grandmother again.'

'That's wonderful, David,' Judy said, and she really meant it, leaning over to embrace him.

'Just wonderful,' Tara echoed, playing with her spoon. 'Another grandchild she'll never see.'

'Who the hell is *Waan*?' Roger asked, adding a few extra '*a*'s for effect.

'Don't be silly,' Judy replied before David could. 'It's David's partner of ... what is it? Must be over a year now.'

David nodded. 'I was seeing her long before last Christmas. Mum met her on Boxing Day.'

'I did.' Judy thought she'd imagined it.

David wiped his hands on the tablecloth, pausing for a moment. 'That might have been the day we had that fight, actually. I think she stayed in the car. Well, anyway, she's having another little Holmes.'

'You sure it's yours?' Judy tutted at Tara's blithe question, aware the whole day sat on a knife-edge and it wouldn't take much to push it over.

David's nostrils flared, and he took a big breath. 'Fair cop, I'll pay that. I have assessed the dates and yeah, it is.' Though his new partner's temper was questionable, he knew her honesty and integrity were not.

Roger and Tara shook their heads at their brother's reply, and Judy for a fleeting moment saw how alike they looked. That hard, fixed chin. Those cold, often expressionless eyes.

Judy worried about her middle child. Parents weren't supposed to have favourites, however she fretted endlessly about David in that petrol station until all hours and how he could be held up by some yahoo at any moment. He'd been such a bright boy, accepted into the Air Force straight from school as an air traffic controller. He should be at one of the big airports by now. Marijuana was his undoing, and who knew what since that gateway opened?

'When is she due?' Judy asked.

'End of November,' David answered. 'And yes, you will get to see this one. All the time, in fact. Getting us a little place. Gonna have it all ready for all four kids so they can come and stay.'

'Where's the place?' Roger picked at the complimentary bread which had arrived, not really caring if he got a response.

'Clarkson.'

'And where is Clarkson?' Tara asked.

'North of Wanneroo.'

'Eurgh,' Tara's nose curled. 'Even I've heard of life up there.'

'You're all south of the river snobs.'

'I believe you were from there as well,' Roger hit back.

'Yeah, and that's how I know what an overrated white-infested shithole it can be. Nothing wrong with bringing kids up in a place where everyone isn't Aryan and privileged.' He looked Roger in the eye. 'Arsehole.'

Judy shushed him as the elderly mother to their left tutted. 'Children, please. Language.'

'Sounds like you're fitting in already.' Tara rose. 'I'm off to the ladies.'

Roger followed his sister towards the restrooms. 'Think I'll join you.'

David laughed. 'Always knew you were hiding something.'

Roger reddened. 'I meant the men's room, you child.'

David grabbed the passing waiter's arm. 'Another beer, cheers. Swanny D if you've got it.'

'Sorry, sir, we don't.'

'Fuck it. Same again.'

'Should you, David?' Judy was well-aware this wasn't his first. 'You do have your car here.'

'You're right, Mum.' Despite his faults, he was always the most obedient of her children. The biggest rebel, forever in trouble at school and with the police, yet always the most compliant at home. He called over. 'Cancel that. I'll grab a black coffee instead.'

Judy relished this moment together. 'Is everything okay, David? You don't look the best, love. Is it money you need?'

'Mother, I'm fine. Thank you, but I'm fine. Got me a place and an honest job now. I'll be off nights from next month. At my age, they're starting to throw me for six.'

She watched him drain the beer. He'd put on weight. Must be all the donuts on the job, she imagined. 'And I wish you'd watch your drinking.'

'I need to drink to sleep. And that's all I was doing this morning. Admittedly, I shouldn't have today of all days, that's another story. But, hey, bugger me, who cares about me? It's Mother's Day. How the bloody hell are you?'

Judy paused for a moment, processing the question. It had been so long since any of the family had asked how she really was. Even at Graham's funeral everyone was so caught up inside their own grief, even those who barely knew him, that hers was forgotten.

She cleared her throat. 'I'm good. I really am. The hardest part of the loss is behind me, and the new hip's working a treat. I feel like a new chapter's opening up.'

'What new chapter?' Tara had returned with Roger. He smelled of cigarettes and was anxiously peering out the window and squinting back and forth at the back door.

'I'm just saying that with your father gone a little while now, I'd like to make some changes and —'

Roger smiled. 'Good for you, Mum. Tara and I were just saying the same thing.'

'Saying what exactly?' Judy enquired.

'That you should make some changes.'

The older lady sank into her chair, realising this wouldn't be so difficult after all. 'Good then, because —'

This time she was cut off by her daughter. 'We've been viewing a few residential villages for you.'

David let out a big belly laugh. 'You're going to put her in a home?' He tucked his chair under the table and sat back. 'Oh boy, this is gonna be a treat.'

'It's not a home,' Tara said as evenly as she could. 'We're actually worried about her wellbeing. Mum, you're not getting any younger. What if you fall again?'

'I am not going to fall again.'

'But what if you did?' Roger reiterated with force.

'I ... I'd do what I did last time and call the neighbours to help me. They really are very nice men.'

Roger's tone softened. 'But next time you might not be so lucky.'

'I'm not planning on making a habit of it. It was your father's boxes that did it. Which I have since gotten rid of.'

Tara took her hand. It always worried Judy when she showed a hint of compassion. It meant there was bad news coming, like she'd crashed the car, or got arrested for cocaine possession, or she'd separated from Antonio. Or she needed money.

Roger laid a stack of glossy brochures out on the table.

'Shit, they've come armed!' David laughed harder.

'How much does all this cost?' Judy asked.

'It won't cost you anything,' Roger said

'Hear that, Mum.' David was loving every moment. 'How could you possibly say no? Roger, you'll be fifty in a few years. Why don't we all jump ship and do it together?'

Judy snapped at them. 'You're not selling my house. That was your father's house. That land's been in the family far too long.'

'And that's the best bit,' Roger leaned in. 'We're keeping the land. Well, some of it. But just look where it is. Look how big it is.' He removed another sheath of documents, this one containing plans and an artist's impression of a slew of double storey flats with that famous view of the ocean each of them knew so well. 'I'm talking eight luxury apartments. We can build them for a few hundred grand each and sell them for five times that when the market picks up.'

'*We*?' David applauded, slowly. 'Oh, this is the best one yet.'

Judy sat up straight, braying for battle. 'I'm not losing my home, Roger.'

'And we don't want to lose you,' Tara said.

'Bullshit!' Judy said it so loudly that all the mothers on all the tables turned to them. 'Bullshit, bullshit, bullshit. You've been planning this since your father was diagnosed.'

Roger reached over and clasped her other hand. Judy found his palm cold and moist. 'We didn't mean to upset you.'

'Well, you have.'

'David, mate,' Roger turned to his brother. 'Help us out here.'

'Why? I don't need the money.'

'It's not about the money.'

'I got my child support payment plan set up. Afford-able little unit. Regular wage.'

'Regular minimum wage,' Tara couldn't resist. 'You work as a pump jockey.'

'So what? It's honest work. Something you two par-asites wouldn't know the meaning of.'

Tara gritted her teeth, trying not to lose her cool. 'And what's that supposed to mean?'

'Come on, Roger,' David turned on his brother. 'It's common knowledge the Bali thing's gone tits up, and you're flat broke. I may not have, how should I say, the *connections* that I once did, but I hear things. So come on, how much money do you actually owe?' The waiter arrived with David's black coffee. He was readying to take their order, but when he saw what he was enter-ing into, he did a swift one-eighty. 'How many times has your phone beeped since you've been here? On a Sunday. How many times have you looked outside to see if your brakes are being cut or if someone's waiting out there to settle the score?'

Roger gripped the table so hard his knuckles turned snow white. 'You are so lucky it's Mother's Day.'

'I can't believe we're related to you,' Tara scoffed.

Coffee spilled down David's chin. He wiped it away with his arm and eyed his younger sibling, ready to burn another bridge. 'Don't make me start on you as well, princess. You're just shitting your designer kecks cos soon you'll have to get a real job. Dreading the day that Antonio finally puts a pin up the backside of your little Frida Kahlo fantasy.' He thumped the table. 'C'mon people, try harder. You're so fucking obvious.'

'Enough, enough, enough!' Judy screamed, no longer caring who heard her, which was everyone in the establishment. She removed her phone from her clutch bag.

'Who are you calling?' Roger asked.

'I am texting Imran.'

'Imran?' Tara was surprised to hear that name from their past.

'Yes. I have been seeing Imran, and he is collecting me. And I want him to collect me now, as I have had enough of this family. I'd had enough of it when your dad was around. The lying, cheating ... cocksucker. And now I've finally had enough of the little monsters we created too.'

'Good for you, Mum.' David gave her a raised fist of solidarity.

'That was never proven,' Roger said, looking down.

'What wasn't?' David asked.

'The cheating.'

'Fucksake, Roger,' David chuckled. 'I was barely out of nappies and even I knew. What do you think the old windbag was doing in those women's houses while we were melting like a pair of Paddle Pops in the car? Selling food mixers?'

'I'm not going in a home.' Judy shoved her phone back into her bag. 'I brought you here to tell you I'm going on a world cruise. Then I'm taking a vested interest in philanthropy where I intend to invest fifty percent of your father's blood money from the trust.'

'What?!' Tara yelped.

'For people who need it a lot more than us,' Judy continued. 'And ... ' For the first time she could remember, Judy had her children's full attention. They were looking at her with respect and more than a little fear. And she loved it. ' ... Imran and I are getting married at sea.'

Both Roger and Tara's faces froze. Their father's assistant was someone they grew up with, yet had never viewed as anything more than a mere flunky.

David was first to speak, in between studying the menu. 'Good for you, Mum. He's a fine man. Gayer than a box of Celebrations — best of luck in *that* department — but good for you.' David lifted his beer to propose a toast before realising it was empty. 'Waiter! Could we have some champagne? Your second most expensive. Actually, seems like those days are gone. Better make it your second cheapest.'

The waiter forced a smile. Two families had complained about their antics and he was already in two minds about asking them to leave. He would refer the matter to his shift manager before uncorking anything.

Judy's phone rang. 'Yes, I'll come outside now, love.'

She got up, lifting her bag, revelling in how good the hip felt. 'You have the bubbly. I'll see you all at Christmas. I suppose we must. And in between then, hopefully you can all get your shit together.'

She walked out past the waiter. 'My children will be getting this one. I am sorry about the disturbance but don't worry, we shan't be back.'

'I'm sorry to hear that, ma'am,' he said, genuinely surprised.

'Thanks for an eventful fifty years.' She wasn't sad. The restaurant wasn't what it used to be. She realised she'd never had a pleasant Mother's Day here. This one was the worst. They didn't even make it to brunch.

Judy walked down the steps. Her children were gaping at her through the glass, still speechless. Roger brooding over how badly the Southern Serpents would beat him once they realised he couldn't pay his share. Tara worrying about how she could afford a flight back to the States, never mind the rent on her Williamsburg apartment, or the lease on her gallery, at least until the divorce went through. And David wondering if he had enough in his savings account to cover a third of the bill, even without breakfast, and wanting to ask if it was too late to cancel the champagne.

Out on the street, the Land Rover waited. Judy climbed in, the hip feeling fine. She cursed herself for wearing a dress which was on the tight side for such a drill, and footwear which made her wobble. Her children had never even commented that she looked nice.

'How was it?' Imram asked.

'Suitably awful,' Judy began brushing her hair in the mirror.

'Just as you predicted then.'

'I told them we were getting married.'

Imram laughed as he pulled out of the car park. 'I only wish I could have seen their faces. I hope you didn't tell them you love me just to get a reaction.'

'Having put up with Graham for all those years, we could both do with some love.' She placed her hand over his on the handbrake. 'Now, let's go and spend his money just like the old bastard would've hated.'

THORNLIE

As fireworks exploded on the big screen, Russ Holt bid farewell to the worst twelve months of his life and vowed that this year things would be different. They sure couldn't get any worse. Russ had been made redundant from his groundsman post at the local high school, and his wife had taken their two kids and left him for the senior mortgage broker at her work.

So when the black sky over the Swan River alighted in a kaleidoscope of colour, and the words of Robbie Burns rang out, Russ did something different. While his friends in the tavern made their toasts and shook each other's hands, Russ sat alone on his corner stool, closed his eyes and recited the Lord's Prayer quietly. Or as much of it as he could remember from his childhood, as he'd never been a religious man.

On the walk home, Russ *did* feel different. He'd been drinking Emu Bitter instead of his usual Export as it was on special at six bucks a can, though he didn't think it was that. He feared it could've been the free barbeque the bar provided and those pinky-grey sausages with the funky taste. Whatever it was, after he got home and drank a pint of water and cleaned his teeth, he needed to go bad. He pulled down his y-fronts, sat on the toilet and pushed. It felt like a bowel movement much like any other, except that after he'd wiped and was about to deposit the paper into the bowl, he caught a glimpse. A glimpse of something incredible. Something life changing.

Jesus.

It was Jesus Christ.

Russ Holt of 114B Forest Crescent had just shat Jesus, or at least faecal matter which resembled the great man's long hair, beard and face. Russ didn't know what to do. But he knew he wasn't going to flush. He'd heard of visions like this happen in exotic places like the Mediterranean, the Middle-East and South America, but not in deepest suburban Thornlie.

He took a picture on his phone. Then he found a plastic bag and reached in and carefully fished it out. Luckily, it was a firm one. He gave it a quick shake and put it outside on the window ledge to dry.

That night Russ had the most peaceful sleep he'd had since living alone. He dreamed of his old home becoming a shrine with pilgrims visiting his sacred shitter from all over Perth, and then from all corners of the globe. He envisioned a media frenzy on the front lawn and saw how impressed his neighbours were. There were whispers of even the Pope paying a visit.

When he woke, Russ felt something else brewing inside. He sat back down on the toilet seat, not thinking too much of it, not thinking that last night's occurrence was anything other than a once in a lifetime fluke. But when he examined the bowl, there lay a turd in the shape of Jesus on the cross. It was small, yet just big enough to detail the crown of thorns and the nails in his hands and feet. Russ Holt felt God's warmth radiate within him. He carefully lifted it out, shook the water off and placed it on the ledge, depositing last night's dried effort into the freezer.

Russ lit a cigarette and sat in his humble bathtub, in his humble bathroom, which hadn't been cleaned since his wife left back in September. And he thought of what to do about this gift which had been bestowed upon him. How to tell the world about this miracle. He simply had to spread the word. This was his mission, his reason for being. After forty-eight years, he now understood God's plan and why he'd been put on this earth.

So, he did.

He emailed the pictures to the *Gosnells Examiner*, *The West Australian*, and every radio and television organisation he could think of. Then he sat back with an Emu Bitter, rolled another cigarette, and waited for the world to arrive on his doorstep to marvel at this visitation from the Son of God.

He considered cleaning the place, giving it a lick of paint, weeding the front yard, but he wasn't sure that's what *He* would have wanted and didn't want to jinx anything. After all, Jesus was born in a stable of modest means, and Russ figured the state of his house would add to the whole authentic experience for which

American pilgrims would only be too happy to cough up twenty-five bucks a throw for.

But the days and weeks and then months went by and the pilgrims never came. Russ received no response from the media. He even set up an Instagram account, though the only followers he got were freaks and weirdos wanting to trade pictures of excrement, until the account was shut down for violating Instagram's terms of service.

The new year carried on pretty much the same for Russ, except he got further behind on the bills, and the house got even dirtier, and he started drinking more and became more depressed.

And yet the holy turds continued to spring forth. There was one of the Virgin Mary and Baby Jesus, another of the wandering star, and a larger, longer one depicting the entire cast from the Last Supper which was a bit of a bastard to squeeze out. There were also more generic ones such as a map of Australia (Tasmania and Rottnest Island included), the eagle from West Coast's crest, and a darker one which looked like the nose of Perth identity Basil Zempilas.

The only thing for Russ to do was empty his freezer box, which was filled to the brim with these little miracles, and mail the actual turds to the press. This would be a sure-fire way to get their attention.

And get their attention, it did. As another year ended and a new one began, he wasn't in the Thornlie Tavern watching the fireworks, nor was he in his home, which had been repossessed. Russ Holt was in Graylands Hospital. The judge thought the mental health facility was a more appropriate place to put someone who had mailed one-hundred-and-forty-nine pieces of their own shit to *The Sunday Times* and *Channel 7* to get them the help they obviously needed.

PERTH AIRPORT

Sudra waited in the customs line. This was the fourth September in-a-row she'd done so, and the queues seemed to snake back further and further each year.

She stifled a yawn. She'd been up since four a.m. and always struggled to sleep on the plane. Her feet were aching in her younger sister's sandals, and she could do without standing, soundtracked by the cries of children around her.

Sudra remembered the first time she came here. Her excitement at leaving Bali for the first time. At being given a three-month trip to Australia, all paid for, and a salary too. No one in her village had ever been to Australia. Australians came to Bali, yes, but not the other way around. She recalled her initial joy at seeing the wide, clean streets devoid of beeping scooters and the oversized homes spread far apart.

That all seemed so long ago. Over the years, her excitement and enthusiasm had waned and morphed into a feeling of cold, hard dread.

First, there was the never-ending amount of work she knew would be waiting for her. Her father had agreed to Dr Findlay and Mrs Findlay's request for her to come to Perth and care for their children during the week and have weekends to herself to discover the city. Instead, when she got here, she was forced to work each and every day, looking after their spoiled children and two large dogs. Plus, cook all the meals, do the washing, vacuuming, dusting and scrub the five-bedroom home, as well as maintain the pool and large garden. She toiled from when she rose until she went to bed. If she didn't, she was threatened that the $500 she earned per week — an impressive sum for an unskilled Balinese woman, but a pittance, she had grown to understand, for someone in Australia doing the work she was doing — would not be wired home to her family.

The line crawled on. Despite her discomfort, Sudra was in no hurry. Dr Findlay would be waiting for her in the arrivals' lounge as usual. He would gripe and groan about the time and deduct the car park fee from her salary, as always. And yet, she liked making him wait. She wondered if he'd drive her to that secluded beach carpark on the way to the house and abuse her again. She was sure that was how she got pregnant last time, but it could have been any of the sixteen times (she had counted) he'd forced her to have sex with him during her stay. It didn't matter now. She'd dealt with it when she returned to Denpasar. She never told Dr Findlay, as she didn't want to give him the satisfaction of knowing he could fill her with life.

She worried about the eldest boy, Hamish. He was twelve-years-old when she first visited, but last year he'd gotten much bigger. He was almost a man. He would leave pornography on his computer screen, knowing she was coming in to tidy. She once found her unclean underwear mixed into his sock drawer. He would insist on hugging her uncomfortably long and close. He looked a lot like his father, and she'd seen signs in the way he treated his younger sister that he could be just as cruel and domineering. She feared being left alone with Hamish this time in that house.

Sudra was close to the front of the line, and her anxiety grew. The customs guard with his olive skin and dark eyes, who looked like he may have been part Southeast Asian, was stamping passports at pace.

She'd asked Dr Findlay to stop, and would get locked in the garage for hours on end in the heat if she persisted. She even tried broaching the subject with his wife. The woman struck her across the jaw with the TV remote and vowed that if she ever said anything like that again, next time she'd strike her with something heavier.

Sudra tried telling her family of the escalating hardship. Not of the sexual assaults — that would be her own shameful secret — but of the bullying. She begged, she pleaded with her father not to send her, though he wouldn't listen. He refused to believe that a man such as Dr Findlay would act as anything other than a perfect gentleman. He was angry with her for trying to blacken the man's good name, a man who had been a fine friend of his for two decades. Who visited their restaurant with his family and associates each night when they holidayed on the island twice a year. A man who had helped them out financially by taking Sudra to Australia and had commenced taking her two younger sisters and her 16-year-old cousin from the village for the remaining months. In them, and only in them, could Sudra discuss her time in Western Australia. It saddened her that they were suffering as much as she did, and how she would see another grain of innocence shed from their sparkling eyes each time they returned.

Sudra was next in line. The guard did not smile or say a word as she stood before him. He perused her passport and tap-tap-tapped on his keyboard. Sudra hated this country with its superficiality, its hollowness, its godlessness. She hated coming here. She prayed each night that her father had never met Dr Findlay and she could have remained poor and simple, yet pure and content in Bali.

A policewoman with a blonde ponytail approached the officer and whispered in his ear, neither of them taking their eyes from her. Sudra tasted the salty perspiration from her top lip. She whispered a silent prayer. The policewoman broke away and approached Sudra.

'Can you please come with us, Miss Sudasra?'

Sudra relaxed. Sarip had warned her there was a chance of getting caught, and she went ahead with it, hearing that Australian prisons weren't bad places, not like Indonesia.

She followed the policewoman into the adjoining room. She thought of those seven kilos of white powder sewn into the lining of her suitcase. She'd probably get less than ten years. That would be ten years in which she wouldn't have to see Dr Findlay and be violated by him or kill his spawn. And at the end she would never be allowed back into Australia, and her own father would likely be dead. She was just willing, praying, that the slit she'd made with a biro in the back of her father's car on the way to Ngurah Rai International Airport was large enough to be found.

SUBIACO

Florence's stomach emitted a low growl. She always ate at six o'clock on the dot, and now it was a quarter-to-seven. He was meant to be waiting for her. The rain was getting heavier. Florence wished she'd worn her fur-lined waterproof instead of this cashmere sweater.

'He should be here,' she told the driver.

'S'alright, love,' he said, thumbing through the paper. 'I'm in no hurry.'

I bet you're not, Florence thought, as the orange numbers flickered and rose on the metre.

She rubbed the mist off the window with her woollen glove and saw her son bound out the building, searching for the vehicle.

'For God's sake,' she muttered. 'It's a London cab. The only car parked here. Driver, toot your horn.'

The driver shifted the pages off the wheel and did so. Martyn glanced over and jogged across. He opened the door.

'Mother, I am so sorry.' He was breathless with a giddy grin and looked like he'd been crying.

'Hmm, very well.'

'Gabby's just out of labour.'

'You should bloody well hope so after a day and a half. Well then, tell us. What is it?'

'It's a girl,' he sobbed, his head falling onto her shoulder. 'A beautiful baby girl.'

Florence reached her arms out to hold him but found she couldn't. 'That's, that's ... congratulations.'

'Thank you, thank you. You'll just love her. She has your eyes.'

'Oh, I'm sure she does.'

'What are we waiting for?' He lifted her handbag. 'Let's head on up.'

Florence gripped the handle. 'Listen, Martyn. I'm actually feeling a little chesty.' She forced a small cough. 'So, if it's alright with you, I'll see her at home when the weather's not so miserable and —'

'Really?' he interrupted. 'Gabriella's entire family are here. Can't you come up and have a peek?'

'I'd rather not, Martyn.' She unleashed a larger cough to end the matter.

'Sure.' Martyn let go of the bag and stepped back. 'Whatever you want, Mother.'

'Oh, and Martyn?'

'Yes. Mother.'

'Be so kind as to pay the man, would you?'

Martyn sighed and removed his wallet. 'How much do we owe you?'

'Eighteen dollars,' said the driver. 'Call it thirty if you want her dropped back.'

Martyn took out two red notes and handed them over.

'Thanks mate,' he said, not offering any change. 'And congratulations.'

'Thank you, Martyn,' Florence said, closing the door. 'Bye, Mother.'

'Onward please, driver.' She tapped the headrest with the wooden point of her umbrella.

The taxi moved, and Florence relaxed. Her hot pot wouldn't have dried up, and she'd make it back in time for the start of *MasterChef*. Eight granddaughters was too much. If it had been a boy, a first grandson, she'd have raced right up there and settled for cheese on toast and hearing about tonight's first episode from the neighbours. But not for another girl with her eyes.

That could wait.

MIDLAND

'You told him I had an abortion?' Donna's head spun sideways from behind the wheel to see if her boyfriend was actually serious.

'Watch that car.' Joey was a good driver, a confident driver. Probably too confident, the judge had remarked when she slapped him with a twelve-month ban for doing doughies out the back of the Mt Henry after drinking all Australia Day. But Joey was not a confident passenger, especially when his girlfriend was at the wheel. 'I needed a solid excuse. One where he wouldn't ask questions.'

'You told him I had an abortion.' Donna repeated the words slowly, her eyes back on the road. Her head was now vibrating furiously on her shoulders in a way Joey didn't think was natural, not quite believing the words he had said.

'Yeah. *And* he didn't ask questions. He just sort of went quiet and a bit beetroot round the gills. He ended up giving me a two-week extension instead of one. He said he hopes you're feeling okay.' Joey clasped the dashboard as she crossed double lines and overtook the Falcon in front. 'Christ, how fast are you going here?'

'So, you told the Associate Professor in a course I just graduated from that I'm already up the duff?'

'No, that you *were* up the duff. He wouldn't even know we're together.' Joey braced himself again. 'You wanna get a bit further up that car's ass?'

Donna let out a scream and veered off the road next to a bus stop. She pulled the handbrake and killed the engine. 'We've been dating since we started uni, you, you ... bag of shit. That's three years. What right do you have to falsely tell anyone, never mind Don Oliver, my number one job referee, that I'm murdering your unborn and very much phantom foetus?'

Joey used to love it when Donna got angry. Now he wasn't so sure. Her moods and her temper had gotten worse since she started this ten-day detox. Then there was the perfume she was wearing these days, which he swore was her step-mother's. He missed the Miu Miu he bought her that did things to his insides, making him want to jump her bones whenever he sniffed it. Then, there were the clumpy shoes which had replaced her open-toe heels and the frumpy dresses. And what was with the bottle-green cardigan she was rocking tonight? He was sure he'd seen her older brother don it. And what about all the fun they used to have together? *Used* to have.

Donna, meanwhile, was more than sick of Joey's shit. Right after she'd agreed to move in with him, he lost his licence. Now she had to drive his ass everywhere. To uni, to work, to see his stupid mother in Butler, not to mention every party they went to. And he used this as an even bigger excuse to act like a bag of shit and get drunker than he ever had before. She didn't want to go to tonight's gathering with his friends, which would inevitably end with them getting stoned and giggling inanely to *Funny or Die* clips.

Both she and Joey were meant to have finished their studies by now and were supposed to be in Europe. That was until the driving fine wiped out his savings. He blamed the stress of the ordeal on his inability to submit his final assignments or study for his exams, and now he had to repeat his final six months. They used to be a team. They revelled in getting in weird and wonderful situations together, never taking life seriously. Driving across the Nullarbor. Backpacking around Thailand. The summer they squatted in the old power station by the river. The nang parties they threw in second year. They were a couple known for their craziness. But these days, those moments were so fleeting they'd almost vanished. And now she had to process this bullshit he'd told the professor about her just because he couldn't be arsed doing the work like everyone else on the course.

A horn blasted, making them jump. It was a bus, the driver waving his arm for them to budge. Donna lifted her hand in acknowledgement. She started the engine, indicated right and drove back onto the road. She couldn't wait to get to the party because that meant the time would be closer to when they could leave, and she could go home and take two Melatonin and pretend all this wasn't happening.

The pace of Donna's vehicle slowed to somewhere around the speed limit, and Joey was bored. He sucked hard on his vape. His stubby of One Fifty Lashes had run out, and he cursed himself for not lifting another for the journey but knew this would have been pushing it with Donna who wasn't drinking this evening. He was so bored that he couldn't be bothered with all this feuding interspersed with bouts of silence. Already a bit tipsy from afternoon beers following band rehearsal, he tried to take Donna's hand which rested on the gearstick, but she pulled away. He was also a bit horny, the couple having not fucked all week due to Donna being tired from working the overtime required to pay their bills. Memories flashed by of when they used to make it in the car when they were younger and didn't live together in a cramped studio apartment and fight nearly all the time.

'Sorry, babe. I love you, y'know.'

Donna kept her eyes on the road. She hated coming to this side of the city as she didn't understand the roads and always found it poorly lit in comparison to nearer town. A problem not helped by leaving her driving glasses in her other bag. At least the roads were eerily quiet for a Friday.

Joey tried again. 'You do know that, don't you?'

She gripped the steering wheel. God, she hated him so much right now. She wished with everything she had that he would grow up or get the fuck out of her life and let her get on with hers.

But as she turned off the main road, she caught his look. Those dark features. Those high cheekbones, puppy dog brown eyes and big cheeky grin that all her girlfriends loved and would've made them do anything to spend these years with him. Something in her ignited as it always did, and she couldn't help the smile spreading across her face. He was a fool almost all the time, getting worse so he was, yet he was her fool. And despite what her family told her, he did love her, and she loved him.

Their eyes met. He reached for her hand, and this time she didn't pull away. She remembered how she fell for his sense of fun and how he never took anything seriously and ...

As the car sped through the stop sign, they felt the bumper crash into something and heard bones crack, followed by a dull thud as the wheels bumped over the shape of a body. A subdued moan echoed out from underneath as the brakes slammed and the vehicle screeched to a halt. The couple's eyes turned from sheer want to sheer panic.

'What the fuck?!' Joey screamed. 'What the fuck have you done?'

'It wasn't my fault, it wasn't my fault.' Her whole body vibrated. 'You saw it, it wasn't my fault. He just wandered out.'

They crept out of the car terrified by what they might find. The road was deserted, partially lit by a dim orange glow emitting from the streetlights. They peeked beneath the Swift. Lying there was a still figure in a long, black raincoat, in spite of the sticky evening.

Donna went to grab the man's leg.

Joey grabbed her arm instead. 'Don't move him.'

'We can't leave him there.' She watched Joey stand there, frozen. 'Fuck you, then. I'll do it myself.'

She did so, yanking the man's arms, pulling him out to the dark side shaded from the lights by an overhanging branch. She turned the man over and his face came into view. He had a greying ponytail and a gold earring and looked somehow familiar. The left side of his body was mangled from the impact. He was bleeding from a deep gash in his head and had lost consciousness.

Donna took out her phone. 'We have to call an ambulance.'

'Wait.'

'What?'

'You just went through a stop sign.'

'So?'

'So, they'll throw the book at you.' He was well-aware that if she lost her licence, then they'd both be screwed.

'What's your suggestion?' She knew he had a point, but she was fast losing patience.

'It would probably be quicker if we rolled him up and put him in the backseat. Drop him off, y'know, anonymously.'

'Right.' Donna wasn't sure, though her mind was too muddled to think of anything better.

'You get his legs.'

Joey grabbed the man's shoulders, and Donna grabbed his feet. He was smaller and lighter and older than they'd guessed.

'Fuck,' Donna said, opening the door. 'You've got all your records in there.' Joey had been meaning to drop off the two large boxes of hip-hop vinyl at his cousin's place in Leeming the next time they passed. He'd agreed to take them off him for $750.

'The boot, then.' Donna really felt uncomfortable about this. Even though it was very much a grandma's car, this was too mobster for her.

'He can still breathe in there,' Joey said. 'C'mon, my back is breaking here.'

She opened the boot and removed a bag of old clothes she'd been meaning to hand to the op shop for forever. She repositioned a sandy beach towel and sun-bleached 2004 UBD to where the man's bleeding head could go. As they squeezed him in, they heard a car and froze, praying it wouldn't be a police vehicle. Luckily, it was a Swan Taxi, the driver in the golden turban paying no attention to them.

They got him inside. Joey was a little too keen and knocked the man's head against the side panel.

'What are you little cunts doing?' The man roused, wheezing through broken and bloody teeth, his eyes flickering.

'We're just ...' Donna stopped as she tried to piece together exactly what it was they were doing.

Joey took over. 'We're taking you to the hospital.'

'You fucking knocked me down.'

'It was an accident.' Donna, too, was having trouble breathing. 'Nobody's fault.'

'Went straight through a stop sign, you bitch.'

'Hang on a minute,' Joey cut in. 'We're trying to help you here.'

'You're past help. Do you little cunts know what you've done? Do you know who I am?'

'No,' Donna almost cried out.

'Why haven't you got me an ambulance?'

'This way will be quicker,' Joey said.

'Fuck off it will.'

Donna got the bags of clothes on top of the records. 'We don't know who you are, but I know you'll be a dead man if we don't get moving.'

'I'm Jimmy fucking Mizon!' He spat blood as his words howled into the void. 'Now get me an ambulance, you little cunts.'

Joey wheeled around, hurling the Chiko Roll he had for lunch into the gutter as he thought about the signature ponytail and that gold earring and the face of the man on the news who ran Perth's underworld in the '90s. 'We're fucked.'

Donna was crying. 'We've killed Jim Mizon.'

'And I'm gonna fucking kill you,' he wheezed, more blood spouting.

A dog barked in the distance. Donna slammed the boot. Jimmy screamed out like a man about to die. There was a block of houses a hundred metres along the street. Donna panicked.

'Let's get out of here,' she opened the driver's side door. She turned the ignition. 'Which way's the hospital?'

Joey sat there, rigid at the reality of what they'd done. His words came slowly, deliberately. 'We could go to hospital … but I don't think he's going to make it.'

'You don't know that.'

'You hit him pretty hard.'

'*We* hit him.'

The screaming was dying out, becoming little more than a rattle.

'I'm just saying, I'm not sure where the hospital is and it could be a waste of time. And it's going to open up a world of pain for us with the doctors and the police and the media and his associates. This is big.' Joey was speaking plainly now, his voice lacking emotion. 'And I don't know where the hospital is, but I know that if we hit the Great Eastern Highway, we're a little while away from some pretty dense bushland, and he's a terrible guy who I'm sure has done some pretty terrible things. And I'm just saying, there was no one around and maybe no one needs to know.'

Donna drove on. The noise in the back stopped. This whole thing was horrible, yet she felt good that she and Joey were communicating again. Planning and scheming like the old team they were. Whatever came of this, that had to be a positive thing.

INGLEWOOD

'And we will never, ever, use your business again, you thick, greasy, wog cunt.'

Dirk slammed down the phone. Today was going from bad to worse. The kid from Romano Printers had told him the brochures for the campaign wouldn't be ready until a week before voting began in the state election. Dirk needed them at least a month before if they were to be of any use to swing the vote. It was tough enough for the West Australian Defence League to spread their message of a white Anglo-Saxon Australia with the mainstream media ban in place without this. The power brokers over east would not be happy. Their investors in America and Europe would be ropeable.

He had so much to do. Speeches to prepare, a website to update, doors of homes and businesses to knock, Greenies to troll. When the phone rang, he left it. It would only be another protestor or some other lefty leech of a journo wanting a quote. Things were so bad that occasionally he dreamed he still had his old job driving Transperth buses. Life was simpler back then, less stressful, dictated by the tight travel schedule. Of course, dealing with Indigenous, migrant and bogan lowlifes had been a drag, but lately even that seemed a breeze to what he had to put up with standing as a member for the WADL.

Dirk closed his laptop. His intern had already knocked off. He wasn't planning on going to the Civic Hotel tonight for karaoke, but he needed some release. He triple locked the office door, making sure to set the alarm. Out in the car park, it was raining hard. His body shrank when he saw the old familiar pile-up of glass on the bitumen. His car windows were smashed again. Fucking boongs was the first thought that came to mind. Or socialist pigs doing it for a wind-up.

Dirk knew the drill. He extended the sleeves of his jacket so they came over his hands and carefully scooped out as much of the glass as he could without cutting himself. He would get the smaller pieces tomorrow with a brush and a vacuum.

By the time he piled into the old Astra, he was soaked. He got his girth settled into the familiar ass groove of the seat. He winced as a shard that he must've missed pierced his cotton business pants. Cheap Chinky shit, he cursed.

Wound or no wound, he was definitely going to the Civic now to cut loose. He needed it before he did somebody some harm.

Dirk shivered on the drive there, the July wind howling through each of the broken windows, cutting through his soaked clothes into his very soul. He was glad to arrive and enter the warmth of the welcoming pub at the top end of Beaufort Street. He ordered his usual lemon, lime and bitters and gave a nod to the other regulars. Jeff, who ran the night. Bob, whose speciality was hair metal. Izzy, a Madonna freak. Roderick, who had hair like a young Rod Stewart and loved singing the sixties, along with the hoard of semi-regulars who came and went. They were congenial, had known each other for years, and yet no one really knew each other outside the hours of eight till eleven p.m. every Thursday. Nobody knew where the others lived, what they worked as, or anything tangible about them, and this was just the way they liked it.

And then there was someone else there. A huge man, bigger than Dirk even. A black man in a chunky red turtleneck sweater. Fucksake, muttered Dirk. This was karaoke. Couldn't white people have just one thing to themselves?

Dirk scribbled down his request. The song he always started with. The artist he always covered. He ordered a bowl of wedges with extra salt to help his throat and watched the others go through their numbers as he primed himself for action.

'And now,' Jeff the compère announced from the sound desk. 'We have Clyde with ''Sexual Healing''.'

Who? Dirk's knees weakened. He had to hold on to the bar to support himself. Marvin Gaye was *his* thing. 'Sexual Healing', 'I Heard it Through the Grapevine', 'What's Going On?'.

The regulars turned to Dirk with a mix of raised eyebrows and devilment, aware that someone was pissing on his territory. He tried to laugh it off, but beneath the shit-eating grin, he was dying.

The intro began. The big guy grabbed the mic, took a deep breath, and let fly.

And he absolutely nailed it.

Even Dirk, as intolerant as he was, had to agree that if you closed your eyes, it was like being in the same room as the Motown God himself.

The lights were dimmed, but everyone in the room appeared to be making 'O' shapes with their mouths. Each of them liked to think of themselves as good, but it was rare, if ever, that someone walked in and was this effortlessly sublime.

'Good luck topping him,' Alan said in his pink chiffon shirt and quiff, waiting his turn to sing Elvis hits all night long.

Dirk wanted to throttle him, but conceded he was right. He was beat. Even if the guy on stage left the bar right after, he would always be remembered as owning Marvin Gaye in the karaoke stakes. And Dirk would forever be known as second best. Dirk was good, of course, but that was just it. He was *good*, and against this pro, that meant nothing.

The problem was that Dirk didn't do any other stuff. He couldn't do any other stuff because he didn't know any other stuff. If he was honest, he didn't really like any other music apart from Marvin Gaye. He was *the* man. His man. Marvin Gaye was what he lived for. But seeing this stranger hitting those high notes effortlessly and with such swagger, Dirk knew it was all over.

Dirk took a final sip of his drink, pushed his wedges aside, and removed himself from the stool. He headed for the car park, knowing he could never come back to the Civic Hotel ever again.

He edged into the cold, wet car and got the engine going on the second attempt. Then he felt the tears come. He needed his Thursday night karaoke. He didn't play footy or golf or have any friends. He had to sing Marvin so bad, so very bad, now more than ever. And now he could never have it.

His phone rang. 'Hi, Dirk,' his fiancé said.

'Hi, Hareem,' he replied, trying not to cry. He wiped his nose with his sleeve but forgot about the glass lodged in there and winced as it scratched his skin.

'Are you okay? I have a bad feeling you're not okay.'

'I'm not,' he blubbered. 'I've had another awful day.'

'You come home now, yeah.'

'Yes, my love.'

'I make your favourite laksa.'

'Okay, my love.'

'I love you, you big jerk.'

'I love you too, babycakes.'

With blood spurting out from his left bum cheek, and now with his nose and lips smeared with scratches too, Dirk longed to be home. After dinner he'd put on Marvin Gaye and sing along on his own mic and dance with Hareem. And try to forget about his awful day campaigning for the WADL and all about how difficult it was getting the party started out west.

Damn that big eight-ball singing Marvin Gaye. Damn the whole universe. Why were people so stupid?

Why was everyone against him?

FREMANTLE

Alberto did not like winter.

'But why?' Luigi asked over coffee and dominoes at Gino's cafe. 'The winter here is good, sometimes like European summer. But the summer, the summer is hell.'

Alberto could not agree. Forty degrees was no problem. Okay, when it got over that it became a bit much, but most of the summer was a joy. This, however, *this* he didn't like. When it was grey and dreary. When the wind whisked off the Indian Ocean and rifled through the old harbour town, skewering right through you. This was hell. Hell for old people. Not the summer, when all you needed was a shirt and shorts, a hat and a bottle of water.

It didn't help that the old men insisted on sitting outside. Then again, the cafe felt the same in winter as it did in summer, always too stuffy, too claustrophobic. He needed to be outside in the air no matter how cold. The others felt the same, watching the traffic and the bluster out on the street. It didn't match his memories as a young boy in Palermo, yet it wasn't a million miles away.

When he left his house, he needed to fill his head with noise. He needed to soak up the light and colour and inane conversation of his Freo with each of his senses so that when he returned to his big, empty and draughty home, he had something to lean on to get him through the long, sleepless night ahead.

Across the street, he could see Bertini's, his old fruit and veg shop. The one his son now ran. Alberto missed his customers, the restaurant chefs and the cafe owners who'd come in religiously, always at the same time, who he'd put his best produce aside in exchange for free coffees, tasty sandwiches and cakes. He missed being known by everyone. Respected. Having something purposeful to do in this town.

It all ended five years ago. His son, Paulo, told him seventy years was too old to be running the store. That mistakes were being made. That the business wasn't growing the way it should, the way it could. Whatever the hell that meant. Alberto was just a semi-literate fruiterer. Yet, he'd done alright for four decades, putting food in his children's bellies, a roof over their heads and providing them with the best education dollars could buy. Still, a deal was a deal. Paulo took over and Alberto was retiring.

Alberto knew from afar it had not gone to plan for his son. The power of the supermarket duopoly was growing. Fremantle rents were on the rise, and with the old man no longer at the wheel, the business lost many of its loyal customers. Alberto tried to advise, he even offered to come back and work for free. But Paulo was adamant he was now running the show, and the old man's services were no longer required.

Alberto looked up from the last of his long black and saw her walking out of the bakery on South Terrace. She was carrying a white paper bag with a seeded loaf poking through the top. In her other hand was a black flute case. She was wearing a thick green camel-hair coat to foil the cold, worn over a short black dress. Her legs would have been cold were it not for her grey stockings with tiny ladybirds on them.

And then there were the shoes. Bright red patent leather kitten heels with a bow on the front and a buckle just above. The girl wore them well, the slight heel elevating her slender frame as she bobbed past the shoppers and beggars, deftly avoiding the litter and the puddles, her long dark hair with the red ribbon blowing in the breeze.

Hearing the music of the 'Tarantella' in his head, Alberto placed two two-dollar coins onto the table, lifted his Dockers cap and set off after her. He looked downwards all the way, careful not to lose those red shoes.

He didn't have to chase hard. The girl had stopped by the side of the pavement to speak with a young guitar player with his hair cropped and bleached, whom she appeared to know.

Alberto leaned against a lamppost. With her back to him, he got a good view of the shoes. They were not new shoes, yet they did not look old. They were shoes that had lived. He could see the heels had been recently rebuilt. The leather near the left toe showed light folds and creases developed over time, but the red polish, freshly applied, gave these imperfections a dignified gleam. Alberto worried what the weather, this dastardly weather, would do to them.

'Now, you look like a man who's seen it all.' A tall boy with a Scandinavian accent, his fresh face looking like it had never met with a razor, towered over him. 'A man who knows. A man who cares. Could I talk with you about Doctors Without Borders for a sec?'

The boy had tried this exact approach twice over the past fortnight and was each time met with the same cool response. Everyone must treat them like this, with disdain. These vultures must get immune to it, Alberto thought. For four decades, Alberto gave his excess fruit and veg to the less fortunate on the streets of Fremantle. He'd done his best to save humanity.

He craned his neck and looked around the boy's slender frame and his blank blue eyes to the busker who was tuning up. The girl was gone. He hurried around the boy and along the street. Damn hyenas trying to rob an old man of his pension. What did someone like him care about doctors in places he'd never been? Finding her was what mattered.

He was cut off by a school group. Thirty young children in matching blue and yellow tracksuits, led by a portly woman with greying curls and a flushed face looking old before her time. Alberto dodged past them, feeling sprightly for a man of his years. Must be a lifetime of greens, he smiled. Thank God he didn't become a butcher or a baker. Things could have been different.

Then his smile died as he thought of his poor wife and how anyone in this cruel world can be dealt a bad hand whether you join the dots or not.

He spotted the red shoes entering the supermarket. He knew it would be best if he waited outside, but the rain had started again.

He walked through the electric doors, the heat bringing life to his tired bones. He needed milk and cat litter. The cat was getting old like him and shitting more than normal. It was softer and lighter and harder to clean. What would the cat be now? Seventeen? He didn't want to think about it. He wouldn't miss all that shit and those cat hairs between his sheets, in his carpets and in his food. But he would miss Donatella's companionship and how she was always there and always listened.

The girl took one of the larger baskets, the ones with the wheels at the bottom. Alberto knew from experience she would be a little while, so he went and got the litter — the clumping kind which Donatella's preferred — then his milk. Milk seemed to get cheaper by the year. He wished everything else would.

Alberto coughed. This bloody damp. Feeling something in his throat, he picked up a small tub of Vicks. His eye then caught his favourite Old Gold chocolate on display — rum and raisin — and he couldn't resist. He'd packed on a few pounds over winter, but wasn't that a good thing at his age?

Alberto spotted distinctive wet footprints on the tiles caused by the shoes' outline and found the girl in the fruit and veg section perusing the mushrooms. It an-

gered him that someone so bright would buy their produce from here. It was overpriced, second-rate rubbish,
sprayed with God knows what.

He purchased his goods at the checkout, always at
the checkout, never those self-service machines which
seemed to be everywhere, and walked out the doors to
wait. He could see her purchasing rolling tobacco at the
front counter. If he'd known her better, he would have
stopped her. Smoking was unhealthy nowadays, unlady-
like, and the reason he had to live the rest of his life
alone. He hoped they were for someone else.

The girl walked out onto the main street, the two
hessian long-life bags by her sides balancing her. She
turned left and Alberto followed, careful to remain at
least twenty paces behind. She passed the old Myer
building, the church, then the site of the ballroom where
he and his wife went dancing. More bland grey apartments were going up in its place. His Freo had altered
so much in half-a-century and was changing even more
rapidly with each passing year.

She stopped at the florists. Alberto waited out front.
It was small in there, even with the absence of other
customers. He took off his glasses and wiped away the
thick drops of rain gathered on the lens.

The girl emerged moments later with a puppy in her
arms. Something small and brown and white. Alberto
hated dogs, ever since he'd been bitten as a child by a
stray mutt. His index finger trailed along the side of his
thumb. To this day he could still feel the beast's teeth
marks. His left thumb could follow where the stitches

had been hastily placed by that nurse.

This puppy was not trained. When she put it down carefully on the pavement, it displayed strength beyond its size, dragging the girl's small body along the street. He winced as he saw the heels skid along the concrete, knowing it was doing them no good.

It began to rain with fervour. The girl fished in her handbag, bringing out a small umbrella, pale green with gold dots, almost like a child's. Alberto pulled up his collar. They said the downpour was to arrive in the early evening, and he had not planned to be out this late until he saw the girl with the red shoes. He knew he should be at home, though as there was no one to go home to, there was little reason to hurry.

He followed her along the back streets. The girl searched her bag again, this time finding her keys. She walked up the steps to a block of units looking onto the old prison. She opened the door, letting the dog in first, and then peeked behind to where Alberto stood. The old man quickly moved behind a tree. He saw her remove the shoes, place them on the doormat, and enter.

Alberto stayed where he was. He could see the shoes lying soggy on the mat. They shouldn't be there, he thought. They should be inside. Should be stuffed with newspaper and left to dry at a safe distance from a heater. It's no good for the leather, for their shape. They wouldn't see another winter at this rate.

The curtains jerked back an inch. Alberto imagined going and grabbing the shoes and taking them back to where they would be safe.

The door opened, and a young man bounded out. He descended the steps towards Alberto. He had a builder's body with broad shoulders breaking out of his sleeveless shirt, the drab weather of little concern to him. It was too late for the old man to flee. He turned the other way, pretending to be preoccupied by something on the other side of the street, although with what he didn't know. The only thing he achieved was getting splashed by a Red Rooster delivery car zooming past, which he saw too late.

'Mister. Excuse me, mister,' the younger man called. Alberto stared straight ahead at the blue door on the house across the street, the colour of the Azzurri.

'You have to stop this,' he came around, blocking the old man's vision. 'You have to stop following her, do you hear?'

Alberto didn't look at him. He walked away, briskly. Maybe the young Australian brute would think he was deaf or stupid. He didn't want trouble. He was no longer strong enough for any trouble.

It was a few hundred metres before he realised he was walking in the wrong direction. Still, he didn't want to go back in case the man was still there. He'd have to walk the long way home.

When he got there, the sky was black, and he was soaked through. He should have worn his Dockers anorak along with his fisherman's jumper. He removed his old loafers and left them by the mat. No one would steal them. They weren't worth drying. The soles were worn away, the evidence there in his damp socks.

He opened the door to his home. He turned the heater on, all five bars firing up. He stripped down to his vest and pants, and put on his thick flannelette pyjamas and dressing gown. He fed Donatella and stroked her gently. She had grown skinnier. He picked up more of the soft shit, trying to ignore the traces of red mucus through it. He'd buried many cats during his time, and it never got easier. As he replaced her litter with the contents of the fresh bag, he said a silent prayer that she would make it through the winter. It was always easier to lose a pet during the summer months when the sun was strong and you didn't rely on them curling up on your lap when it was cold. Alberto wondered if he would get another cat. It would have to be an older one. He was well-aware he wouldn't outlive a kitten.

He scrubbed his hands before reaching towards the fridge and removing a half-can of minestrone that was left in a Tupperware container. He reheated it, scooped it into a bowl, and sat in front of the heater with the soup perched on a tray. *Today Tonight* was still on. Something about a window cleaner who they'd caught on camera stealing his customers' underwear. What was happening to the world?

Alberto dozed, tired from walking, not wanting to hear anymore, and not in the mood for eating. The cat lay on his lap, feeling much the same.

Alberto saw his wife in his dreams, as he often did. Dancing the 'Tarantella' on the ballroom floor. Drunk with love and happiness and hope for what lay ahead here in the New World. Before they got married, had children and became weighed down by the business. Before she was old and gone.

The phone rang. He jumped, scaring the cat who clawed his pyjama bottoms before scurrying under the couch for safety. Alberto cursed it as he examined the new pull on the soft fabric. He answered. He guessed who it would be. The only person it ever was.

'Hello, Gina.'

'Hello, Dad,' his daughter's voice sprang down the line. She sounded tired. He could hear balls bouncing off walls and thundering footsteps in the background and knew she was at indoor soccer with her children. Her husband was probably working late at Bertini's in Coogee, the new store Paulo had given him to manage. Why didn't he get *him* to oversee it? Alberto knew about the business. Steve was a mechanic. A South African mechanic. What the hell would someone from there know about fruit and veg?

'Are you well?' she asked, more out of habit than out of love or curiosity.

'I'm good. What's wrong?' Gina only ever called when something was up or she needed money, which was often.

'Dad. The police have called again.' The old man sat back down. 'You have to stop this. You have to let it go. The couple said next time they're going to prosecute.'

Albert paused. 'I . . . I, I don't know what you're talking about.'

'It's been two years now, Dad. You have to clear out the rest of her stuff. I can help.'

'No. No, it's okay.' His eyes stung. 'I'm sorry. I stop. I'm just old and silly. I get confused.'

'Promise you won't go to that girl's house again. Promise me, Dad.'

He sighed. He felt a heavy sadness he hadn't experienced since the day of the funeral. 'Yes, yes. I stop.'

'Promise me.'

'I promise.'

'Good, then.'

'Is everything alright? The kids, they are good?'

'They're fine.'

'You need some money?'

'We're okay this month, thanks.'

'Can I see you? The children?'

'This week isn't great.' A whistle sounded down the line. 'I have to go, Dad. Remember what we talked about? Remember the promise?'

'Yes, yes, I remember. I love you.'

She'd already hung up. The cat sat on the armchair across, licking herself and purring contentedly. Alberto moved towards the bedroom. He had not slept there since the ambulance took her and she never came home. He had not been in there since Gina had made him take something, anything — in the end, those red shoes — to Saint Vincent de Paul.

On his way, Alberto removed a box of bin liners from the bottom drawer in the kitchen. He entered the bedroom and switched on the light. It still worked. There was a musty smell from the lack of fresh air, but everything was much the same as they'd left it. The framed poster of Pope John Paul II on the wall. The still life picture of the bowl of pears her departed brother had painted. The bed was still made, nice and tight like his wife had learned during her first job as head house-keeper at The Esplanade.

Alberto opened the wardrobe door. There was a thin layer of dust on the handle. Inside were fur coats and ball gowns and dresses of every colour. His Fran loved clothes, making many of them herself.

He carefully lifted a handful of shirts and cardigans on hangers and placed them into a bin liner. Memories of dances and evenings filled with passion flooded back. He took a handful of the colourful silk scarves and posi-tioned them on top.

He lowered himself cautiously to his knees and ex-amined the shoe rack. The first pair was missing, but there were another two-dozen pairs. High heels, boots, sandals, all handmade and well looked after. He lifted them and placed them into a bag of their own.

He filled three black bags to the brim. He would take them to the High Street's Saint Vinnies first thing.

He was tired, yet felt for the first time in a long time that he'd achieved something, that he was getting some-where. He didn't know why he'd let it get to this. Didn't know why he'd waited so long. The girl's boyfriend, the police, Gina, they were all right. It was unfair to put this on the young girl. He should have given away more than just the red shoes. He should have given away the lot to let more women put his wife's clothes to good use.

Alberto glowed inside at the joys of what the changing seasons would bring as he watched the girls of Fremantle ghosting around the old harbour town.

MARANGAROO

'It's gonna be a bit weird, but ... '

'He's our mate.'

'Yeah, who we haven't seen in a year.'

'It'll be the same as it's always been.'

'Only not,' Neal said, checking his phone. 'He's ten minutes late. He was always early. Always the first one here.'

John polished the head of his one-wood with vigour. He shared his friend's anxiety at seeing Carl again, but didn't want to show it. What had he been doing all year? Why had he cut himself off from them? And yeah, why was he late? He worried about the state they might find him in, and how much he might be suffering from the death of his wife, Eleanor, who he'd lost a year ago to breast cancer. And just why he hadn't returned their calls.

The two men waited in the car park for Carl. And they waited ...

'This is rubbish,' Neal said, checking his phone again. 'I gotta meet Cath in Bunnings at two.'

'What's she wanting this time?'

'A new pergola.'

'What's wrong with the one we fitted last year?'

'That was five years ago. It's not long enough now and doesn't go with the new garden furniture she's got in for Christmas.'

'Shit the bed. Life sounds a riot round yours.'

Neal shook his head in agreement. 'Mate, you don't know the half of it.'

They cut their losses and went in, making a start on the round. They figured Carl had probably been waylaid by another wave of grief, or he didn't have the cash or something.

'I'll go round there when we finish,' John said. 'See if there's any movement in his old joint.'

Just as John lined up his well-buffed club to drive the ball up the fairway, they heard a car hooning into the carpark, beeping its horn. They looked and saw a vintage red Alfa Romeo Spider with its top down parking up. 'I'll go third, fellas,' shouted the driver.

It was Carl, only it didn't quite look like Carl. For starters, his hair had grown back.

'Good,' John said, surprised.

'Great,' Neal agreed.

By the time they teed off, Carl was with them. His hair looked real enough. A spray tan covered his toned, hairless arms and upper chest. He was wearing a Hugo Boss shirt and tartan pants, the type they used to rip the piss out of anyone brave enough to wear them on the course. And he was dragging new Callaway Apex clubs, which wouldn't get you much change out of a couple of grand. He'd also shed about twenty kilos.

'Brothers,' he declared, pulling them in for a hug. They'd all been friends since they were apprentices and yet they'd never, ever hugged, not even at weddings or funerals, always preferring a firm handshake. 'How've you been?'

'Good,' John said.

'Great,' Neil added.

Carl rested his buggy, put on a pair of leather gloves fresh out of their wrapping, pulled out a one-iron, then hit as sweet a drive as had ever been played off this hole. It sailed straight down the middle, landing nice and tight to the flag.

'Fucking hell,' John said.

'Not bad for someone who hasn't played in a year,' Neil agreed.

'If only, fellas. Was playing every day in the Med when Naomi and me were travelling. And since we've been back, I've been getting coached by the pro up at Lake Karrinyup.'

'Who's the pro?' Neal asked.

'Who's Naomi?' John followed.

As they putted through the first few holes, Carl told them how he'd met Naomi at a spa soon after the funeral. She was a beautician, younger, in her late-thirties. So, when he got a million-dollar life insurance pay-out, which he wasn't expecting, unaware that Eleanor had bumped it up before she fell sick, they decided to go sailing around Europe.

'Where've you been since you got back?' John asked. 'I pass your house every day. And I never see you in the shops or the tav.'

'I bought an apartment off St Georges Terrace. Yeah, Naomi swore by city living.' Carl putted for par. 'You know me. We're kids of the 'burbs, right? But Perth is really something now. The quality of cuisine is quite phenomenal. And those new small bars are vibing.'

Vibing? John glanced at Neal with a raised eyebrow and then back at their old friend, standing there with his hair and his tan and his new golf wear, his fruity aftershave pollinating the breeze.

There was little doubt that Carl had played a heap of golf. While the other two were taking five, six and sometimes seven shots to putt, Carl was more often than not achieving par. On the seventh hole, he even got a birdie. He was usually the poorer player of the three, but by the fifteenth hole, he was sitting on an impressive five-over.

'What's your new chick like?' Neal finally asked, landing the ball in the bunker on his second shot on the 16th.

'She's got my whole life on track,' Carl replied. 'It's exactly what I needed.'

'Just a bit surprised you shacked up so soon,' John said. 'I know after twenty-five years of marriage I'd at least want to play the field for a year or so. See what's out there.'

'It's not like that with Naomi. She's so ... so open.'

'How'd you mean?' Neal asked as they strolled down the fairway.

'Well ... ' Carl looked around to check no one was listening, despite there being no one in sight. 'We have an open relationship.'

'A *what*?' John's old trolley got stuck in a divot, causing him to stumble.

Carl whispered. 'We visit this swingers club twice a month, so I feel like I get the best of every world.'

Neal stopped dead. 'You mean you get to poke other women?'

'Countless other women. Much younger women too.'

Then John stopped. 'You mean you let her poke other blokes?'

Carl walked on, either not hearing or ignoring the question. 'I tell ya, fellas. Heaven? The man upstairs can keep it.'

John and Neal followed, a geyser of thoughts and questions bouncing through their heads.

Carl turned. 'Have you guys ever made a porno?'

Neal's toe hit a rock, and he fell face-first onto the turf. John kept walking, pretending he hadn't heard.

By the 18th hole, both John and Neal had got their fairly typical twelve and fourteen over-par respectively, while Carl had beaten them with a cool seven-over.

'Tripp won't be happy,' Carl said, zipping the covers back on his clubs.

'Who's Tripp?' Neal asked.

'My coach. I got a six-over at Karrinyup yesterday. But I did have my own caddy. Plus, it's such a smooth course. Not like this goat track. You fellas will have to come down and play. It's members-only, but I can sign you in.'

They headed towards the clubhouse.

'Beer,' John told them. 'We always have beers.'

'I can't, no,' said Carl.

'How come?' John asked. 'You're not working on a Wednesday. We never work on a Wednesday.'

'Didn't I tell ya? I retired. Sold the business. Gotta pick Naomi's dog up from the groomer.'

'How much you sell it for?' As they were all butchers with their own shops, John was keen to know.

'I can't remember. Around three hundred, I think.'

'Three fucking hundred?!' John's business had been up for sale for $230,000 for the past 18 months and he hadn't had any offers approaching two-thirds that.

'I was lucky,' Carl said. 'Got out just in time.'

'But three hundred? Fuck me.'

'Yup, fellas. Things have been real good for me lately. But then, you have your wives. I'm the one who's really missing out.'

He gave them both another hug and promised to call within the month and book them in for a round at Lake Karrinyup. John stayed quiet about the idea, always preferring to stay within the safe confines of his local public course as a matter of principle, no matter how shabby its greens were.

'Isn't it awesome to see him doing so well?' Neal said, watching Carl speed off, tooting the Alfa Romeo's horn.

'Just wonderful,' John replied.

'There we were fearing he'd turn up a shell of a man, and he's killing it. Like a new bloke.'

'Hmm, ain't he just. You coming in for one or what?'

'Nah, I'm already late for Bunnings. Then we gotta see a new councillor for Miles. ADHD the school reckons. They're threatening to kick him out.'

'What happened to us ... ?' John trailed off, asking no one in particular.

'Sorry, John Boy. Next time for sure.' Neal lifted his bag and threw his clubs into the back of his rusty HiLux. 'Remember your tartan pantaloons for the country club. I'd better not bring this shit bucket, I won't get within ten clicks of the joint.' He winked, tapped the bonnet of the ute and drove off.

John entered the empty clubhouse and ordered a Crownie. He thought about his butcher's shop. A good business, lots of passing trade. It was as good as — if not better than — Carl's up in Joondalup. And yet, he couldn't even give it away in the current climate. He was the better butcher too. He'd always been more talented in all pursuits.

He ordered another stubby and gazed out at a mob of kangaroos which had emerged from the bush. He pictured quitting the shop and losing his beer gut. Getting a coach and playing golf every day for a year. He could probably turn semi-pro.

His phone rang. It was his wife. He ignored it. She knew better than to call him on a Wednesday. This was his time. He saw there were four texts from her about picking up dog food on the way home, collecting their youngest from a friend's place in Alexander Heights, about how the washing machine was leaking again, and how another brick had come loose on the side of the house and asking when he was going to get that rendering quote off his apprentice's older brother.

John sat and thought about his wife and the weight she'd put on since the children, and how they hadn't made love all year. He thought of her and imagined her getting sick. How the kids would be sad for a while, but how they'd eventually get over it, and how it could really open up a new world for him. She was as strong as an ox though, rarely even got a cold, and her parents and sisters were the same, acting like they would go on forever. Then he remembered his apprentice had got tipsy during Saturday drinks and told him he knew a few shady people who would be only too happy to bump someone off for a slice of the profits.

John ordered another cold Crownie. He smiled as he ignored the latest text from his wife and daydreamed about just how good the next chapter of his life could be.

RIVERVALE

She took her coffee out onto the decking by the pool just as she did every morning before she left for work. She sat back on the wonky sun lounger and gathered her thoughts, letting the much-needed buzz from the caffeine wake her stiff bones. Today was Christmas Day, yet it was unseasonably cloudy with a distinct lack of warmth hiding in the breeze.

Christmas Day.

She turned to the swimming pool and remembered when they'd bought it and how happy they'd all been. It had been a dream of theirs to have one for the kids when they emigrated from Ireland.

Then, there was the day it arrived on the big truck with the crane after the digger had made way for it, up-rooting those rose bushes she'd liked so much. She remembered how the kids wouldn't get out of the pool that first summer, having to be bribed with party pies and ginger beer to have a rest. Kids from down the street too. Kids she'd never seen before.

Good times. Sunscreen and chlorine. Chilled white wine and barbecues. So many good times. So many good Christmases.

Róisín sipped the warm coffee. Her mind grew lucid, allowing her to remember. Another child came along, one they didn't plan and didn't need. But she had it, and they loved it. And the others loved little Niall too. And how he loved the pool. He would squeal and flap his short legs and flutter his little arms from the get-go. Their only Australian-born child, they swore he came into this world with the ability to swim.

Chlorine and white wine. Barbecues and sunscreen. She no longer drank, but she could go a large wine right about now. A nice sav blanc.

She remembered that last Christmas. They'd been swimming all morning and into the afternoon. She'd been cooking and drinking. She needed a lie-down. She should have told her husband and went to bed. Instead, he took the older kids inside to set up the PlayStation. She thought he had Niall. He knew she did. She sprawled out on the lilo in the warm sunshine. And with a wine in her hand, she fell asleep.

Sunscreen and barbecues. Chlorine and white wine. She awoke to screams. Screams from her husband and children. And another low guttural noise which she could never forget and had never been able to place.

The paramedics did all they could, but that didn't mean much. The coroner said Niall was under for eight minutes. They thought he could swim. They were wrong.

Róisín finished her coffee. She looked at the drained pool, bone-dry, its base showing a furry layer of green moss, its edges eaten by black damp. She hadn't wanted to come back to the house, but no one wanted to buy it. They'd all seen the news. When she eventually got out of the psychiatric unit, there was nowhere else to go and no one to go to. Her husband had remarried and moved down to Bridgetown. Her kids had grown up and settled over east.

Sunscreen, chlorine, barbecues and white wine. She lifted her mug and walked towards the sliding door, away from the outside. She tried to remember in every gorgeous detail the laughter and good times the family had out here. The times which came to an end ten years back.

But she couldn't, she never could. Whenever she tried, that noise overcame everything. It seemed to stem from between her ears. And the only time it really gave out was during her shift manning the switchboard at the State Operations Centre, helping other poor souls who needed it.

Work was the only thing that could shut out that noise.

BOORAGOON

Vincent didn't drive. When he was seventeen and his friends were on their P's, his dad wouldn't let him learn in his prized Jag that he'd gotten from his own father, so Vincent just never got round to it. He also had environmental and ethical concerns. Not to mention that he was a keen reader, and the absence of a car allowed him to devour every horror paperback he could get his hands on.

But the main reason Vincent didn't drive was because he loved public transport. He knew the 160 bus timetable to the city by rote and looked forward to lazing on the backseat each day, soaking in the views of the Swan River from the Narrows, and reading or re-reading his favourite authors. Simple joys he wouldn't get to experience if he was crouched over a wheel, strung out as part of the rat-race.

However, as Vincent moved out of his teens and left the cosy confines of tertiary education, he discovered that catching public transport was frowned upon. He had qualified as a pharmacist, yet every job he applied for required the same:

You must have a C-Class driver's licence.

He could never work out why as he would be work-ing solely within the premises and getting there via pub-lic transport was no trouble for him, it was a pleasure, in fact. Still, no matter how many times he reiterated this to prospective employers, they never listened.

Then, there was his extended family. At every gath-ering they'd fret about how he was going to get to and from whoever's house they were attending.

'You're going to walk to the bus stop in *this* heat?' his chubby cousins would sneer, despite the stop being at the end of the road.

And then there were girls. Whilst friends would rip him about his love for public transport just for some-thing to do, the same couldn't be said for the dating scene. At first, the particular member of the fairer sex might find it quirky that their new interest would bus and train it to dates and parties. But eventually the joke would wear thin and they'd be embarrassed, especially when their friends were around.

'So, seriously, when are you going to get a car?'

No one noted how he could already afford a deposit on a unit with the money he'd saved on car repayments and fuel costs, or that Perth had one of the best pub-lic transport systems in the country. Vincent considered moving to Melbourne or someplace like London, New York or Tokyo where commuters shared his passion for PT, and those who drove were considered the odd ones out, but he knew it wasn't a long-term solution.

Unable to secure a job in his chosen field, or find a steady girlfriend, Vincent was forced to hold on to his casual post at Timezone in Northbridge, and he became depressed. He knew there was only one solution. And so, he took his savings and used them to buy his own small car, paid for lessons and bade farewell to daydreaming across the Swan River and reading Clive Barker novels, trading them for the *Drive Safe* handbook and Mix 94.5 like everyone else.

Vincent was a competent driver and took to his new life seamlessly. He quickly secured a position in a pharmacy in Yokine and found himself a steady girlfriend in one of the shop assistants, a young Canadian traveller who didn't have a car, so that worked out well.

It was on his way home after dropping her off after dinner and a movie that Vincent's time on this planet expired. His Nissan Micra was mashed into the parapet of the Narrows Bridge by the back-end of an out-of-control 160 bus whose driver, two months away from retirement, had suffered a heart attack at the wheel. Vincent died instantly, the Transperth vehicle bursting into flames upon impact. A mother on the left-hand back seat of the bus suffered third-degree burns and died a week later. An East Timorese exchange student on the opposite side was thrown so hard, she obtained a spinal injury and doctors told her she'd never walk again.

It was the 23:25 bus from the city, the one Vincent would have been on, sat on one of its rear seats had he still been at Timezone and not learned to drive and not got that job as a pharmacist. All those girls and all those pharmacies who turned him down wouldn't have made that connection, but the irony of it all gave those family members who felt guilty some solace as they drove to the funeral service.

SPEARWOOD

Andy checked his GPS again, cursing at how the thing had a mind of its own and how he still couldn't figure it out.

He was in the City of Cockburn. They'd been in Australia eight months, yet he'd never ventured this far south of the river before. All the jobs that came through the housing authority were up near him, Joondalup way. The bosses ran it like that so you didn't spend half your day in your van driving around. Recently though, there'd been a big spike in repairs that needed doing all over the metro area. One of the other carpenters mentioned it was to do with Christmas having just been and gone. That and the heat. This maddening heat which seemed to send everyone over the edge, their houses bearing the brunt of it one way or another.

Andy didn't much like the northern suburbs. His wife said it was where all the British migrants went, so that's where they headed. Affordable housing, close to the beach, surrounded by your fellow country folk. But it wasn't for Andy. Andy loathed it. The stifling weather, the flies, how the Australians failed to understand the

Glaswegian accent, or worse, the ballsier ones — oddly, it was always women — who would mimic it. Then there were the Brits themselves. Rejects the lot of them, dragging their old problems and shitty working-class habits 12,000 miles away with them. Most having no new experiences, just poor imitations of old ones in warmer climes.

Andy was already feeling adrift down here with a wife desperate for them to pay off the mortgage and climb the ladder (what ladder?), a thirteen-year-old daughter who had taken to hanging around the local boys at the shopping centre, and a ten-year-old son who was getting mercilessly bullied because of his autism.

And there were no pubs. The nearest one was a ten-minute drive from him. Not on the street corner, but a *drive*. Plus, the price of a pint was near double what it was in The Baird, where he drank in Scotland. Sharon wasn't a fan of him drinking at home either, limiting him to a mere six-pack and one bottle of wine a week, to be consumed between them during weekend meals. She defended her reasons saying she wanted things to be different here. Didn't want him on the piss all the time like back home.

Sharon had said a lot of things to get them to come out. She said they'd have a pool. There was no pool. Said they would visit Scotland once a year. It looked like many years before they would get that kind of money together, despite the favourable exchange rate. And she said that with his experience in the building game, he'd be sure to be a manager or a supervisor and wouldn't be anywhere near a hammer. Yet here he was, driving a van and on the tools, doing odd repairs for undesirables courtesy of the public housing department.

The GPS informed him he was in Spearwood now. He turned down a side-street. With its older cars, run-down bungalows and a squad of mean-looking FUBU-wearing teens on BMXs, this part of the suburb, even to Andy from Glasgow's east-end, looked rough. At least Sharon hadn't moved them here.

He pulled up in front of the address at the end of the street and let out a sigh. It was the worst he'd seen since he'd started. There were children's toys and broken bikes spread out on a barren lawn which had lost its battle to the cloudless sky and incessant sun long ago. In the driveway an old Ford was stripped of its windows and engine, perched high on bricks. Fucksake, Andy thought. He should be back at home doing his old job, doing the flooring on new builds. Tonight Celtic were playing Aberdeen at home. He'd have been going. Having a few beers in The Baird on the walk there. A few sneaky more before he walked home. And yet here he was in an area the likes of which even his wife's family wouldn't piss in.

He opened the van door and grabbed his toolbox, making sure to lock the vehicle. He read the job sheet as he walked towards the doorbell. *'Yuralla family - broken front door'*. Andy was face-to-face with it. It wasn't broken. It was taken clean off its hinges, kicked in by the looks of the boot marks near its base.

'Hello,' Andy called in, knowing a knock would send it crashing to the floor. He waited. No answer. He got to work, unlatching the toolbox to see if he had new hinges that would fit. He took out a cordless drill and removed the old set attached to the frame.

'And who are you?' boomed a voice from inside.

'The milkman,' Andy couldn't resist.

A big, black, bearded face appeared from around the corner. Andy had never met anyone Aboriginal before. Or, at least, *this* Aboriginal. He believed that men like this man only existed in the desert. The big, black bearded face stared at him. And then it broke into a laugh so fierce Andy feared he might pass out, as the man gripped the door frame to keep from wobbling over.

'The milkman. The bloody milkman,' he cackled. 'You're alright by me, chippie. Beer?' The man with the big beard and even bigger gut held out a red can of Hammer N Tongs.

'I'd better not, pal. On the job and that, y'know.'

'Course, mate, course. Important to maintain a professional air at all times when you're on the clock.' He squeezed past Andy onto the veranda, parking himself on the faded floral couch that had seen more than the occasional spill. 'Mind if I smoke?'

'It's your place.'

'Actually, I think you'll find it's *your* place.' He lit a roll-up he had prepared and inhaled, satisfied. 'Or is it Homeswest's? Or the government's? Who can keep up? Ah, who even cares. However, I do appreciate the sentiment.'

'Nae bother,' Andy said in between the squeal of the drill.

'You Scotch?

'Scottish, aye.'

'I ain't ever left these fair shores, but I can always tell an accent. Been here long?'

'Since June.'

'Like it much?'

'You want an honest answer?'

'I'll have to settle for whatever answer you give.'

'I don't. No really, no.'

'And why not, Scotch?'

'How long've you got?' The bigger man laughed again. Andy continued. 'Miss my family, my pals. Everything here is just different. I mean, it tries to be the same. But it comes across as ... I don't know, not European, not Australian, just .... shite. Doesn't seem right.'

The other man stared off, lost for a moment. 'Doesn't it just.'

'I miss the football.'

'We have football.'

'Real football.'

'Ours is better.'

'I don't get the rules.'

'Easy as piss. Well, best explained over a game. Bulldogs are my team back home. Played 193 games for the seniors before the knee started playing up. And before this took over.' He nodded to the beer he cradled.

'I'm sure it's fine. Just with the way I'm feeling, I'm no in the mood for the place, y'know?'

The man sipped his beer, delicately, Andy thought, for someone his size. 'And your family feels the same?'

'I think if they were honest, then aye. But we're each in our own way putting a brave face on.' Andy sanded down the edges of the door in preparation for the new hinge. It wouldn't look perfect, but it would close and be lockable.

'You know,' Andy went on. 'You're one of the very few Australians I've spoken to. Definitely the first Indigenous boy.'

'And I think you're the first Scotchman I've ever spoken to. Poms, they're ten-a-penny. Paddys too. But not the Scotch. Not down this way.' The man opened the esky positioned by his feet. 'Have a beer with me. You can still do your work.' He held a cold one out to Andy. 'Go on.' He waved it about as he peered up at the tall gum tree swinging in the breeze with a kookaburra singing up top. '*It is a beautiful day in the City of Cockburn,*' he sang along to the bird's tune, pronouncing the name of the suburb phonetically.

It was after midday. It was Andy's lunchtime. It was Friday, and Andy was thirsty. 'Ah, go on then.'

'Good man.'

Andy held the icy can in his palm. He opened it, the bubbles dripping heavenly onto his lips before they slid onto his tongue and down his throat. He hadn't had a drink since he'd finished his weekly allocation of beers on Tuesday night.

'I'm Bill,' the man cheered him.

'Andy.'

'This is meant to be blackfella land, but I don't feel like I belong either.'

'How's that?'

'This ain't my country.'

'I was told it was.'

'There's about five hundred nations of Aboriginal peoples in what you mob call Australia.'

'Shite.' Andy felt embarrassed not knowing this, thought it should be compulsory for new arrivals.

'My mob aren't Noongar. They're from up the north-west way.'

Andy nodded. He'd considered applying for a job in Karratha as a caretaker for a high school, but Sharon wouldn't move that far out.

Bill looked out at the busy, airless street unkindly. 'We're salt water people. None of this traffic and pollution and shit.' He looked at his beer and for a second gave it a filthier look. 'No grog.'

'So why are you drinking?'

'To deal with the traffic and pollution and all the shit.' Bill laughed his big tobacco laugh, coughing at the end.

The door was nearly done. It wasn't great, but then again Andy was never told to do great work. Just the old in-there-out-there-plaster-over-the-wound job. The reason being limited funding. Plus, the understanding that whatever repairs there were, they'd be called back out soon enough to do them over again.

'You want another beer?' Bill crushed his can and struggled up. Andy checked his watch. He knew he had nothing on for an hour, this side of the city. He was enjoying the man's company, the lack of pretension. He'd been told by guys on the job to avoid Aboriginals if you wanted an easy ride, yet was finding this not to be the case.

'Ah, go on then.'

'Right answer again.' Bill handed it over and they cracked the beers. Andy took a seat on the worn wicker chair across from the man, careful not to break it.

'I'm sorry about the door,' Bill said.

'Gotta earn my wage some way.'

Andy had also been told during his first-day briefing not to converse with tenants as to how their property got damaged. This was not their job.

Bill took a healthy sip. He was tipsy, though he handled it well. 'She brings me down all this way. I can't get work. I don't know anyone. And then she locks the doors on me. On the one night of the week I go out. And now she's gone to a refuge. Takes the kids from me too. Says she can't live with a volatile man. Whatever that means.'

'Right.'

'What do you do with your woman, Scotch, when she plays up?'

'Marriage is a series of capitulations.'

Bill laughed and swung forward, cheersing him again. 'Ain't that the truth.'

'I dunno. Mine wants to make a go of it here. Try something different. I can see why.'

'What about us, though?' Bill jabbed his thumb into his own chest. 'What about us?'

'I'm still working that out.'

'Me too, Scotch. Me too.'

They drank. The kookaburra had stopped serenading them. The men enjoyed the silence, at ease in each other's company.

Bill stubbed out his butt and cleared his throat. 'I hated Perth twenty years ago. Was here with my cousin who was working. It was then that I met her. The first thing I did when I knew things were serious was tell her we had to move to my land. She agreed on the proviso that we'd come back to Perth when her old dears' time was nearing its end.' He finished his beer. 'And we did when they got sick two years ago. And they're still holding on, and we're still here.' Bill reached into his cooler. His hand reappeared empty. 'I'd offer you another, but I'm out. I can head to the bottle-o?'

'No, pal. I best be going. It's my buy, anyway. Next time.'

'Yeah,' Bill grinned, a hint of mischief in his eyes. 'The back door's hanging off its hinges. Don't think it'd take much to pop these cracked windows, either.'

'Is that right?' Andy smiled.

'Yeah, might be nice to get you down here for a few days. I'll help you tidy the place up. I'm a handyman as well. A nice lick of paint. New sofa from the Salvos. It might bring Bron back.'

'Sounds like a plan. I'll log it before I finish if you want?'

Bill winked. 'Now you're talking.'

Andy thought it would be nice too, instead of heading to those dodgy drug dens where he had to keep both eyes on his tools rather than the job at hand. Or those staid government buildings dealing with all those broken souls in shirts and ties. Plus, there'd be a few beers in it, not too many because they'd be working and he'd be driving, but a couple wouldn't hurt. And a bit of conversation along the way.

The men shook hands. 'See you, Bill.'

'See you, Scotch. A fine job you've done here. And I'll need to take you to a real football game one Saturday.'

'Indeed, you will.'

Andy unlocked the van, putting his toolbox in the back. He drove off, waving all the way on the road out of Spearwood, which, in actual fact, was far more pleasing to the eye than he first thought. He wasn't thinking of Scotland. He was thinking what a genuine bloke Bill had been, and how nice the day was turning out, and how the evening would be even better. He'd take his daughter and son to the beach tonight for a dip then fish and chips, as they were always asking him, but he could never be bothered. Tonight would be different. You had to make the most of all this. Embrace it. This country, the weather, these times.

That Celtic game would've been fucking freezing.

PADBURY

Angie felt the sun kiss her skin as the cool breeze from the Fremantle Doctor soothed her. She liked this weather. Sure, she preferred the vast majority of what Melbourne had to offer. Its liberalism, its passion for the arts, its superior coffee. But Perth in May was a welcome change. In a short floral op-shop dress, matched with a light burgundy cardigan and sandals, she was thankful she'd escaped the cold, damp and grey for this weather. It was worth coming all this way for.

She found the house she was looking for. 11 Breer Place. House and land package. Pajero and boat out front. It was everything she'd spent her entire life pushing against.

She took a deep breath, pressed the bell and waited. The sound of high heels approached from down the hallway.

'Hi, Angie. Long time.'

Angie was greeted and kissed by Jen Edwards, an old school pal, or rather Marcie's old school pal. Having a mutual best friend meant they had to pretend to like each other, and they'd always done a passable job of this. Angie noted that Jen had put on weight, but this was offset by a seriously impressive amount of jewellery, topped with lavish hair extensions and fragrance. Angie suddenly worried she was underdressed for the occasion and was thinking she should have had a shower when she got off the flight rather than head straight out.

'Be careful you don't slip.' Jen told her. 'I just had the floors steamed.'

Angie followed her through the double doors. They passed brass Buddhas and random wooden sculptures of animals and idols Angie couldn't make out. Probably from Bali. Every time Marcie spoke to her, she seemed to say Jen was in Bali.

'No one's here yet. You're a bit early.' Jen led her out the sliding doors to the garden. They sat at the wicker setting sheltered by an umbrella, surrounded by large burners either side turned on full-blast despite the temperate conditions.

'I thought Marcie told me three p.m.,' Angie said.

'Really? I told everyone four. She has a lot on Saturdays. Not that it matters.'

'I brought a bottle.' Angie offered it, wrapped in a plastic bag.

Jen forced a smile. 'Oh. Okay. It's not really a boozy day. We thought it wouldn't be fair to Marcie.' She reluctantly took it, placing it at the end of the table.

'Good thing I didn't bring a case of Passion Pop,' Angie laughed.

Jen didn't. 'Why would you do that?'

Angie realised it was her and Marcie's party drink of choice and couldn't remember Jen ever getting involved in their drunken escapades. 'Sorry. I wouldn't know how these things go.' None of Angie's Melbourne friends had kids, most weren't even in steady relationships.

'Well, as you've noticed, I've had a few baby showers of my own.' Jen rolled her eyes good-naturedly towards the far end of the garden. Angie hadn't noticed, but there were three white-blonde children by the back fence playing swing tennis. A boy was trying to smack his younger sister with the ball. 'Play nice, you lot,' Jen shouted half-heartedly.

Jen poured them both a glass of red punch which had brightly coloured chunks of lemon, lime and orange floating amongst the ice. 'And what brings you back from Melbourne? Apart from this, of course.' Jen would have noted how Angie hadn't ventured over for the baby shower of Marcie's now three-year-old. Angie had only met little Ray once. That was when Marcie's husband was over for work, and they came with him, squeezing in a play park visit.

Angie felt her skin prickle under all this heat. She shuffled to a softer spot on her seat and took a sip, wincing as her nerves were attacked by all the sugar, with no alcohol to settle them. 'My dad,' she finally answered.

'Is everything okay?'

'He's sick. He has, ah, motor neuron.'

'Fuck, I'm so sorry,' Jen put down her glass. 'That's still, like, really, really bad, isn't it?'

'Yeah, pretty much. He's at home at the moment. But mum's not around anymore and my brother's ... you know, so ...'

'So, you'll be back for a little while.'

Angie tried to smile. 'I'll be back for a little while.'

She brought out her pouch of tobacco, like she always did in anxious situations, and began rolling. It wasn't until she put the cigarette between her lips and produced her lighter that she noticed Jen's look. 'Sorry... can I smoke?'

'Of course, you can.' Jen tried to remain cool. She searched around. 'We don't have an ashtray. Maybe use this.' She lifted a plant pot from next to the table, placing the tray from under it before Angie as carefree as she could.

'Thanks,' Angie turned to blow the smoke over her shoulder despite the children being a good distance away.

'And if you could try to keep it off the plants too, that would be helpful. We had those imported from Far North Queensland.'

Angie felt queasy and stubbed it out. 'Actually, I had one when I got out the airport. I'll probably be alright for a bit.'

Angie had struggled to connect with Jen ever since Jen started hanging out with them — or rather, Marcie — when they took business studies together back in Year 11. Spending any time alone with her had always been ex-cruciating and now, over five years since their last meeting, this was even worse. Angie hated Marcie for doing this to her and would tell her when she saw her.

'So how is Melbourne?' Jen asked, not topping up the drinks despite both being dry.

'Melbourne is Melbourne,' Angie replied.

'You're in Carlton, right?'

'Coburg.'

'Oh.'

'You been much?'

'I'm more of a Sydney gal, to be honest. I do like Chapel Street, though.' Angie tried hard not to grimace. 'What can I say? I'm a child of the sun. Melbourne always seems a bit dreary. A bit dirty and unsafe.'

'It's not for everyone,' Angie answered, wanting to add *thank God* at the end of her sentence.

'I don't know how anyone with kids could live there.' Jen wasn't letting it go. 'But then, I'm not an artist like you.'

Angie wasn't sure if this was a compliment or a dig. Angie hadn't appeared on TV for years, not since *Play School*. She wasn't sure if Marcie had told her she'd left the theatre company and was now a teacher's assistant in the drama department of an inner-north Melbourne high school.

A roar came from inside. 'Eagles Dockers today.' Jen gave her signature roll-of-the-eyes, pretending not to care. 'Who's your team?'

'I don't really have a team.'

WA's obsessions with AFL astonished Angie. In Melbourne, the home of the game, she rarely caught sight of it. Few people seemed to talk about it or even care for it unless it was Grand Final day. But here, every home you went into, every bar, it was always on with a hoard of meatheads gathered around the screen grunting like gorillas. Angie couldn't think of anything worse to do with three hours of her life and had always avoided guys who were the sporty type.

'We probably won't see Trev and the boys,' Jen said. Angie hoped not. She didn't even want to ask about Mr Tacchi. She didn't want to know. 'Trev's good,' Jen went on as if Angie had asked. 'He's deputy head now.'

'Convenient.' Angie immediately regretted her bitter tone. 'I mean, it's just around the corner.' Angie dug at the side of her empty glass with her bitten nail. It had an old kiwi pip stuck to it, which the dishwasher had failed to dislodge. She hadn't wanted to discuss their old maths teacher, Mr Trevor Tacchi, who Jen started seeing at the end of Year 11 when she was sixteen and he was twenty-eight. This went off and on until graduation and then, when the whispers got too much, he left Padbury Senior High. Or rather, he was told to. Marcie told her shortly after she left for Melbourne that they'd got back together, married and stayed that way. And in that decade, everyone eventually came round to the idea of them being a couple. Including Marcie. Even the school took him back.

But Angie never could. She never would accept it. She sensed her spine go rigid as she remembered the way he would leer at her when she was still a child. The way he would stand over her, making her stay back after class for one of his famous 'pep talks' about how she could improve her grades in a subject area she didn't give a shit about. She was too young to realise he was trying it on, and she wasn't the only one. She'd heard stories of him driving girls home, giving them cigarettes and Stollies, going to eighteenth birthdays after they'd graduated. Jen was the only one stupid enough to settle down with him. Angie hoped the game would go on all night, and he wouldn't come out and join them. She couldn't handle that without a smoke and cracking that wine.

'Marcie should be here soon,' Jen said after Angie checked her phone again. It was ten minutes past four.

'Who else is coming?'

'It's real small, this one. It's always bigger for your first, more of a novelty.' Angie nodded along. 'A couple of girls from Marcie's work. I don't know them that well. And Chantelle. She was a couple of years younger than us. Oh, shit!' Jen slapped the table excitedly. 'Guess who's coming with her to watch the footy?'

Angie pursed her lips and gently shook her head, bracing herself for what was coming, trying to remember if it had been three days or four since she last washed her hair.

'Dale. Dale Stephens.'

Angie froze. 'Dale. Dale Stephens. Right.'

'They're engaged,' Jen added.

'Wow. Hmm, sorry, where's your bathroom?'

'Up the hallway, second on your right.'

Angie moved as briskly as possible without making a scene. Crowd noises emitted from the door on the first left. Through the gap she saw that unmistakably large head she used to see the back of when he was writing equations on the blackboard, which she never grasped. It looked lighter on the top. He was flanked by two beefy bodies, one in yellow, the other clad in purple, ogling a screen the size of the ones at Cinema Nova.

'He's open!' came a call from the sofa to the screen. 'Feed him. Fucking feed him!'

She tiptoed along and found the bathroom. She locked the door. She reached into her bag and located her tobacco pouch. Then she noticed the window locks and knew she couldn't get away with it. She put it back in her bag and found two dexies resting at the bottom. She needed something to get her through the afternoon. She swallowed them and then flushed for no reason. She washed her hands. She opened the door and slammed straight into a beer gut protruding from a wide-chest. She bounced back fearing it was Mr Tacchi, then remembered he was never this tall. She looked up and saw it was someone worse.

It was Dale.

'Oh, hey ... sorry,' he stuttered.

'No, I'm sorry ... you look well.' She said this without looking. She'd lied. Her ex looked awful, stood there in thongs, ¿ length cargo pants and a black Tapout t-shirt. He was a good thirty kilos overweight, his face, much like his gut, was blotchy and bloated. This was her first love, her first love who lived for techno, and always went on about how much he hated Perth and how he was moving over east the first chance he got. Here he was, two decades on, still living in the area and attending parties thrown at their most-hated teacher's abode.

'So do you,' he blushed. He didn't look quite as tall or as confident as how she remembered. 'I've just gotta go quick.' He edged past her into the bathroom, careful not to make contact.

'And I gotta head back to the girls,' she said to the door which had already closed.

She'd missed his body. His smile. His confidence. His zest for life. She'd measured every guy she'd dated since against him. She now realised that those traits, that guy, were gone.

Angie moved on quickly past the cinema room door.

'I tell ya, rental properties are more work than they're worth,' she heard a high-pitched voice whine outside. Angie emerged and saw a girl with long, straightened, bleach-blonde hair, and breasts so prominent in the tangerine boob tube she wore that they must have been enhanced. She'd never seen clothes like it since she last lived here.

The girl spun around, and a smile ripped across her face. 'Oh, my god! Angie! It's been so long.' She wrapped her arms around her. Angie was sure she'd never met this person. 'Sorry. I was just saying what a nightmare our new tenant's been in one of our rentals.'

Angie gave a knowing smile, despite not knowing a thing about having a 'rental'. All she knew was that she had a strong disdain for anyone who owned them as these people contributed to the housing shortage, pushing up the cost of ever buying a first home for her and her friends and people like them.

'Cheers,' the girl grinned, clinking her glass with Angie's, presenting a wide, toothy grin. So this must be Chantelle. Dale's fiance. A girl three years — or was it four? — her junior. Angie had never encountered someone this happy. 'Anyway, all that is *so* boring. I heard you're this kick-ass actor now.'

'I've done a few stage productions.'

'And you did the soaps.'

'A couple of minor roles. *Neighbours* and *Offspring* back in the day.'

Chantelle lowered her voice reverently. 'Did you know Heath Ledger?'

'No. I, um, can't say I did.'

'How about the Hemsworths?'

'Um ... friends of friends, I guess. Not my friends, sadly.'

'That is *so* cool. We should grab a coffee while you're here. Would love to pick your brains about some stuff.'

'You're an actor?'

'I do voice-overs for on-hold advertising. But this year it's my mission to branch off into film.'

'You have an agent or anything?'

'No!' She turned to Jen about to burst, instead punching her sweetly on the arm. 'See, this is why I have to talk to her!' She swung back to Angie. 'I'm teaching, that's my primary income stream.'

'Oh, right.' Angie did not want to discuss her teacher's aide post, which barely earned her the living wage.

'I'm head of drama at Padbury. Trev put me up for the job.'

I bet he did, Angie thought. This girl was a drag, but strangely Angie damn near wanted to hug her. She tried to resist the urge to pace the pavers or jump up and down. She hadn't had dexies in a while, didn't think they'd be this good, and knew it was because she hadn't eaten. She remembered Marcie and her used to neck five at once before heading to Northbridge to dance all night long. She didn't think two would be worth it, yet she was already giddy.

'So, you're thinking of moving back to the old hood?' Chantelle asked.

'I'm just here for a bit.'

'It's great for kids. You don't have kids, do you?'

Jen, who was texting, stepped in. 'It's so nice to be near your parents. Or *parent*. We couldn't have had three if the olds weren't around the corner.'

'You and Dale have kids?' Angie was curious.

'No, but we will. I'm so impressed with you not having children at your age. Still having your life. *And* not having a partner. I mean, I love Dale, couldn't imagine being without him, but sometimes you just wanna *Sex in the City* it up a bit. Am I right, or am I right?'

'Yeah, right,' Angie managed, unconvincingly.

'Wait a minute,' Chantelle stopped short, remembering something. Surely Chantelle was on amphetamines too. No one was this much of a natural livewire. 'You dated Sam Bruckley, didn't you?'

'I don't know if Angie wants to talk about that,' Jen said with a half-smile.

'Sam's a good guy,' Angie said, really not wanting to talk about him. 'It's just ... yeah, anyway, he's a good guy, let's leave it at that.' He was a good guy until he got drunk and cracked her in the throat, nearly bursting her windpipe. No, she didn't want to talk about her other ex, no matter how many Emmy-nominated HBO shows he was now on, or how many Hollywood A-listers he'd banged. Especially not to the fiancé of her first love, pills or no pills. She was paranoid about the look Jen shot her. No one knew why Sam and Angie's relationship really broke down, except for her dad, who could no longer speak. And Marcie.

'Hey, that's cool. You're in Melbourne, hey?' Chantelle appeared unable to focus on one topic for more than three seconds. 'You should totally appear on *Real Housewives of Melbourne.*'

'But she's not a housewife,' Jen answered for her again.

The conversation was interrupted by two women from Marcie's work quickly dropping off gifts of a changing table and teepee. They couldn't stay as they had another baby shower to go to. People everywhere over here were either having kids or planning kids. Chantelle confided, loudly, that she was coming off the pill right after her wedding in October.

The punch jug was empty. The shouts from inside

became louder, meaning the match had reached some dramatic juncture. Angie grinded her jaw, wishing she'd brought some Juicy Fruit, the type you could still drink with. She needed a cigarette. Where the hell was Marcie? She looked at her watch. She had to go. It wasn't like she had a choice. Her dad was due his medication before dinner, and the nurses didn't visit on weekends.

'I'll have to leave you guys.'

'Oh, no,' Chantelle whined again, really meaning it.

'I'm sorry about Marcie.' Jen got up, not trying to stop her, 'It's really unlike her. Did you drive here?'

'No.'

'Trev!' she called. 'Is the game done?'

'Pretty much.'

'Angie needs a lift.'

'No, really, I don't,' Angie pleaded.

Trevor appeared like a bolt. Angie had to hand it to him. Unlike Dale, he looked almost exactly the same, if a little thinner on top. 'Angie, so good to see you.' His arms extended, and he brought her in close. She wanted to curl up and die. He pulled back to get a good view, staring deep into her eyes. She shuddered, remembering this look. She hoped he had changed, that he didn't still give young girls this same look each day at school. 'You look terrific.'

'I've had a couple of beers, but I can still drive,' Dale said, appearing behind him.

'Oh, I don't mind that you used to date. I trust you.' Chantelle put her arm around her fiancé and giggled.

'Just no handjobs if you get stuck in traffic like old times, hey?'

Angie and Dale shared a brief, mortified look.

'I can take her,' Trevor said, laughing and giving her that old leer. 'I need to swap the gas bottle, anyway.'

'No, please,' Angie insisted. 'It's lovely of you all, it really is, but please, I'm fine. I walk all the time in Melbourne.'

'Yeah,' Trevor's smile faded. 'Never have understood that about the place.'

'Or I get the tram.'

'Good luck doing that here,' he laughed again.

Angie backtracked down the hallway towards the front door. 'Thank you for everything,' she announced to no one in particular.

Just then the front door opened and Marcie struggled in. 'I'm so, so sorry.'

She looked radiant with the basketball-shape pushing out from her belly. She rushed over to Angie and hugged her like the old friends they were.

'What happened?' Angie asked, knowing something was up.

Marcie rested her hand upon the wall. 'Ray picked up a spot of food poisoning from daycare. I thought I had it too, so we went to emergency and I forgot my phone. But it's all good. They just checked us out. I'm totally fine now. Poor little Ray-man's feeling a bit sorry for himself so I can't stay long. Mike's taken him home. Total nightmare.'

'Oh my god,' Chantelle appeared. 'Our Maltese terrier ate a half-bag of peanut M&M's at Easter and was so sick. Isn't it just the worst?'

'Come and sit down.' Jen took her arm. 'I'll get you a water.'

'I could murder a cheeky glass of red.'

'Of course. You still have to go, Angie?'

'What?' Marcie saddened. 'Please don't.'

'Oh well, if —'

'She says she has to give her dad his medication,' Jen said with some finality.

'I'll drop you there now and you can run in,' Marcie offered.

'It's late, I really should go.' Angie knew it was for the best. She didn't know if she'd be able to politely reject another ride from Mr Tacchi.

'When will we see you again?' Jen asked. 'The Christening?'

Christening? Angie couldn't get her head around how everyone here seemed so Christian all of a sudden just because they'd married into it. Weren't you supposed to become more godless the older you got? If the church knew what half the girls in her school had gotten up to before they had a ring on their finger, they would never let them or their children within a ten-K radius of God's house.

'How about my hen's in Bali?' Chantelle almost squealed with excitement. 'Us *bi-atches* are hitting the road.'

Angie didn't know where to look.

'I think Angie's got enough going on in her life right now,' Marcie smiled, trying to help.

'Or a girl's night?' Chantelle tried again.

'You bet,' Angie replied. No matter what this girl said or did, she didn't have a bad bone in her.

'Such a shame you never got to meet my kids. Bloody iPads.' Jen nodded to the end of the hallway where the three children were now crowded round a screen, barely breathing.

'I'm not much of a children person.' Angie blurted it out and immediately felt bad, as she knew how awful it sounded. 'I mean, I just don't have that much experience with them.' It was at this point Angie realised why the *Play School* producers never called her back, or why she'd never contacted them.

'Thought you were a teacher?' Jen said.

'Yeah, I am. Sorta.' Angie didn't want to explain the gap between being a teacher and a teacher's aide. She just wanted out of there. 'Well, next time for sure.'

Jen pressed the plastic bag into her hand. 'Here, take your wine.'

'Please, you keep it.'

'No, honestly, we're not big merlot drinkers. It would be wasted.'

Angie wasn't arguing. 'It was great to see you all.'

'You too,' Jen said, already walking away. 'You know where we are. Don't stay a stranger.'

Angie opened the front door and headed out. Marcie followed her onto the porch. 'How you getting home? You can't walk. It's miles.'

'One-point-nine kilometres. Twenty-three minutes, apparently. It's gonna be a beautiful night.'

'I'll get you an Uber. Or I'll drive.'

'Marce, I'm fine. It's the only exercise I get back home.'

'You are home.'

'You know what I mean.' Angie had wanted to remind her that they used to walk these roads all the time back and forth to each other's houses.

'How's your brother?' Marcie asked.

'Don't ask.'

'How's your dad?'

'Definitely don't ask.' Angie realised she was fighting back tears. 'Not today.'

'And how are you?'

'It's weird living in my parents' granny flat when I never got round to actually making them grandparents. Or ever having a granny flat for them.'

Marcie held her tight. Angie had missed this more than she realised. 'We'll have a proper catch up during the week, yeah? You be careful walking home. I'm so glad you're here.'

Angie tried to say something similar in return, then found her throat tightening. She turned and drifted away from the Pajero and the boat in the drive. She was about to give a final wave when she heard a door close and saw nobody was there.

Angie hit the footpath and began the walk to her family abode. She avoided the sprinklers firing water onto the path. She plodded past oversized bungalows which all looked identical and had the same oversized TVs lighting up the lounge rooms behind the blinds. She would be late giving her father his medication, but that would have to be.

She thought of Melbourne. Her new neighbours were having a flat-warming. There'd be lazy Sunday beers around the bars of Brunswick. Monday was taco and quiz night with her housemates. She would miss that the most.

Angie was grinding her teeth, still enjoying a pleasant buzz from the pills. She unscrewed the wine and took a generous mouthful. Jen was right in handing it back, it was cheap gutrot, but it was hitting the spot.

She lit the roll-up, feeling better about herself. The sun had gone, and it was almost completely dark. The breeze on her back had become a chill, and she wished she had worn tights and boots. Still, the weather was kinder than over east at this time of year, at least until Perth's unforgiving summer reared its head. For the next few months, this would be one of the few things there'd be to enjoy.

PERTH II

I hadn't been in church since leaving Kal. Christ knows, I'd passed this one enough times since we moved down here, and Syd's liver started giving him grief. I kept telling him not to drink with it, kept telling him it was his fault he was pissing blood. But deep down I had a feeling, just a feeling, mind, that the thing was buggered to begin with. Syd was always going to get a dud one when it came to it. I bet you some sherry-sipping prick in Peppermint Grove got the good one and ain't going through half of what he is right now.

Anyway, I don't know what happened to me. All I know is it was cold, and it was June, and when I came out the hospital, the cathedral was right there as it always was, only this time it looked so inviting. I felt this warm sort of glow looking at the spires up top and spotted the little guy hanging there, and I thought bugger it. Bugger Arsehole Aaron behind the bar and his happy hour. The grog can wait. I'd had a skinful the night before and a few in the arvo on the way into town anyway with Syd's sister, Pam, who's down for the week. So, I just thought, I'll go in here and maybe say a few prayers. I can remember some of them. The Hail Marys and Our Fathers. Bits of them. I was baptised Catholic. Dad was a Mick. It's not like there'd be anyone at the door checking and complaining that I hadn't done my Communion because Mum moved us away. Or that I'd been rooting since I was 14 and divorced twice. Well, I didn't think there would be. God's door is always open, isn't it? Until you die and he flings you to the fire.

So I went in, and my God, it was beautiful. A load of young fellas in their pea green blazers were singing in the corner. A mob of Chinese or Japanese or whatever — they're all the same to me, and I mean that in a nice way — were lighting candles. There was an old couple, Italian-looking or something, who were praying with their heads down the way the old nuns at the home used to. And a few other randoms milling around, looking at the statues or taking pictures and smiling at me. And I just thought it was divine. Way better than that tin shed we used to have to go to mass in. Might've taken to it all if they'd built a place this nice. All regal and shit. Fit for the Pope so it was, fit for the Pope. And way better than Bar at the Barracks and its happy hour.

A baby was there with its parents, and they were talking to a nun. I didn't know these Indians and Pakis were Christian, but there you go. Always nice were the nuns. Never met a bad one, honest. Met enough nutty ones. You'd have to be not to have a man. Or would ya? When you look at the mess they've got me in! Nah, nah, but to not have your kids or your freedom, I dunno if I could do without all that.

The priest came out and talked to the choirboys. Stiff starched collar, stiff expression. Probably stiff everything, if you know what I mean. A few parents were gathered, and he started to go on about doing their sacraments. They weren't doing their Communion, they were doing the other one whose name I could never remember. The one my cousin May went on and did. Never really got the point of that one, no matter how many times she explained it to me. About the Holy Spirit being inside you and all that. Sounded like another excuse to shift more tickets and pack the crowds in.

The priest seemed okay. Youngish bloke. Local. I thought this was weird cos most of the priests I see around now are African or Asian. But this fella had a bit of personality, and whatever he was saying must've been good because they were all smiling. And those boys seemed like good boys, all listening and respectful and thoughtful. Warmed your heart, so it did. Made me think of my kids and how they coulda turned out had I brought them here. Probably a darn sight better than they have, but they never had the opportunities these tackers had. It's good to have a God, but you need a little rub of the green in life as well.

Pam reckons I'm a grandmother again. Says Jessie had a little girl, not that she bothered to tell me. Maybe there'll be hope for this one. Then again, the church and God packed up and left that town long ago. Long before I did. I can hardly blame The Man Upstairs for giving in. It's too hard. It's the devil's country now.

I thought I'd go and light a candle and say a prayer for Syd. He drives me up the wall most of the time, but I'd still miss him if he dropped off the perch. I have done the past few weeks. He says I'll be fine if he checks out of this world, that I'll find someone else, but I dunno. I think this is it for me. I hope so, anyway. God's good. He'll be right. I love his bones. Just wish his shitty liver wasn't rotting away.

The candles were replaced by little lights that you had to pay money and press a button to light up. Now that don't seem right, mixing bloody capitalism with technology in order to send a message to the heavens. Call me old-fashioned, but I'm sorry. The church seems all well and good going into this century, but that seemed a bit off.

I got down and rested my knees on the puffy little cushion. 'Dear God,' I said. 'I'll come to this place every day, well ... every week at least, coz even though I've retired I've got a load on with this and that and what have you. I'll bring Syd too, though it's not his thing. He had it bad with the priests back in the day, not sex stuff, like, just beatings. But I'll get him to come, and we'll give our thanks if you make it better. Might even volunteer our services. I could teach these kids a thing or two about the world. Some people who volunteer get real well looked after, from what I hear. I've heard they can get cars and housing. I don't want much, I wouldn't need all that. A shiny new car would be nice, though.'

It started to get a bit cold in there. I mean, it was June after all, and I didn't have me coat, so I knew

I should probably go. When I was leaving, I saw there was a poor box. I was gonna put in a dollar or something. If I had one, I would have. The lid on it was loose. There was a twenty and a five sticking out. I could see a few shiny gold nuggets too.

I knew it was a sign.

Christ, there ain't nobody poorer than me at the moment. Especially until Syd gets out. And Jesus himself did go on about helping the needy and all that. So, I had a quick check to see if anyone was looking cos I know what people are like, and I helped myself to some of it. All of it, granted. But desperate times call for desperate measures, you know how it is.

As I exited through the big creaking door, the wind nearly knocked me off my feet. I looked at my old Nokia. 5.49 p.m. I could still make happy hour, wouldn't even need Arsehole Aaron's tab. Syd would probably be dozing, anyway. I could always go and visit him tomorrow, he'd understand.

CLOVERDALE

'We are gathered here today to farewell a man, a good man by all accounts, who touched the hearts of many.'

Keith looked around the chapel. He was the only person present apart from the priest perched high on the altar reading from his notes, and the men from the funeral company sat at the back. There was the grey-bearded one doing a crossword, the younger one cleaning his ears with a carefully rolled up tissue. The organ player hadn't even bothered to show up. Bob's old work-mates must've been late, Keith thought. Perhaps his ex-wife had something else on.

'Bob Bennett was a warm-hearted man known for his generosity,' read the priest.

Keith saw an old Chinese man with a flat cap enter the squeaky side door. Keith was surprised, as Bob was a few degrees to the right of being a mere casual racist and had no other friends apart from Keith, that Keith knew of, never mind ones who weren't white. Sure enough, the Chinese man whispered something to the older funeral director, who pointed in the direction of the Anglican Church around the corner.

Keith thought about what the priest said, and how Bob never bought a round unless you pulled him up on it. How Bob was always stopping by his house, making sandwiches for his tea with Keith's bread and cheese because he was too tight to do a shop himself.

'The type of man who stuck up for his friends.'

Keith thought back to when Bob was getting aggro in a pub down Freo way one night after a Docker's game, aggro caused by Bob making a comment to a Kiwi guy about his pink shirt, and how Keith had reluctantly intervened only to get a slap in the mouth from the Kiwi guy's mate. When he came to, Bob had fled to the toilets where he stayed until security removed the assailants from the premises. The police were going to charge Keith with homophobic harassment, before they realised he was the wrong guy.

'A man with a terrific sense of humour.'

Sure, Keith rolled his eyes. Bob loved nothing more than practical jokes and relentless name-calling, or 'banter' as he called it, until the joke was on him. Keith remembered soon after he started at the factory where, after four months of piss-taking regarding his limp caused by a bike accident as a youngster, he signed Bob up for the Mormons on April Fool's Day. A pair of pasty students in pressed white shirts and *yee-haw* accents, and who looked about thirteen, visited him at work much to the delight of the supervisors. Bob didn't speak to him until Christmas.

'A man who encouraged others to follow their dreams.'

A few years back, Keith wanted to go for his pilot's licence but was talked out of it by Bob, who told him it was a waste of time and money. Then two years later he found out Bob was taking skipper lessons on weekends and had bought himself a tinny.

'Yes,' the priest continued, 'it's fair to say that here lies someone ... um ... Bill Butler,' his eyes strained as he looked closer at his notes. 'Sorry, *Bob Bennett*, who will be sorely missed.'

Keith had heard enough. He got up, lifted his coat and walked out, finally realising all the years he'd wasted on his supposed best friend. The priest and funeral directors didn't even notice.

Keith headed to the library across from the park. He was going to research flight schools and get that ticket. Then he'd go to the pub and order a middy or two and call Bob's ex-wife and ask her out. He'd always liked Phillippa, always respected her for leaving Bob when she did. And he completely understood why she wasn't here today after everything Bob had put the poor woman through.

Keith's legs bounced along the pavement like rubber pistons, faster than they had since Bob Bennett barged into his life. Today, this week, this month, this year, the future itself was finally his own. And the Bob-less world he now inhabited felt wonderful.

NOLLAMARA

Vedad's house is such a ballache to get to. Over the border of Ravenswood Drive into Nollamara. It's weird, when I was on the gear every cunt and his nonna seemed to be holding. Good shit too. Sometimes didn't even need to cross the street. Great times, but you ain't gonna live long playing it that way.

I had fun alright, but I done me best and kicked it in the cunt like everyone who gave a shit about me told me I should. Problem is, now I'm smoking the green and drinking like a bastard. And the bigger problem is that nowadays weed is hard to come by. Ice, that A-class life-wrecker is easy. But that mellow-as-fuck, keep it real, keep it on the down-low shit, you have to go out the suburb to get it. Out of Balga too. Well, for good stuff anyway. I've smoked so much and been smoking for so long that I can't be doing with cheap imitations. And Vedad's is far from a cheap imitation. It's cosmic space-age shit, man.

I walked across the park, regretting wearing my Lakers jacket. Fuck, it was hot. Couldn't wait to get this errand done, get some Red Rooster, get back to the unit, strip down, pour a Bundy and Coke, light the Scooby Doo bong and watch *Vice-Principals*. Fuck, I love Danny McBride. Love that other cunt who played that drag queen in *Sons of Anarchy* too, in a non-homo way. Funny as all-fuck.

This trip would've been a lot quicker if I'd taken the bus, but my dole doesn't come in till tomorrow. It's too fucking expensive anyway, even with concession. No wonder every cunt in this city drives. I would too if I could still afford it. I will again, soon as I get a job.

I was at the edge of the park when I saw this little kid going down the slide. Cute little boy about six or something with a blonde bowl cut and a Socceroos shirt. Should've had a hat on as well in this heat, the play area isn't shaded. I was walking past them. His mum was sitting on a bench texting or something. His mum was... fuck, his mum was...

'Crystal?'

'Trav?'

She'd been my girlfriend. Grew up two streets away. Our step-mums were besties. We went out for most of high school and on-and-off for a good while after. She was my first root. Fuck, she was my only root for years.

'Your kid?' I nodded to the boy who was now on the roundabout. 'Looks like you.'

'Yeah, he is,' she said, head darting about, not keen on making too much eye contact. Made it more awkward than it was.

She looked a million bucks. She had her hair dyed blonde properly. She'd always been a dirty blonde.

Big expensive sunnies — well, they looked expensive, could've been from fucking Bali for all I know about fashion. I mean, look at the state of me standing there. Under the jacket I had my Cypress Hill singlet showing, the faded one that I'm pretty sure I had back in school. The only fashion I know is Nike and NBA shit. I hadn't showered yet or shaved in a long while.

'What brings you back?'

She put her phone down. 'I'm going to a home open.'

I hadn't seen her in fuck knows how long. Last I'd heard, she'd enrolled in a business course and moved to the coast. Round here was getting posh if the likes of Crystal Barnes were moving back in.

'It's just for investment,' she continued. 'My ... my husband, he deals with that sort of thing. We're just waiting for him.'

The little guy moved to the swings, and she got up to push him. She looked good, great even, if a bit too grown up. Nah, she looked real good with a smart blouse and a sensible skirt on. She wasn't a girl anymore. She dressed like a woman.

As she pushed her little boy, I saw a little bulge peek out over the top of her waist. I didn't want to mention anything just in case, but it didn't look like a potbelly from a weekend on the piss, if you know what I mean.

'How are you doing anyway, Trav?' She only ever used my name when she was dark with me.

'Getting by.'

'You working?'

'Not anymore. Got made redundant. It's still tough now after the downturn.'

'Yeah, so they reckon.'

'Trying to get it together to go to TAFE. Do graphic design.'

'You should. You were always good at that stuff.'

'Worked out alright for you there. Got you out of here.'

She gazed out at the busy road as a cement truck thundered past. 'It's not so bad here.'

'Mustn't be. You're back buying up the joint.'

She smiled at this. For a split-second, we shared a cheeky look that took me back to that place in a different lifetime. When we were together, and everything was okay, and things didn't seem so heavy and nothing else mattered apart from us having each other.

'You still smoke?' I asked this just as something to say. I don't know why I said it. It was like a brain fart. I immediately regretted it. She just gave me that old look when she's mad, where she pushes her lips together and her nose points up. She turned to her boy. Of course she doesn't smoke. And you don't say that in front of someone's kid.

'Sorry,' I said. 'I bet you don't miss this life.'

She looked back at me, her expression relaxing. She was still beautiful, a different kinda beautiful, whether she was happy or sad. 'I'm not ashamed of where I came from and what I did.'

I heard a car horn and looked over. A shiny, white Chrysler had pulled up and an Asian dude in a shirt and tie with deadly aviator shades and slicked back hair, maybe a couple of years older than us, got out.

'That's Darren. Let's go, Alfie.' She took the kid by the arm. On the way past, he did the cutest thing. He gave me a big smile and came and shook my hand.

'Pleased to meet you,' he said. I nearly died inside.

'You look after yourself,' Crystal told me.

'Yeah, you too. Nice seeing ya again. See ya, Alfie.'

And with that she was across the road, kissing the bloke and heading into the townhouse with the big *For Sale* sign, where another suited bloke at the door waited to usher them in.

I got back to walking. I was late. Vedad hated it when I was late. He's super punctual for a stoner.

As I crossed Ravenswood, I started thinking of Crystal and how long it had been since I'd had a root. Maybe four or five months ago off that backpacker chick in Mullaloo. I kept thinking how I'd spent the best part of a decade on and off with Crystal and how that never wavered. It was always special in that department. I got to thinking about the last one we had in this very park on Australia Day six or seven years ago. And how I swear Alfie had that exact same blonde bowl cut I had when I was his age and that same crazy glint in his eyes.

WOODVALE

He called her phone again. There was no answer.

The young barmaid with the cleavage on show served the young man next to him. She hadn't noticed or didn't care that Frank was here first. He let it go. He was all set for his two p.m. slot. He'd be hard-pushed to fit in his pre-show cigarette now. He reasoned this wasn't such a bad thing. He'd been limiting himself to five-a-day. This meant he could have one later, when he left the hospital and made that long and lonely drive back up the coast towards home.

The barmaid served the man next to Frank his cider and two sparkling wines. Then, she turned to the opposite end of the bar, greeting a friend who was cradling a baby. Where the fuck was Paddy? Frank thought. Women of a certain age complained about being disrespected, disregarded even, by society. Eileen noticed this when she passed fifty. Frank felt that being a sixty-three-year-old man was much the same. Too old to matter to young women, not old enough to enter the domain of kindly old man. Although with his potbelly, thick greying mutton-chops and sailor-inked arms, he doubted if he'd ever fit that description.

'Excuse me,' he called over, his voice raised, but level. 'Can I get served here?'

The barmaid threw him a stare. A man with a full-forward's build shot out from the back office. His body was squeezed into the same grey polo shirt that Paddy wore.

'Can I help you?' he asked.

'Pint of Kilkenny, please,' said Frank.

The younger man poured, avoiding eye contact. 'Twelve dollars.'

'I'm performing.'

'What?'

'I'm the act. The cover act. Paddy gives us a couple of free pints.'

The man craned his huge neck around the pillar and noticed the amp and the black Martin semi-acoustic set up in the corner. 'Paddy's not here anymore.' Paddy had started booking Frank a decade ago. He paid him well, looked after him. 'I'm the new manager,' he said, his pecs arching above Frank's eyeline. 'Where've you been the past two months?'

'Just away.' Frank's attention was drawn towards a table of ladies making a noisy toast in the corner. Frank didn't want to confide in anyone, much less this stranger. 'My wife ... she's not been well.'

'I can give you that, but that's it.' He placed the pint before Frank. 'You got a contract or anything? Paddy never mentioned you.'

'God, no.' Frank took a sip. 'Never been a need for anything like that.'

'Talk to me when you're finished. We'll have to sort this out.'

Frank wiped the froth from his lips and forced a smile. He lifted the drink and walked to his corner, avoiding stray chairs, handbags and children. He hadn't wanted to come here today. He'd wanted to stay by Eileen's side. But eight weeks is what he'd agreed with Paddy, and fair's fair is what his wife had told him. They had a trip to Tasmania to save for. That's all this gig had ever been for him. Back in the day, he'd work his nine-to-five for the council, which paid the mortgage and the bills. Then he'd play two, sometimes three gigs a week around the northern suburbs. This put their kids through Catholic school, took them to Disneyland once and back to Ireland every two years. But the shows had dwindled, and now all he was left with was this. Still, with the kids grown up and gone, it sent the couple somewhere nice and closer to home twice a year.

He didn't want to go to Tasmania. He felt as if he'd already been there as everyone told him it was like Ireland, and he was long over that place. But Eileen wanted to, and he wanted to be with her. What he really wanted more than anything though, was for the chemo to end and the cancer to go away.

He tried calling her again. No answer. Maybe there'd been a visitor. Maybe one of the kids had come over to surprise her. He switched his phone off.

When he picked up his old guitar, he realised this was the first time he'd performed on a Sunday after-noon without her. Eileen was always in the front row with a lager shandy, occasionally with their neighbour Anne if she wasn't minding the phones at the RAC. The weeknight shows he used to do alone, but Sundays had always been theirs. They'd have a drink afterwards, a proper session, and then a Sunday lunch. Paddy and his wife would join them and they'd stay till late, Frank sharing stories of Limerick, Paddy of Glasgow, and then cab it home.

Onstage, he held his hands up to the mic and watched his fingers tremble. It couldn't be nerves, he'd been doing this since he could walk. Maybe more to do with the half-bottle of Tullamore Dew he'd tanned in front of the box last night watching the *Carry On* box-set his son had got him all those Christmases back, trying to somehow remain cheerful.

Frank gave the guitar a strum. He looked out. It was busy, but he could see none of the regulars. There was no Old Hugh on the stool by the bar. Or Cathy up the front with her man, the Greek fella whose name Frank could never remember. In their places was the girl with the baby, and a table of tradies in high-vis shirts, their grubby nails pinned to their smartphones, and their eyes on the big screen showing some footy game with the sound thankfully turned down, preoccupied on spending their overtime cheques.

'Hello, I'm Frank McCann,' he said as he tuned. 'This is a song from the old country. This is 'The Irish Rover'.'

Frank had played this song a million times, and it always got the same foot-tapping, sing-a-long response. This afternoon was different as the table of women briskly lifted their handbags and ice buckets and clopped into the lounge. Two of the tradies didn't bother looking up from their phones and the other two, with what Frank thought were Dublin accents, sneered at him, smirking at a private joke.

When the song finished, Frank crouched down and finished his pint. He still had another forty minutes to play before his break. He wished he'd gotten two pints or perhaps a chaser to go with it. Paddy would have sorted him out mid-set, no problem. He looked to the bar. The girl was talking to a man in a British Lions jersey. He saw the new manager's shadow in the doorway of the back room.

'Thank you, thank you,' Paddy said to the applause which wasn't there. He stumbled into the mic, knocking it in the direction of the speaker, sending off a shard of feedback that made the crowd wince. 'Sorry about that, folks.' At least it shut up the table of tradies. Maybe he didn't need that drink after all. 'Here's some more tunes to keep you feeling fine, or make those end-of-weekend blues fly far, far away.'

He eased into the classics in the hope of getting the fifty or so people in the room feeling something, any-thing. 'Dirty Old Town', 'Whiskey in the Jar', 'The Fields of Athenry'. The tradies rose and headed to the bar, jok-ing loudly about some bet one of them had won.

Frank relaxed. He'd never needed a set list or a chord or lyric sheet. He'd been doing this so long he could do it in his sleep. But tonight, he lacked his usual swagger. He sensed no vibe from the crowd. He missed

Paddy. He missed the regulars. He missed Eileen. It was because of her that he played 'One'. He'd never much liked U2, though he didn't mind this song. It was his wife's favourite.

As he strummed the quiet chords, he heard the phone ring in the back office. The barmaid didn't notice as she served the tradies shots of something clear, which they threw back and slammed down like gunshots on the bar top.

The manager answered it. He mouthed the word 'Who?' Then he turned to the stage and to Frank, who sang the chorus.

Frank knew. Frank just knew. He'd been waiting and dreading this for so long.

'One life, we gotta carry each other, carry each other...'

He looked down to his empty pint glass and his mobile phone, which was turned off. He thought about the holiday in Tasmania, and how he wouldn't have to go, and how he no longer needed this gig. He thought about the children he no longer knew and imagined how he would tell them. He didn't know where they were anymore. He didn't know how to reach them.

GREENWOOD

She parked in the driveway. She didn't open the car door, she just sat there. The house looked different. Bright red gutters replaced the old, peeling green ones. There was a new beige garage door. Yet the garden, the street and the suburb surrounding it were much the same.

She tried to think of the last time she'd been here. Boxing Day. Four years ago. After that, Danny didn't want to. Especially when his real habit crept in.

She remembered their last year of high school. She used to spend most nights here. In his room, drinking homebrew, smoking cones, watching Wes Craven movies, listening to Queens of the Stone Age. Making love. That was fifteen years ago, yet it felt like a lifetime.

'Mummy, when are we going in?' her six-year-old, Hunter, asked from the backseat.

Mikhaila lit a cigarette. She immediately regretted it as Val would smell it on her and add that to her shit list. She was already wearing a black, sleeveless top that couldn't hide the love heart tattoo, which Val had never disguised her disdain for. The one *her* son had inked on her.

'In a minute, hon.'

She reclined the seat and took a drag. She might as well finish it now that it was lit.

Back in high school, she was seen as a good influence. Their Daniel had never got anything but D-grades. All he wanted to do was skate. And then she came along. Pianist. President of the student council. Plans to study medicine. Singer in an up-and-coming band. Danny's marks moved up to a C. His parents liked her. For a little while, she felt.

'Mummy, I'm thirsty,' her four-year-old, Courtney, whined.

Her band got signed. Got on the North American festival circuit. She didn't want him to come. It was work, after all. But Danny did. And with a lot of time and a little money on his hands, the soft drugs became hard.

Then, quick as it began, the band ended. Artistic differences, youthful arrogance. Their visas expired. She and Danny returned home. Settled down. Somehow their relationship rolled on. They had one kid, then another.

She wanted to get married, she wanted to take his name. She knew this would make *them* happy. She saw how they treated Jess —Danny's older brother's wife — once they'd married. She couldn't even have kids. But then Lauren was a respectable primary school teacher, not a former frontwoman of a failed synth-pop band who flashed her legs (and occasionally her tits).

Danny always had an excuse ready and loaded about not conforming. She even got the blame for not baptising the kids Catholic, even though Danny said he'd take care of it. She wasn't even Catholic, but she wanted to do this. She knew how it would make his parents happy and her life easier.

'I'm hungry,' said Hunter.

'I'm bored,' said Courtney.

They moved down south. She got a job in a clothes shop. His tattoo venture didn't get off the ground, and he couldn't cope with the normality of just existing. Of being a father. A partner. A son. His addiction took hold and knowing he was failing at all that mattered, he chose to take his own life on the one night she'd come back up to the city to have dinner with her remaining friends.

'Mummy, can you hear us?'

Last month in the Family Court it all came out. Val said it was Mikhaila who had turned her son onto the pipe. That she was unstable. That she was an unfit mother. Val claimed it was Mikhaila's fault that her son had ended it all with a leather belt wrapped around his neck.

Val didn't mention how Mikhaila had never touched serious drugs. How Danny had lost them the home she paid for, her car, her job. And left her a bereaved single mother at age 31.

The judge gave the grandparents one weekend of visiting rights a month.

The front door opened. Mikhaila stiffened, quickly put out her cigarette and opened the window. But it wasn't Val. She saw the dark greying features. The prominent jaw. The dignified gait. It was Brian, Danny's dad. Almost exactly how Danny would have looked if he'd made it to retirement.

'Hello, love.'

'Grandad!' the children squealed, racing out the car to throw themselves at him.

'Hello, Brian.'

She'd always liked Danny's dad. He wasn't a strong man, but he was a nice, quiet man who, in his own way, and faced with great adversity, had tried to stick up for her. Mikhaila saw the curtains twitch and spotted Val's stern features gazing through the gap. Her eyes bore right through Mikhaila and then softened when they settled on her grandchildren.

'You doing okay?' Brian asked.

'We're getting there.'

He reached into the back and lifted Hunter and Courtney's backpacks. 'I'll drop them to you Sunday night.'

'Thanks.'

'I know it's hard, but it's important we do this. For the children.'

The kids waved and disappeared through the door. Mikhaila started the engine and reversed down the driveway. She drove down the quiet street, parallel to the one she grew up on, and made it out of the suburb. The humdrum suburb where nothing ever happened, which she'd tried her whole life to escape, but never could.

It wasn't until she hit the freeway that she realised she had nowhere to go.

BECKENHAM

Rob parked the van in the customer car park as he'd been told. A quiet Wednesday, a little after one p.m., there was just enough room to position it between a pair of people movers.

With no sign of Corey, Rob removed his lunchbox from the glove-box. In it was a Tupperware container filled with tuna salad, a nut bar, a Pink Lady apple and a note from Christie. It read:

'Love you so much, sweet cheeks. Can't wait to see you at home.'

Rob grinned boyishly. He'd never been in love before, and it felt good. Good to wake up next to someone, good to come home to somebody. He'd only ever lived with his mum. Christie got him saving his wages instead of pissing them away down the pub. She'd got him going to the gym three nights a week. He'd lost twelve kilos since he'd moved into hers.

Yeah, life felt good for Rob Dawson. He felt good being thirty, being older. It felt good to be away from Gosnells and closer to the city. Somewhere different, where he didn't know so many people and they didn't know him. Of course, he'd never get rid of the boys. He'd always be tethered to the place in that way. Mates for life is what they said. They had the *GOZDOGS* tattoos on their forearms to prove it.

And that's why he was here.

He heard a bus pull up on the road behind. He put down his half-eaten salad, surprised at how healthy food filled you. He looked in his wing mirror and saw Corey get off where there wasn't a stop. Corey shouted something to the driver, then stuck up his middle finger. As he approached the van, Rob noticed Corey had his baby girl attached to him on a sling, her head facing inwards. Cara, Clara, what was her name? It had been that long. Rob worked out that he hadn't seen his friend in the six months or so since she was born, when Corey had fixed him up with a job at the couriers. He'd called Rob yesterday and said he'd been caught up with the breakup, and moving out and the custody battle which followed, and he needed a hand with something.

As he came closer, Rob thought Corey looked awful. He appeared smaller and thinner, wearing a filthy Chicago Bulls singlet and torn jeans. It must have been the stress of fatherhood and the relationship troubles. Deep-down, though, Rob knew Corey was back on the gear.

Corey opened the van door and climbed up, manoeuvring himself into the passenger seat clumsily with the baby still attached.

'How are you, bro?' Rob gently squeezed his bony arm. 'Long time.'

'Shut the fuck up,' Corey whispered harshly, ignoring Rob's outstretched hand. 'Been trying for two hours to get her to sleep. She was howling on the bus worse than that dumb cunt mum of hers. Had to tell two old fucks to mind their own business. They were going on and on about winding her. I told it, ''I'll wind you if you don't fucking leave me alone''. Then the driver started on me. Good thing for that cunt I was getting off, and I had her with me. Good fucking thing.'

Corey was no longer whispering, forgetting his child who was gently snoring. With unsteady fingers, he reached into his pockets and removed a packet of Drum and rolled one. He lit it. 'Want one?' he asked, lobbing the packet into the grey upholstered space between the seats.

Rob shook his head. Christie had helped him quit four months ago. 'Should you be doing that?' Rob pointed to the baby, who made a little sigh in her sleep. She looked a bit like Corey around the eyes. Back when he was a kid, before his innocence was peeled apart.

'Don't you fucking start. Babies' lungs are the strongest they'll ever be at this age. Everyone knows that.'

'It's just ... the van,' Rob mumbled. 'They told us not to smoke.'

Corey looked at Rob. Looked at his hi-vis shirt and nametag. 'Nice shirt ... Robert,' he smiled without warmth.

'There's already a Rob who works there.'

'Sure there is, mate. And where's the beard? Did you do the old landing strip as well?'

Rob turned straight ahead, brushing his smooth chin. He hated Corey when he was in this mood. 'Thought it would be a better look for deliveries.' This was partly true, but the main reason was Christie hated beards. Her ex had one. It made her happy the day Rob got rid of the facial hair he'd had since school.

'How is it working for Uncle Will?'

'I mainly report to Rich, the other bloke.'

The baby let out a little cough from the smoke. Corey rolled down the window some more. She turned her head inwards and went back to sleep. 'Who the fuck's Rich?'

'Richard. Will's business partner. Nice guy.' Rob glanced at the baby girl and leaned in with a smile. 'Funny story. He comes from a massive motocross family. They've all won trophies and represented the state. He has four older brothers and no sisters. All his brothers went and had boys. So, he gets married, and she gets pregnant, or maybe she got pregnant before the wedding. Doesn't matter. And what does she go and have? A girl! Still, it's not the end of the world, and about a year or so after they have another bash cos he really wants a boy. So, out it pops, and what is it this time?'

'A girl,' Corey said, staring at the Baby Bunting store facing them.

'A girl! So Rich is just devo. Wants to go again. But his missus, she's all ''nah, nah, I only had one sibling growing up, same with both me parents, my sister has just the two, it's how we do things, it's what we agreed on''. So that's that. Only he keeps at her. After seven years he wears her down and pops the condom or whatever, and she falls pregnant. And what does she have?'

Rob looked to Corey, who was still assessing the store, the pause telling him this was where he was expected to jump in. 'I don't fucking know. A horse with five cocks.'

'Twin girls!' Corey cracked up. 'And now all his brothers are off to the motocross every weekend, and he's braiding hair and going to netball. Worst luck ever, right?'

Rob laughed. Corey didn't. 'And what exactly's wrong with that? You saying something's up with having a girl?'

'Nah, there's nothing wrong. Nothing at all. It's just, y'know ... four girls.'

'I'd love to have five of the cunts. You don't know what you're missing.'

'Sure mate, sure.'

Rob suddenly felt that the cab of his delivery van was much too small for the three of them. Especially when 'Rocket Man' came on the radio.

'What the fuck is this shit?' Corey said.

'Um, Billy Joel. Or Phil Collins. Can't remember.'

'What fucking channel is it?'

Rob didn't want to tell him. 'It was on there when I got in this morning.'

'Gets the fucking Js on.' Rob tried. He typed in 99.3, but the Aussie hip-hop track was coming through fuzzy. 'Ah, shut it off,' Corey told him. 'Piece of shit.'

Rob did so quickly, not wanting to rub his friend the wrong way any more than he already had.

Corey rolled another. He returned to staring at the store.

Rob cleared his throat. 'He says you can still have a job there.'

'Who did?'

'Rich. And Will too.'

'I know I can. He offered it to me first.'

'I mean ... as well as me working there.'

'I can't with my illness and all.'

'Didn't they take you off disability?'

'Doesn't mean I still haven't got depression. Just means they're insensitive fuckwits at Centrelink for not acknowledging it.' Corey blew a smoke ring. 'Working's a mug's game, anyway. Just look at the state of you.'

'Rich says he'll teach you how to drive.'

'I can drive. I had an accident. I'm damaged.'

'Rich says you reversed into a bollard.'

Corey's eyes narrowed, and his voice raised. 'He left the car in gear. The thing was going at speed. At-fucking-speed!'

Rob glanced to the people carrier next to him and its *BABY ON BOARD* sticker. He reached down, lifted the tub and continued on his salad.

Corey smirked. 'Fucking rabbit food.'

'I've been training. Getting fit, y'know.'

'I can see. Thought it was that. Or cancer.'

'Me and a few fellas from the warehouse are playing indoor soccer. Got a team together in Leederville.'

Corey's head arched back. 'Soccer? In fucking Leederville?'

'Yeah. You could join us if you want. Got a spot.'

Corey's eyes returned to the store. 'Can't. I'm taking this shit serious. Single father now.'

They both looked out. A woman with a pram came out of the automatic doors and walked towards the people carrier to their left. A young male shop assistant with a Baby Bunting lanyard followed her, carrying a large box with a picture of a bassinet on it.

'Corey,' Rob said quietly. 'I've only got fifteen minutes of me break left. Gotta drop a load of plant pots off in Alfred Cove by two-thirty.'

'Right.' Corey answered, not looking at him.

'What's this all about?'

'You owe me.'

'For the job?'

'Yes, for the job. And a heap of other stuff.' He turned and fake-smiled, showing Rob his chipped front tooth. 'Like, I dunno, saving your arse on the inside. Making sure you didn't get bent over and your face rammed into a fucking shower head every morning.'

This was somewhat true. Casuarina was a harsh place, and Rob with his weight problem and soft nature was an easy target for inmates to dominate. Corey, though, had been at juvey with some of the ringleaders and used these connections to ensure Rob's three months in the slammer weren't nearly as uncomfortable as they could have been.

But what Corey forgot to mention was that he was the reason Rob was put in there. He got him involved as a driver for a Lebanese crime syndicate who were robbing factories at night. The job helped fund both their habits when they were using every day.

'Yeah.' A lump caught in Rob's throat as he thought back to those days, that old life. 'And thanks for all that, I do owe ya.'

'Fucking right.'

'And ... how exactly do I repay you?'

'By helping me on this job.'

Rob didn't like where this was going. He knew Corey too well. And he knew that tone in his voice, the tone he could never say no to during their twenty-five years of friendship that had got him into all that trouble.

Rob said nothing more, waiting until Corey did.

'I'm gonna hold up that baby store.'

'What?' Rob almost screamed. 'C'mon, you said those days were gone.'

'I've told you before,' he hissed even louder. 'Keep your fucking voice down! If you wake her up, so help me fucking God.'

'But you did, though,' Rob whispered.

'That was before I had child support to pay.' He looked down at his daughter, no longer smiling. 'And everything else that goes with this thing.'

'But ... a baby shop?'

'Look at the amount of people who've drifted in there in twenty minutes. And y'see what they're coming out with? No expense spared.'

Corey had a point. In that time around twenty people had walked out with trolleys loaded full of goods to pack into their four-wheel drives and wagons.

'And,' continued Corey, taking out a handgun and wiping the grease from the handle onto his jeans, 'as well as the money, it means I can grab a few things on my way out. Left the fucking baby bag Kailee gave me on the bus with all her shit in it for the next two days. And I can kit out her room.'

Corey rolled the window back up again. Rob watched as the people carrier indicated onto the road.

Corey glanced at Rob and smiled a genuine smile, the first Rob had seen from him in years. 'And that, my good friend, is why I need the van.'

Rob tried to process this. He thought of the delivery he had to do in Alfred Cove, a place he'd grown to like. And the dinner he had planned with Christie. Salmon night it was. Then, the indoor match the boys had against the bottom team, which meant they would surely, *surely*, get a win. It made sense to Rob why Corey had contacted him, his old friend who never said no. But he didn't understand why he was doing this right now. He looked at the sleeping baby. 'So why have you brought her?'

'You're my out. She's my in.'

'Your what?'

'Everyone loves kids in there. No one's gonna start shit with her latched onto me. The hero count will be zero.'

'No way.' Rob had heard a lot of wild schemes from his old friend, but this was the wildest yet.

'Yes fucking way. Bring the car up to the front exactly two minutes after I go in. I'll race out. We'll load the car and off we go. Job well done.'

'You've ... you're losing it here.'

'Listen,' Corey's tone softened. 'No one thinks of hitting these joints. It's always servos and liquor stores. That same old shit gets you nowhere. Seriously, what am I gonna pick up? A fucking king brown and a packet of beef jerky? That shit's no good to me. Not anymore.'

'But ... she's a baby.'

'Aren't you a bright one.'

The baby stirred. She opened her bright blue eyes. She edged her head up and looked at Rob, giving him a tiny smile. Rob had no experience with kids, but his heart skipped.

'I mean,' Corey looked down at her, tears welling in his eyes. 'Who could say no to this little face? They'll probably see her and hand me the shit for free.' Corey opened the door and got out. 'Now remember the old drill. See you in two minutes and not a second more.'

'Corey,' Rob was sweating, the twitch where his left eyebrow randomly leapt up had returned for the first time since he met Christie. 'I really don't know about this.'

Corey stuck his head back in the car and fixed his stare on Rob. 'You don't have to *know* about this. There is no *know* to it. You've owed me for too long, and I'm calling it in.'

'But . . . the kid.'

'My kid, ain't it? They haven't challenged that one yet. Kailee can do what she wants with her five days a week, and I can do what I like the other two.'

Rob could only watch as Corey walked into the store with the baby still strapped to him. He wished for once he'd stand up to Corey, put his point across. He never could before. He thought he would be able to as they got older, but now he realised that he never would. His friend couldn't be told. His mind raced towards him losing Christie, losing it all. The life he'd battled so hard to turn around was about to be run off the rails once again by the usual suspect.

When Corey reached the front doors he stopped. Then he made an about-turn and almost ran back to the car. Rob breathed easier, believing Corey had seen some sense as he opened the door, gagging.

'Ah, shit,' he coughed.

'What?'

'Fucking smell that.'

Corey held up his daughter's back-end. Rob inhaled. He caught something like off-milk, but he'd had a cold last week and his nasal passages still weren't clear.

Corey was getting the full brunt of it. 'That shit's unreal.'

'Change her, I guess.'

Corey ripped off the sling. 'I fucking can't, can I? The nappies and wipes were in that bag.'

'Well, get some more.'

'I'm fucking trying to, aren't I!' he yelled. The baby gave a little jump then cried into his face. Corey screamed back at her. 'Shut up. Shut the fuck up. I don't need this shit right now.'

'Settle, mate.'

'You fucking settle. You try and settle when you're in the hole I am. Have you seen the price of nappies? A fucking wrought is what it is. No wonder the government wants you to keep having the little cunts.'

Corey yanked the baby loose as she cried on. 'She's blown it now. Can't go in there with her like this, screaming and stinking up the joint. They'll want me to shoot her instead.'

Rob felt for his keys. 'Let's just go. I'll drop you at the station.'

'Fuck that. I come all this way. You did too.'

Corey handed the crying child over to Rob. 'What are you doing now?' Rob realised he'd never held a baby before, not even his own nephew. His sister never seemed comfortable when her ex-con brother was around her son.

Corey tore off the sling and repositioned the gun where his belt should have been. 'I'm going in anyway. Piece of piss. I can grab more shit without her.'

Before Rob could argue, Corey was off towards the entrance, disappearing inside. Rob looked at the little bundle of joy in his hands. He held her out to get a better look. The closer he got, he wasn't sure if she looked all that much like Corey. Her hair wasn't blonde, and the smile and dark eyes were those of her mother's.

The baby stopped crying. Her eyes focused on the face before her. Her lips ever so slightly curled up at the edges.

Rob remembered. 'Ciara. That's it. Ciara.' He felt a surge of warmth inside that he'd never experienced before. He also felt a strong dampness coming from the girl's bum and finally got a deadly whiff of what Corey was complaining about.

Rob wound down the window. He reached into the glove-box, picking out a wad of tissues. He put them down on the rest between the driver and the passenger seats and sat the girl down. She snuffled back a pocket of snot. Then she launched forward and made a grab for his salad.

'You hungry?' He opened the tub. He was pretty sure babies were allowed a few crumbs of tuna. He held it out, and she gobbled it up messily, smiling and showing a small front tooth which had just broken through.

'You want some music?' Rob turned on the radio and tuned the dial back to 94.5. Daryl Braithwaite was singing 'Horses.' Rob was sure this was the second time he'd heard it today. Little Ciara seemed to love it though, waving her tiny hands.

Rob looked at the clock. It was two p.m. His designated lunch hour had ended. There was one minute to go before he had to collect Corey. But he couldn't do that now, surely not. Not with the kid not strapped in.

'Daddy will be here soon,' Rob told her, in hope more than anything as she let out a sneeze, shooting a chunk of tuna onto the dashboard.

Just as he said it, Corey ran out, a gun in one hand, a bag of nappies in the other. Right behind him was the employee with the lanyard. He took a running leap and both his hands caught Corey's skinny midriff, taking him down. The gun and the nappies scattered. The heavier guy easily got his two knees up onto Corey's shoulders, pinning him to the tarmac. Two women in Baby Bunting uniforms emerged, the older one pushing a number on the cordless phone in her hand.

It dawned on Rob what Corey had got him involved in once again. An accomplice to armed robbery. Also, there was a child involved. And who knew how many children and parents inside that Corey had waved the pistol at. Rob shook his head, furious at himself for never saying no to Corey, for sliding back down into the deep, dark hole he'd only just emerged from. He couldn't get dragged down all that way with him. Not now, not again.

He turned the ignition. He picked up the baby and plonked her between his legs. He drove on carefully past her father, lying face-down on the gravel. Ciara giggled and gripped the bottom of the steering wheel as police cars screeched past in the opposite direction.

As he accelerated, he saw the beanie she was wearing had little rabbit ears sticking out the top. He'd always wanted a boy. Boys were supposed to be easier going, or so he'd heard. Maybe it was Rich who'd told him that, he couldn't remember. But this one seemed alright. She seemed to like him. She had to. He was all she had at the moment.

He wondered if Ciara had ever been to Alfred Cove. It was a nice spot. He wondered if that ice-cream van would be riding around at this hour. He thought about where he'd take her after that and realised he had no idea. But he knew Christie was going to be pissed with him whatever he did.

LANDSDALE

She folded the newspaper and slotted it into the brick letterbox. She moved slowly on to the next house.

Ana wondered how many copies of the *Wanneroo Times* she'd delivered in the fourteen years since she'd arrived in the country with her son and his wife and their baby. Since she'd taken the only job which her age and lack of English would allow. The load had started with three-hundred papers, give or take a few, every Tuesday night. The area had since expanded and the delivery grown to around six-hundred. The total amount she'd delivered could amount to as much as 300,000. Quite a sum. She might be from humble rural stock, but her maths was proficient. Her father taught her the importance of that after the war. Nowadays, this job, along with playing the horses every day except Tuesdays and Sundays, helped keep her mind sharp.

She folded the newspaper and slotted into the aluminium letterbox. She walked carefully to the next house, avoiding the hose stretched out on the barren lawn.

Over the years, the paper had gotten heavier. Ana was always hearing how print media was dying, how everything was going digital and paperless. And yet *The Times* was getting heavier. Glossy adverts for TVs and fridges. Flyers for swimming pools and reticulation. Business cards, the occasional fridge magnet for security alarms and pest controllers, all bundled between the centre pages.

Ana had never missed a Tuesday delivery, even when she was battling sore throats or the odd cold or flu. She never missed a house, either. Frederick, the driver who dropped the run off at her door each week, told her of unscrupulous types who became deliverers, mostly kids who either through spite or an inability to do the task, hid the papers in garages, or threw them in the lake, or dumped them in the bush. Ana understood that people needed their local press. They relied upon it. It was a source of pride to her to have this role in her adopted country. None of the local homeowners or tenants would ever have cause to complain about her.

She folded the newspaper and slotted it into the brick letterbox. She crept across the shrub of a vacant lot towards the next house. The sheer bulk of delivering the newspapers through the years had made it difficult for her arthritic hands to lift and angle them into the small, never-changing slots. The increasing load also made it cumbersome for her to lug the papers into her large wicker basket and wheel them around the suburbs on the cart her son made for her. She could no longer do the job if it wasn't for her grandson, Elbar. She watched the boy at the end of the quiet road. Already over six-feet tall at just fifteen, with a wide back and light, easy features, he had helped her for the past five years, delivering the papers with pace and precision.

She folded the newspaper and slotted it into the timber letterbox. She hurried to the next house, her ears ringing and heart racing from the large, grey dog barking through the gate.

Across the street from where Elbar was delivering, two boys sat with a girl in an old boat docked by the side of a plain house with busted fly screens and peeling window frames. Ana saw them pass a cigarette between them as the boys laughed and taunted her grandson. They knew his name. They must have been from his school, Ana thought, though they looked smaller.

Elbar ignored them. He lowered his head and continued on. He was blessed with his grandfather's even temperament. Anna's husband, Elbar Snr, had been a big man, but he was not a violent man. Despite the ethnic quarrels which flared often in their border village when the couple lived there, he was always the first to break up any trouble rather than take a side.

She folded the newspaper and slotted it into the brick letterbox. The searing sun still bearing down upon her from the cloudless sky, she wished she hadn't worn a cotton undershirt as she shuffled stiffly on to the next house.

It saddened her that the suburb had changed. When they moved here, it was surrounded by bush, as the locals called it, a drier, less colourful form of countryside compared to back home, yet still quiet and peaceful. Now this was gone, with newer suburbs surrounding Landsdale. British, Africans and Asians had moved in. Aside from the shopping centre and fast-food outlets, there wasn't much for the children to do except hang around the park and smoke and spray-paint crudely written words that she couldn't decipher onto walls and fences.

She thanked God that Elbar had his basketball three nights a week along with the paper round. She'd told him she earned $120 delivering the paper and halved this with him. In fact, the sixty dollars she gave him was the full amount she earned. She'd done this since he'd started, and she didn't want him to know the truth knowing he'd refuse it. Ana had little use for the money. Her son never accepted a cent for accommodation, her horse racing habit usually paid for itself, and her pension covered her meagre outgoings. She didn't socialise as it was rare for her to meet anyone from Eastern Europe, her son and daughter-in-law choosing to mix with Australians.

She folded the newspaper and slotted it into the stout, stone letterbox. She tripped on a rock and grabbed a dragon tree branch to keep her balance, scratching her hand on its prickly edges. Ana cursed. She looked over and saw one of the boys throw a brown carton of flavoured milk at her grandson. He ducked, and it struck the wicker basket. It exploded, brown bubbles gushing onto the papers.

'Swine!' she hissed, though they wouldn't have heard as they were already pedalling away on their bikes. Elbar quickly removed the Master's Choc and the spoiled papers. Luckily, there were always extras stuffed down the sides.

Ana would have stopped doing this long ago if Tuesdays hadn't grown into a ritual for them. She would collect Elbar from school, and they would go home together and cut the string on the papers and carefully load them into the baskets. They would ensure the carts were oiled, and that they had water and hats and sunblock when it was warm, and tea and coats and umbrellas when it wasn't. Then they would head out. Sometimes, when the additional ads in the middle pages were few and their loads light, they could get a whole run completed in three hours and be home in time for the late news. Other times, usually in the lead-up to Christmas when there were multiple pamphlets stuffed between the pages and the weather was hot, it might be almost eight p.m. until they were done. But no matter what time, they always finished at Chicken Treat for a meal. It was here that the quiet boy would open up and confide to her about his parents and friends,sport and school. It was this half-hour, their half-hour, that made the aches and pains in her back and in her joints — pains which could last almost a full week — worthwhile.

She folded the newspaper and posted it into the brick letterbox. She felt faint and clutched the edges, taking a moment to collect her breath.

Elbar had finished his side of the street and started on his grandmother's. The girl hadn't followed the boys and was now talking to him. She had brown hair over her shoulders matching her skin tone, with long, limber legs stuffed into denim shorts, which, despite her thin build, looked tight on her. The girl was young, yet already aware of the hold she maintained over the opposite sex as she confidently looked down on the boy from the vantage of the boat.

Elbar's movement slowed, and he could only manage fleeting glances of eye contact. With his strong body and striking smile, Ana knew why the girl was with him.

The girl smiled back and skipped inside the house. With his shoulders arched back and an added zip in his step, Elbar quickly delivered the remaining three newspapers into the slots before Ana had a chance to put in one.

'Are you okay, Baba?' Elbar was suddenly next to her, holding her up by the arm.

'Of course,' she answered.

'You're out of breath. You're trembling.'

Ana hadn't noticed. The boy sat her down and gave her a drink from his water bottle.

'The air is hot,' she said. 'I'm just a little dizzy. We finish now, anyway.'

'Yes.' The boy looked over at the house with the boat. A door opened quickly with a clang.

Ana sipped more of the water. 'I be fine. We go for food now.'

Elbar chewed his lip. 'Maybe tonight you go home. You're sick, Baba.'

They always went to Chicken Treat afterwards. Always. 'Okay. We get takeaway. We eat at home. We watch TV.' She struggled up.

The girl exited her home and approached them. She now wore sandals and a skirt which touched her knees. Her long brown hair was tied back.

'I'm going to go without you,' the boy said. 'I heard they have jobs advertised there. They need young people to work weeknights. They pay good.'

The girl was almost beside them, flashing a confident snow-white smile. Ana felt her dizziness return. What about his basketball? What about the papers? If it wasn't for Elbar, what would the people do for their local news? Or if they needed a new TV, or their fridge stopped working? What if their pool leaked, or they wanted to install reticulation? What if they were robbed and needed an alarm, or if their house was eaten away by termites?

What if ...

MIRRABOOKA

Spencer wandered around Mirrabooka Square. He saw all the different faces and ethnic stores selling clothes and furniture in the brightly-lit shopping centre, and he thought to himself, *this is living*.

He'd been in Perth all of his twenty-four years, but only for the very occasional hockey match did he ever venture north of the river and never for very long. And certainly never to anywhere as blue-collar and multicultural as Mirrabooka.

His schoolmates at Trinity would take the piss out of poorer areas like it, saying they were full of 'boongs', 'coons', 'slopes' and 'terrorists'. Yet, his Syrian-born girlfriend, Aisha, who he'd met whilst studying at UWA, swore by it. She'd been raised in the area and had since bought one of the newer apartments here. Despite affordability no longer being a prime concern for her, she said she couldn't see herself living anywhere else. Sure, Mirrabooka had an edge to it and was still one of the lower socio-economic suburbs in the city. Nevertheless, Aisha loved how it was one of the most diverse areas, boasting over fifty nationalities, with a smattering of white faces sprinkled in between.

'Are you lost, my friend?' a South Asian man wearing a red turban and a thick gold chain, asked.

Spencer realised he'd stopped walking and was stood in the middle of the walkway. 'I was told about this really good Punjab place.'

'Ah, yes, beautiful, beautiful food. My brother-in-law, he owns it. The food hall is down the corridor on your right. You tell him Ranbir sent you.'

'Thank you so much.'

The man smiled, and Spencer smiled back. In Nedlands, strangers did not help each other. They did not stop to talk to each other.

Spencer found the restaurant and ordered a feast for twelve dollars, thinking how you'd be hard pushed to buy a sandwich for that where he grew up.

He tucked into the dish. The chole bhature was fresh and delicious. Spencer reminisced, the food taking him to another place. He hadn't enjoyed a meal like it since he'd travelled North India during his gap year with his best friend, Marcus. Lost in the moment, he gnawed through the chickpeas and flatbread, letting the fragrant flavours transport him to another place. Around the food hall he saw families, mainly African, Arabic and Southeast Asian, happily do the same.

This is living, thought Spencer, as he departed the shopping centre, his stomach satisfied. There was an African drummer by the door performing a spectacular array of twists, turns and tricks along to the pounding tribal beat. As he turned a corner, a Mongolian performer with dreadlocks expertly juggled four flaming sticks. Spencer meandered back to Aisha's apartment, bursting to tell her how right she'd been about Mirrabooka.

Once there, he checked his phone. Aisha had texted to say Royal Perth needed her to work overtime and she wouldn't be back until after ten p.m. He strummed the acoustic guitar in her bedroom, the first time he'd played since high school. Then he scribbled down an idea for a short story, where the son of a Federal Liberal Party MP falls in love with a refugee and moves to the northern suburbs.

Spencer put on a record of hers, some Arabic ambient soundscape that could have been a soundtrack from a movie. He peered out the front window at the flickering street lights and graffitied fences and donut marks on the road, and Spencer again thought, *this is living*.

Stuck for an ending to the story and being a Saturday, Spencer fancied a glass of wine. Aisha didn't drink, so he'd have to venture out. It was dark now, and the pleasant sea breeze had cooled the suburb. As he retraced his steps back to the Square, he noticed the street performers had gone. Instead, there were hooning cars doing burnouts, and teenagers shouting insults and hurling glass bottles in the car park next to McDonald's.

Spencer paid for the Chilean red and exited the liquor store. He worked out he would be quicker walking around the back way. He was looking forward to getting to the apartment and finishing the story before Aisha returned. They could even order a takeout if she was early. He was getting peckish again as he imagined what the other restaurants in the area had to offer.

'What's in the bag, bro?' a young accented voice shot out the shadows.

Spencer ignored him and walked on faster, only to see more faces ahead.

'Fucking give it me, cunt.'

As Spencer was floored with a punch from behind, he thought of Mirrabooka and the food and the families and the music and unpredictable beauty of life in these parts.

On the gravel, the pain throbbed in his cheekbone as a boot cracked open his ribs. Spencer felt his Spanish loafers removed from his feet as he drifted in and out of consciousness.

Still, he couldn't help smiling as he understood for the first time in his life that *this is living*.

FORRESTFIELD

She always watched the news during dinner. Or listened to it, rather. Almost all the blind people she knew didn't bother with television, preferring the radio. But Lorraine liked the news on the telly. It meant that when she travelled on the bus to the shops or to the library, she could talk about the same topics and issues that others did. Of course, she couldn't see the pictures, though it was hardly difficult to follow.

Lorraine's parents insisted on watching it when she was growing up, along with *The Don Lane Show*, and *Hey Hey it's Saturday*, as well as soaps and movies, and they never considered changing their ways just because one of their children was vision-impaired, believing it was good for her.

She would often sit and daydream that she'd feature in a news piece. Lorraine spent her days organising and fundraising for Blind Citizens WA and wished that one day the cameras would come and interview her. Then she could sit down at home and hear herself on there. And all the people around town would notice her and acknowledge her when she tapped around with her stick and her beloved Labrador, Fyfe.

Lorraine tucked into her baked potato with beans and cheese that she had made herself and relaxed in front of the TV, enjoying her favourite part of the day.

'And news just in,' Susannah Carr said, interrupting a piece about storm damage in Busselton, 'we're receiving reports of an armed man holding State MPs hostage in parliament. We'll cross now to our reporter Geoff Parry, who's live at the scene.' Lorraine dropped her fork, goosebumps spreading up both her arms. 'Hi Geoff, can you tell us what's happening there?'

'Yes, I can, Susannah. A man allegedly stormed the building at the end of a fresh debate on Roe 8, strapped with explosives. Witnesses claim he shot dead one of the guards shouting, "Allahu Akbar".' Lorraine's pulse throbbed so hard she watched it bopping through her wrist. 'He has since identified himself as Abdullah Amasi.'

Lorraine gripped the armchair as she felt it spin like it had dropped from space.

'Sources say he's a twenty-three-year-old Australian-Pakistani citizen who claims to be a member of ISIS.'

Richard. Her beautiful baby boy, Richard.

The phone rang, making her jump. Her dog shuffled and lifted its head before going back to sleep. She wanted it to stop. It rang and on and on. She switched the TV on to mute and nervously lifted the receiver. 'Hello.'

'Hello, Mrs Amasi?' came the voice.

'I'm not Mrs Amasi.'

'You're not?' She heard a hand cover the receiver, followed by a forced whisper. 'She says she's not Mrs Amasi.'

'I'm Ms Webber.'

'Rhys Sneddon here, *The Australian*. We were wondering if you could provide us with a few quotes regarding your son's actions?'

'I really don't think I can.'

'But you don't condone them, do you?'

'Of course, I don't.'

'Did you raise your son to be a jihadi?'

'Of course, I didn't.'

'I'm at Parliament House right now. The police have the area surrounded by snipers. Would you object to them taking out your son if it means saving innocents?'

'Oh, my lord,' she wept. 'You … you … what are you asking me?'

'Mrs Amasi.' She could no longer correct him. 'Mrs Amasi, are you still there?' He paused. 'We'll call you right back.'

The line went dead. With dread, she turned the TV back up as the dog snored. Geoff Parry was still at the scene. 'The terrorist's demands are for a helicopter, the removal of all western troops from the Middle East, and for Western Australia to become an Islamic Caliphate. And twenty million dollars.'

Lorraine thought of her beautiful boy and how this didn't make sense.

There was a knock at her door. She froze. Fyfe leapt up, barking in its direction.

'Ms Webber?' It was a woman's voice. 'Ms Webber, are you there?'

Lorraine thought of her beautiful boy who hadn't seen his Muslim father since he left when the boy was fourteen-months-old. Lorraine had tried to keep young Richard in touch with his heritage by cooking halal and taking him to the mosque on occasion, though he'd never shown much interest. Then everything changed when he left for Pakistan, shortly after failing his Year 12 exams, to search for his father. He never found him. But what found him in a big way was fundamental Islam.

'Ms Webber, are you still there?'

She stayed quiet as the dog barked. 'It's Louisa Radic, here from ABC Radio. We were wondering if you could give us the lowdown on your son. What was he like? Who was he? What got him into this mess? We want to give you a voice.'

Her beautiful, shy, intelligent boy who went over there on her dollar and returned as someone she no longer recognised. In traditional clothes and with a wife who spoke no English, whose face she still hadn't seen to this day.

Richard was now to be called Abdullah. He had no patience with her blindness, saying God must have cursed her for her wickedness, forgetting she'd been born blind. He would throw her food in the bin and smash her wine bottles in the sink, telling her she was unclean. He moved her furniture around when he knew her home was her only sanctuary from the chaos outside. And he would push her and strike her for no reason, turning on poor Fyfe with his feet when the dog tried to stop him.

She could take it no longer. She got her brother to remove his belongings from the house and changed the locks. It broke her heart, yet she had no choice. She told her son she would always love him and she would allow him back in the house when he changed. He spat in her face, screaming that she would live to regret this.

That was a year ago.

'Are you sure it's this house,' the reporter asked a colleague behind the door.

'I can't see the numbers,' a male voice replied.

'Look how lovely this home is. How green the grass is. This person isn't handicapped. I think it's that old shack across the street.'

'Let's go.'

Lorraine breathed again. Fyfe came and lay by her feet.

'Good dog. It'll all be okay now. It'll all work out now,' she said, almost praying, her nails digging into the leather sofa.

Her dinner was cold, though she was no longer hungry. The news had changed to footy. The Dockers were in the finals this Saturday. Maybe that meant things would be okay. Maybe it would all end peacefully and her son would get the help he needed.

'Raghead wankers,' came the shout from a car racing down the road followed by a heavy object careening through her front window, sending shards of glass flying.

She smelled the petrol and felt the heat from the flames. She regretted what she'd wished for alright. As her dog barked, she knew if she made it out of the house, away from the inferno, that she would regret the moment her fifteen minutes of fame arrived.

CLAREMONT

Lachie Stott sat on the same park bench he did every lunchtime during the warmer months. Under the same eucalyptus tree. Wearing the same Roger David suit with the pockets he'd never gotten round to unstitching. Eating the same cheese and ham, white bread roll from the school canteen he always ate, smoking the same Champion Ruby roll-ups.

For Lachie Stott, every day was the same these days. But what Lachie Stott didn't know was that his life was about to change forever.

Lachie Stott had been living like this for ten years, since he'd accepted the role of payroll officer at Christ Church Grammar, the school he'd once attended. When he graduated in 2001, he swore he'd never set foot back inside the place unless it was with an uzi and a suicide vest.

He joined a punk band as a bass player (putting five years of clarinet tuition to some use), backpacked around Europe, tried and failed to write a Beat novel, and worked in bars and at restaurant sinks to make ends meet.

When he returned to Perth, his girlfriend became his wife, and they had a daughter and it came time to settle down. Being one of the few students at Christ Church who hadn't been particularly academic, he had no qualifications. So, he enrolled at TAFE as a mature-age student in the only course he'd been good at in school — business studies. And a year and a bit later, due to his father's Masonic connections with the deputy headmaster, the advertised job was a formality, and all memory of his past indiscretions, much like that flare he threw into the staff room on his last day of school, went up in smoke.

Lachie Stott kicked a large damp leaf off his shoe and stared at the vast river where a solitary black swan paddled by. Four Year 12 boys were smoking a joint on the bench further along. He recognised them by their leavers shirts, but as he wasn't a teacher, they probably didn't know who he was. And even if they did, they wouldn't care, just as he wouldn't have when he was in their lace-ups and was wifeless and childless and mortgage-less and wasted two decades ago.

As he wiped down his shoe with a tissue, Lachie Stott was struck by how everything in his life had turned out exactly how he hadn't wanted it to. He couldn't remember the last time he'd seen a band or bought a record, been on holiday or got drunk or high. He wasn't entirely sure why as time wasn't a factor. His wife had kicked him out, and he only saw his daughter once a fortnight. But the childcare payments and the mortgage for the house he no longer lived in meant he was still here, grinding away at the school he'd attended since age five.

Lachie Stott watched an elderly lady wander across the bank, gripping a walking frame, wearing a nightie with a heavy, home-knitted strawberry-coloured pullover. Another older lady with an exaggerated stoop was propped up by a young Indian carer wheeling a drip, the pair slowly approaching the jetty. Behind was a local respite home, and the residents who weren't overly incapacitated would visit the water for fresh air and their daily exercise, some assisted, most not.

The staff and school teachers Lachie Stott spoke to hated coming to this part of the river, choosing not to spend their break times haunted by the spectre of illness and ageing, and the reminder that life was finite. Lachie Stott wouldn't say he loved it, though he didn't hate it either. It may have been the quiet and the stillness that made him feel somewhat balanced here. If he was honest, it was more to do with how he could smoke and get away with nobody from school noticing that brought him back here each day.

An old man with a wooden cane, featuring a brass handle with a lion's head, hobbled out the gates of the home. He was freshly shaven with lustrous Brylcreemed white hair and a tailor-cut dark-blue pinstripe suit. Unaccompanied, he shuffled along the path. Lachie Stott could smell the Old Spice and a hint of urine as he passed.

The man perched on the park bench nearest. He relaxed his old bones on the wooden slats. He lit a thin cigarillo and took a satisfying puff. Then he leaned back, closed his eyes, and released what Lachie Stott and his old school accomplices would have referred to as a 'right royal ripper'. Tree branches jerked wildly above. Magpie's shot out of nests and up into the skies. The swan backpedalled as quickly as its legs could carry it.

The old man's hunched shoulders settled, and he smiled. The smile of a man who knew that the world would never get any better than this. That simple random pleasures such as these were what life was all about and what he'd miss most.

He stubbed the cigarillo out with the toe of his polished wingtip and patted down his trousers. Bones creaking, he rose and made it back through the gates to the old home.

Lachie Stott sat up and smiled. The smile of a man who hadn't smiled in a long time. The smile of a man who realised he had the rest of his life in front of him.

He binned the other half of his ham and cheese roll. He removed his tie, draped his jacket over his shoulder, and walked past the Year 12s and the respite home, in the direction of the train station. Away from the school, away from the suburb, away from this life he knew all too well.

He figured it was about time his wife's new partner started paying half of the mortgage, anyway.

MOUNT HAWTHORN

Wayne Clegg was sure he'd lived in the suburb longer than anyone else. He remembered back in the sixties when Mount Hawthorn was just a regular patch, full of battlers. Proud working-class families, yet battlers all the same. Fast-forward half a century and the place was overrun with fancy cars and babies' prams the size of Russian tanks. Men in skinny ties, women drowning in silver and gold, and young people showing too much flesh, with hair which looked like it had been ironed.

Wayne did not feel part of it at all, and all the newcomers let him know it. Crossing the street when they saw him, shielding their children from him when he walked through the park. Partly because his was that big old property with the garden he could no longer maintain, which sliced a good $25K off everyone else's townhouse.

Wayne was a born loner. He'd been on disability since he was of working age and walked with a crutch after contracting polio as a boy. He'd never had friends. He didn't need these folks who now called his suburb home, and he certainly didn't want to be their friend. He just wanted to be acknowledged. He'd gone his whole life being ignored and now in his sixties, with his body entering its final act, he wanted to feel a part of something. Wanted to feel like he at least mattered. That he existed. Yet, every year, as house prices went up, the level of respect that Wayne received diminished.

And Wayne had had enough.

Across the street from the old house his parents had died in and left him was an empty corner block. Empty as long as he'd lived there. With two large gum trees and a wild mass of shrubs, it had never been used by the public, so he was never sure why the council kept it.

Then one day, at the tail-end of another endless and unforgiving summer, a couple of guys in Ned Kelly beards, flannel shirts, tight jeans and R.M. Williams boots began clearing the weeds and chopping down one of the trees which had rotted. More joined them, and reticulation was fitted, a mesh fence erected and seeds planted. Soon the area turned a lush green. Come springtime, a neighbourhood market was in operation. Locals congregated on Saturday mornings to choose from a rich array of pumpkins and silverbeet, cabbage and carrots, as their children ran amongst the bountiful rows of thick produce.

Wayne wasn't happy. He realised he loved that vacant block and the natural solitude it offered. Now his quiet street was inhabited by tattooed men and bra-less women, laughing and tilling, watering and planting. And on weekend mornings it was overrun by passers-by purchasing their overpriced vegetables. And not one of them so much as offering a friendly 'hello', 'how are you?' or a 'kiss my arse' to him. Even when he went over there one time to purchase a banana (they didn't have any), he was treated like a leper. Wayne had had enough of the suburb and everyone in it, and the local market was the tipping point.

A creature of the night, he began jumping the fence in the small hours to get a closer look at what all the fuss was about. He didn't get it. He didn't get why people would go out of their way to buy here when the Woolies down the road had cheaper stuff which looked a lot shinier.

It was in the new gardens late one night that Wayne had the sudden urge to urinate. Must have been all that Kole Beer he'd had during *Neighbours*. And so he did. He took it out of his Stubbies and urinated. Right there on the red chillies. He should have held it in and gone home, he really should have, but boy it felt good spraying it about like that. An almost seismic release of piss and pent-up tension.

So much so that this became a nightly thing. In the dead of night, every night before bedtime, he would cross the street and carefully relieve himself on the produce. Wayne would then giggle on Saturdays as he peered out his front window and saw the locals sniff and sample all that he had touched and buy it by the box-load.

Another night he was there, he had a shit boiling in his bowels. It felt natural for him to do it right there, much more natural than doing it in a porcelain bowl and flushing it out to sea. Double-checking to make sure there was no one around, he dropped his shorts and laid one right next to the beetroot. He knew this wouldn't be quite so easy to get away with, so he dug a small hole next to the root with his bare hands and rolled it in there, making sure to cover his tracks.

Then, one hot summer night, when taking a walk amongst the zucchinis, he was thinking hard about *Xanadu,* which he'd re-watched for the hundredth time on his trusty VHS player. Wayne wasn't exactly a sexual being. He was a virgin, he would always be a virgin, and he couldn't remember the last time he masturbated. And yet here he was, lost in the moment, naked, rolling around in the dirt thinking of Olivia Newton-John in all that white satin, and blowing his beans from here to the heavens. Or, more specifically, all over the eggplant.

Wayne had finally found something to live for. His days were full of expectation and anticipation as he whiled away the hours waiting until darkness fell, and he could urinate and defecate and ejaculate over the produce which now occupied that old corner block.

The market grew in popularity as hoards from the suburbs and surrounds visited. They extended the opening hours to seven days a week. Reviews appeared in the local paper about how delicious and fresh the vegetables and herbs were. The reviewers couldn't work out how they did it.

Wayne was happier, relaxed and more fulfilled than he'd ever been. As he wandered around his suburb, he sensed something familiar, a sort of indefinable connection with everyone he met, and he began to smile instead of scowl. And people responded in kind, no longer crossing the street and shielding their kids. Instead, nodding and beaming and saying 'hello' and 'how are you?' and really meaning it. He began to see himself in the eyes of his neighbours and experience a genuine connection.

And things only look like getting better.

Unless, of course, he's ever caught going about his business on one of his late-night escapades. All the good vibes will go out the window then as the smiling hipsters castrate him and hang him from the fence line. But until that time arrives, Wayne Clegg feels wonderful.

MOUNT PLEASANT

'You'll love them, trust me.' Scott took her hand. She was still raw at him from the fight they'd had in Kuala Lumpur when he bought that camera lens. Just another skirmish in a long-line of battles. He had half-a-dozen still in their boxes back home, and he'd used their limited funds to buy it. *Her* money, part of the advance from her publishing deal. Not his money, as his photography start-up hadn't gotten any work yet. And her money had to last them for the three weeks they were in Perth until they returned to London and could start earning again.

Kisha lay her head on his strong upper-arm in the back of the cab. It wouldn't pay thinking of the č429 now. She was here in his homeland, about to stay with his people, and she knew no one. It was her first time away from Europe, bar a solitary family trip to the Caribbean. Now was not the time to fall out.

She smiled a tired smile. She hadn't slept since Heathrow and regretted all that red wine. She was apprehensive about this, all of this. Especially meeting his family. His father, the insurance exec, his mother the bored homemaker. His brothers and sister, which Scott had warned her were so very different to him.

Landing in Australia was not like she imagined. It was cooler than she expected for December. The endless blue sky which Scott talked about all the time in London was instead overcast, the sun failing to get much change from it. His family was supposed to be here to greet them at the airport, but Scott said they must have forgotten or got tied up, so they caught a cab instead.

Kisha stared out the window. The highways and roads seemed excessively wide, though the traffic was light, made up of gas guzzling vehicles, the likes of which she'd rarely seen back home. The houses were large and bland, mostly beige and brown and grey with huge gaps between them, making them appear cold and unwelcome. Australia lacked any of the warmth or colour she'd expected.

'I hope so,' she finally replied, squeezing his arm. This was the first Christmas she would miss with her large, close family in South London. She hoped it — hoped *he* — was worth it. She felt a stab of guilt that she still questioned this after three years together.

She turned to Scott. He, too, was staring out the window and wasn't smiling. He'd been so stressed, especially when his short film didn't get anywhere at the festivals he'd submitted to. He seemed worn-out from London. She realised he needed to come back and recharge. See his family, his friends, the beach. She wanted to get to know him, the real him, in his natural environment.

Kisha thought of her prospective in-laws and their Facebook profiles she'd stumbled over. The constant reposts his father made from that ginger-haired Australian politician which he seemed besotted with and who seemed so hateful. The 'Ban the Burqa' and 'Stop the Mosques' campaigns his mother obsessed over. The stream of Aboriginal and Muslim memes his older brother posted.

'Alanna's moved back in with Mum and Dad,' Scott said suddenly.

Kisha remembered the name from Scott's past, though it took her a while to place her in the scheme of things. 'Your ex?'

'Yeah.'

'Why?'

'She broke up with her boyfriend. They built a place together, and she had nowhere to go. Mum didn't want to turn her away.'

'When did this happen?'

'A few months ago. But they just told me.'

A few months ago was when they booked the trip. Scott should have been told. *She* should have been told. At the very least, he could have told her at the start of the trip. Alanna wasn't just any old girlfriend. She was Scott's girlfriend from when he was fifteen until he was twenty-six. His fiancé for that last year.

Kisha didn't want to fight. She needed them to remain tight. She thought of Uncle Sol's Christmas reggae mixtape she'd be missing, and Aunty Marisha's macaroni pie that went down so well with the turkey. She thought of how much they loved Scott and claimed him as one of their own.

The taxi pulled off the main road, into a narrower suburban street with cookie-cutter front lawns and four-wheel-drives out front.

She pulled a stray braid back from her face and tried to smile. She snuggled in close to him, peered up, and through the rear-view mirror she saw that same stony expression of fear in his eyes.

GOOSEBERRY HILL

Caitlin expected Drew to be here. She still would have come if she'd known, she had to, but it would've prepared her.

'He's gone back to Japan,' Sadie told her, standing there in her fur vest and long gold chain, using a broom to dust imaginary cobwebs from the corners of the high ceiling while Caitlin sorted the last of her father's books into boxes. 'You should know that. I don't know why you don't know that. It's not my fault you don't speak and you don't know that.'

'We do speak, Mum.'

They did, always had. And since their father's lengthy illness, and the weeks following his death, she'd spoken to her brother almost every day. Drew told her Akari was struggling with the kids on her own. She must have called him back to Kyoto sooner.

Caitlin knew Drew didn't want to do all this. She may have been closer to her father, but being three years older, he had more memories, more bad memories, from the family home in the hills.

Caitlin leafed through a hardback copy of *My Brilliant Career*, the one she remembered reading as a child. She put it in her cardboard box to take home. The removalists would not be taking this to the op shop.

Her mother scrubbed at the door handle vigorously, almost angrily, with the dry, green scourer, careful not to let her blue gel nails get in the way. 'You know Drew has work.'

'I have work too, Mum.'

The older lady bit her lip so hard Caitlin saw it lose its colour. Caitlin knew it had always bugged her that her only daughter completed a carpentry diploma, abandoning a degree in corporate law. And how Caitlin had moved away to Albany with her girlfriend Stacey, who she'd been with years before Drew met his wife.

Caitlin skimmed through the dusty collection of unblemished Jackie Collins and Nora Roberts paperbacks. 'Do you want these kept?'

'No room in the condo,' Sadie replied, almost cheerfully. 'Everything must go.'

Caitlin didn't understand why, aged just sixty-six, her mother, who still walked these hills and swam every day, and had a body firmer and fitter than her daughter who was half her age, would want to live in an old people's home. Or a *Community Condo,* as the website called it.

Caitlin put this bundle of books in an empty box to be taken away. She fingered through a selection of Lessings, Fitzgeralds, Hemingways and a first-edition of Anaïs Nin's *A Spy in the House of Love*. She placed them into another box. They were reminders of her father, the shy man of few words who tried his best to teach her that life could be tolerable, and at times even beautiful.

While she listened to the overgrown branches of the old oak tree brush against the window, one of the removalists, a girl, entered and lifted the new box.

'Oh, no, not that one,' Caitlin said, carefully taking it from her, their fingers coming together for a moment. The removalist smiled shyly, showing a row of crooked front teeth which somehow suited her, making her awkwardness endearing. Caitlin looked into her eyes and saw a delicate soul trapped in a cumbersome, clumsy body. A brief spark flashed between them, and Caitlin felt ten years younger. The carefree way she'd been before she met Stacey. Caitlin could tell the girl hadn't yet come out.

'These are my father's books,' she said, lowering the box. 'Have you read Anaïs Nin?' She held up the frayed, browning pages, showing her.

'I'm not much of a reader,' the girl said, distracted by Sadie standing at the edge of the room, her eyes boring through her. Flushed, she quickly lifted the next box and left the room.

Sadie resumed dusting the fly screens, dead mites and small crumbs of dead leaves dropping onto the ancient floorboards. Caitlin had hated living here in the hills. This parched, faded town on the edges of civilisation, far from the bright lights of the CBD, or the cool breeze of the ocean and those with minds wide-open.

This study, this library, had been her salvation. The only room her father, Malcolm, could relax in with his books and his jazz records and his red wine. Where she could have a break from her mother and all her despair, and drink creaming soda and scoff lollies. Where they would kill time together, doing nothing in particular. Something her mother never understood. Despite having left this house fifteen years ago, she had a sudden urge to gather up the six hundred grand and buy the old weatherboard home her grandfather had built after the war.

The bookcase was empty now. Caitlin had shifted across to where a bundle of framed photographs lay, mostly wedding ones, and others of Drew and her growing up. There was a picture of a family holiday, probably Rottnest or somewhere down south. Their old neighbours Victor and Susan were in it. Caitlin remembered something her father had mentioned. Something she'd been meaning to ask her mother.

'Doesn't Victor live in that retirement village?'

'*It's a community condo.*' Sadie rammed a scraper into the corners of the window with a clunk. She took her time to answer. She appeared to be choosing her words carefully. 'Victor does, yes. He's a dear man who's had a hard time of it and done a lot for me over the years. A darn sight more than most when I needed them.'

Caitlin's father was the only GP in town when she was growing up. She wondered if this was still the case. If the doctor here had to tend to the sick, resuscitate car-crash victims, tell families that their loved ones weren't going to make it. She tried to remember a time when he was in the house and not asleep or desperately trying to unwind from it all in his antique leather wingback. She realised she couldn't.

It was in this room that Caitlin had read and learned about life. First through literature and the collection of long gone *Encyclopedia Britannica*, and later the internet on the home computer. It was here she found out about periods and babies, boys and then girls. Subjects any other daughter would be uneasy discussing with their father, subjects she could never broach with her mum.

The girl entered and collected another box. She gave a quick smile to Caitlin, blanching slightly. When she retreated, Caitlin felt a glare from her mother and knew it was because she had booked the firm. Not a firm with wide-torsoed, strong-armed, meat-eating men, but one that employed females. Dykes at that. Caitlin understood this because she'd felt that same glare growing up when she'd told her mum she wanted to play football instead of take ballet, do carpentry over law, sleep with girls instead of boys.

'That's me, I'm done,' Sadie said, downing tools and stretching her neck to iron out a creak. Caitlin wasn't sure why her mother had come. The cleaners were booked for tomorrow ahead of Wednesday's settlement.

Sadie collected her handbag and gave Caitlin a perfunctory peck on the cheek, the kind where there was zero body contact aside from her thin, cracked lips. Caitlin could never imagine this woman wiping her bottom when she was a child. Caitlin couldn't imagine doing that for Sadie should the time come, like she'd done so many times for her dad. Her kind and gentle dad who did so much for these hills and couldn't even stand or utter a sentence or take a shit on his own when the slow, sad end came.

'I'll be seeing you then,' Sadie said. 'Text me if you need anything.'

Sadie walked out of the study towards the front door. Caitlin didn't know when she would see her mother again. Drew had no reason to return now. Over the past three years, she'd only seen her mother during hospital or hospice visits.

Caitlin steeled herself and stuck her head out the study doorway. 'Mum,' she called down the hallway to the woman's back. 'I'm pregnant.'

Sadie paused, then turned. 'How ...? Have you left ...?' The words wouldn't come, a million questions vying for answers. 'Is it with a man?'

'With Stacey. With a donor. We've wanted this for a while. Stacey's busy with the business. It was easier for me to do it.'

Her mother's face remained expressionless. 'Well, as long as you're sure.'

Caitlin heard a car engine pull up out front. 'I'm eleven weeks. I'm not supposed to tell anyone.' Caitlin wept, the first time she'd cried in front of her mother since she was a child. She didn't want to admit that she'd told her father the news the day before he died. That he understood and smiled and was proud, pulling her in close to his deathbed and telling her so.

Caitlin swore she saw a hint of a smile gather across her mother's face. That there was a glint of moisture in her eyes. Sadie swayed forwards. Caitlin thought she might retrace her steps and really kiss her, perhaps hold her, and mean it. Instead, her mother stood tall and threw her handbag over her shoulder. 'That's nice. Be sure to call me if you need anything.'

The door closed. Caitlin looked out the study window. There was a silver Mercedes tucked in behind the removal truck. She saw one of Victor's signature cravats dangle over the steering wheel as her mother got in beside him. They kissed, and the car pulled away down the hill.

Caitlin heard the removalists bumping and heaving through the front door. This was the noisiest she remembered the house ever being. Through the reflection of the window, Caitlin saw the girl come back into the study. She crouched down and put all the photos on top of her mother's books. 'Shall I take these?' the girl asked.

'Please.'

Caitlin turned. Their eyes met. Caitlin hoped the removal girl had the guidance she lacked growing up in these hills. The type only a woman can provide. She knew that if she was still here, if she wasn't with Stacey, that she could be the one who showed the girl the way things were.

LEEDERVILLE

'We need to get out of here,' Sebastian said, shaking his tortoise-shell head from side-to-side from the safety of the top of the fridge.

'What do you mean?' Geoffrey replied, shushing and trying to usher the Rottweiler out of the lounge towards the laundry.

'What do I mean? I can't believe you let this happen.'

Geoffrey got the door opened wide, using his feet as the dog turned and they wrestled. 'I didn't know she had a dog."

'Horseshit, you didn't.'

'Well, I didn't think it was this big.'

'This is so typical of you.'

Geoffrey took a step forward and tried to corner the hound. It sprung back and then lurched forward for him, its jaws gaping, fangs snatching at his sleeve. Geoffrey squealed and drew back, the dog hanging off his red Bunnings shirt.

Sebastian paced the fridge-top. 'Gouge its eyes. Squeeze its nuts.' The cat shook its paw. 'Kick it in the dick!'

Geoffrey drew back. He took one look at Sebastian and screamed and threw himself at the beast. The dog retreated, took a few steps back, and Geoffrey's momentum got it inside the laundry.

He hastily shut the door, breathing a giant sigh of relief. He collapsed onto the sofa. He took a tissue from the box on the table and wiped the saliva from the sleeve, showing a toothmark-shaped rip. 'I'm going to need a new shirt. My supervisor will not be pleased.'

'You need a lot of things.' Sebastian watched as Geoffrey lifted the bong from the table. 'And you need to stop doing that.'

Geoffrey took a deep draw. 'Why? This is the reason I'm talking to you. You never said a word till I started.'

The tomcat licked the dust off his paw and leapt gracefully down from the fridge. 'Yeah, well, I'm still not sure that's the answer to your predicament.'

Sebastian hopped up onto the sofa and stretched out, relaxing now that the dog was behind the door. Despite it still sniffing and growling, the threat had subsided.

'When's that wench home?' he asked Geoffrey.

'Don't call her that. Her name is Gwen.'

'When's that wench Gwen home?'

'An hour ago.'

'And you're okay with that?'

'With what?'

'She could be with him, you know.'

'Who?'

'No one.'

'She's at work.'

'You know she's using you.'

'Stop saying that.'

'Elsbeth said it too.'

'Don't bring mother into this.'

'I'm just saying.'

'Just don't.'

'I'm just saying what she said before she died. That the wench would take half of everything.'

Geoffrey needed air and removed his Bunnings sweatshirt. Then he leaned between the folds of the corduroy couch, letting the smoke take hold. 'That hasn't happened yet,' he said, with barely a whisper.

'So you're saying that it is going to happen.'

'No, I'm, it's ... please, can we leave it? I'm on the early, and I need to relax. I've had a full day of people haranguing me about nuts and bolts and ... rakes.'

The cat recommenced licking its paws. 'We used to relax every evening back in Roleystone. I miss that place.'

'I do too,' Geoffrey mumbled, his eyelids heavy.

'I miss the garden,' Sebastian frowned out at the balcony which faced away from the city, towards the suburbs.

'So do I.'

A Harley accelerated down Oxford Street below. 'I miss the quiet.'

'Hmmm.'

'I miss the creaky wooden floorboards and all that space, and not having to watch your back every moment in case you get snapped in half by that animal.'

'This is nice though, isn't it?' Geoffrey almost whispered, barely awake.

'It should be like this all the time,' Sebastian replied. Geoffrey said nothing. 'It could be, you know.' Geoffrey had drifted off. 'If we killed her.'

Geoffrey's eyes opened. He lurched forward. 'What?!'

'What?' Sebastian playfully rolled onto his back.

'What did you say?'

'I said, "If we left her".'

'Oh,' Geoffrey pulled back. 'That's alright then.'

'So, we will?'

'What?'

'Leave her?'

'No.'

'Why not?'

'Because I love her.'

Sebastian sneezed. 'You hate living here.'

'I wouldn't say that.'

'You hate the lift that never works. You hate the noise and how the pollution plays games with your asthma. You hate living on top of a hundred people with another hundred more above. You hate having to drive to work. You hate —'

'But there's a wedding.'

'Two years since the engagement, Geoff, and it hasn't been mentioned.'

'And the trip. That's why I'm here, saving up for the trip round-the-world.'

'You hate flying.'

'I've only flown once. A mystery flight twenty-five years ago to Broome. Might like it now.'

'And you might freak out. You might hit a flock of seagulls. You might get held up by terrorists. You might run out of fuel and crash.'

'Stop it.'

'And even if it turns out peachy, what am I going to do while you're snapping pics of pyramids? Hmm? Stay here with that brute?' Sebastian hissed at the door and the dog whined.

'There are catteries.'

The cat glared at him. 'They're like prisons. Colombian prisons. Mother would be turning in her grave if she knew what you were doing to me.'

'Please stop bringing her into this.' Geoffrey searched for the cone-piece, feeling the need to de-stress once again.

'I might as well be dead as it is,' Sebastian paced the floor. 'No fresh air. No exercise.' He took a pinch of his excess flab in his paw. 'No ABC Classic FM. Just stiletto toes in the balls from her, and the constant threat of bombardment from that thing.' The dog scratched the door and growled. 'I might as well do it.'

'Don't say that.' Geoffrey lit the bong.

'If you don't do it, I'll be off that ledge seeing if I can fly like that cat on YouTube we saw.'

'You can't fly.'

'You didn't think I could talk either, and that theory went out the window pretty quickly.'

Geoffrey took another hit and pondered this.

'So, are we killing her?' Sebastian asked.

'What?' Geoffrey coughed.

'I said, "Are we leaving her?"'

'Where would we go?'

'Where do you think? Home of course. The house hasn't sold yet. Do it before it does, and she gets her hands on the loot.'

'I don't want to be alone again.'

'And this is living, is it?' Sebastian looked to the melange of pinks and frills in the cramped apartment. Geoffrey didn't even have a place to put his keys.

Geoffrey cleared his throat, moving the gluey phlegm which was lodged there. 'It's how most people live.'

'She won't even give you your own drawer in the bathroom. There's four of them. Big ones. You have to wrap a plastic bag around the handle and put your toothpaste in there.'

Geoffrey reluctantly nodded. 'That is true.'

'She gets to come and go as she pleases. You're kept on a leash. You're not even allowed to bowl anymore.'

'That was my idea. It's too far.'

'From here maybe. But not the old joint.'

'I'd miss the companionship.'

'Yeah, the separate beds, the dearth of conversation, the complete lack of intimacy.'

Geoffrey closed his eyes not wanting to hear anymore. Sebastian leapt onto his knee. 'I miss mother,' Geoffrey whispered.

'So do I,' said Sebastian, snuggling into his lap.

'I'm not happy here, am I?'

The lift in the lobby pinged.

'We're not,' Sebastian agreed. 'I miss the old house.'

'I miss the bowling club.'

'I miss the garden.'

'I'm not sure I love her.'

'I know.'

'I'm not killing her.'

The cat looked up. 'Who said anything about killing her?'

'We could just move out.'

'Or you could kill her.'

'What?!'

'Nothing.'

'You said I could kill her.'

'Probably easier killing her is all I'm saying. All that sitting down and explaining, then breaking her heart and dividing your things.'

'No ... no ...'

The cat licked its paws. 'Just saying, a soft nudge over the balcony, who would know? Our little secret.'

'No.'

'Could keep this as a city pad. Should probably kill the dog too.'

'Don't be so cruel.'

'She's the one who's been cruel.'

'I don't know about that.'

'She doesn't love you.'

'She might.'

'She told you so.'

'You didn't hear that.'

'Do you think there's someone else?'

'How do you know that?'

'I read her email.'

'You can't read.'

'Oh, we're back there again, are we?'

'I'm not sure.'

The cat looked his owner in the eye. 'She's having an affair.'

The lift pinged again. Geoffrey held his breath. Sebastian turned to the door and the fourteen-pound bowling ball next to it. The footsteps came closer, then stopped. A key entered the lock. Sebastian moved towards the door. Geoffrey got up. He nodded. He knew what to do.

DIANELLA

On the drive to the family home for his sister's thirtieth birthday party, all Nick had ringing in his ears were the words from his parents in the lead up. All about how great a guy her new boyfriend was, how much he did for Melanie, and how he'd have to meet him soon. And how they'd apparently attended school together. Joshua Drysdale, they said. It didn't ring a bell for Nick, and he'd been far too busy with his new role to visit before this.

He hadn't thought much about it as he parked up and entered and said hello to his aunts, uncles and cousins who he only saw when someone was getting married or buried.

After he'd crouched down to kiss his sister in her wheelchair and wish her a happy birthday, he realised he'd never seen her so vibrant, so confident and happy. He gave her a gift. A comedy one of a *Dawson's Creek* paperback he found at a garage sale, in homage to the show they used to religiously watch as teens. Then, a serious one of a one-night stay at Crown. Overjoyed, she hugged him again, tighter. She then called her partner over. And it was then that it came flooding back.

Joshua Drysdale.

JD.

Hot Lip.

He was standing there, not in a Metallica t-shirt and Rollers, with oily and unruly hair and a bumfluff goatee. No, instead he was in a button-up shirt tucked into ironed chinos, and a neat side-parting up top.

'I'm Joshua.' He held out a chunky right hand, that old scar above his left-eye still visible. 'I've heard so much about you.'

Nick shook it. 'Yeah, likewise.' He searched his face for a hint of recognition, but there was nothing except a broad smile from bright teeth.

Nick's mother appeared with a glass of champagne. 'I'm told you two went to school together?'

'I went to Morley High very briefly, Mrs Mrdja. Kept a low profile.'

'I don't believe that for one minute,' Nick's mother teased, smitten by her prospective son-in-law.

'Josh, there's someone else I want you to meet.' Melanie took her fiancé by the hand and let him wheel her towards the front door where a group of her girlfriends had entered.

'He's been so good for her,' Nick's mother said as they viewed the pair. 'Done wonders for her self-esteem.'

Nick remembered Joshua. And bullshit had he only been to Morley High briefly. He went there for years.

'He doesn't care about the disability thing at all,' his mother continued. 'He's already had ramps and rails fitted in his home. This must be serious.'

JD was a lone wolf who bullied and tormented all the smaller boys, the weaker and gentler ones, with his particular ire set upon Nick and his Computer Club buddies. The abuse was so bad it forced Nick's best-friend, Tang, to switch to Chisholm halfway through Year 9.

'He has his own courier company,' Nick's mother continued. 'Swam to Rotto last month to raise funds for MS.'

JD used a variety of tactics to terrorise Nick's group. Royal flushes, wedgies, extortion, down to a good old-fashioned flogging. But Joshua's pièce de résistance, which he reserved for Nick and Nick alone, was far more sinister.

Hot Lip.

Each time he bumped into Nick, in the toilets, in the corridor, by the canteen, out on the oval, anywhere in fact, JD would swiftly lick his middle finger, squeeze it down the back of his black jeans, force it up his own arsehole, then remove it and smear it across the space between Nick's nose and mouth, screaming 'HOT LIP!' much to the horror of everyone around.

Even after he was expelled at the end of Year 10 for dacking the sports teacher in Noranda Square during late-night shopping, for the next two years everyone still knew Nick as 'Hot Lip'. It was even documented as his nickname in the yearbook. And because of this, getting any girl or boy in school to go anywhere near his lips was an impossibility.

Nick saw Joshua pass his sister a bowl of dip as they chatted to his Aunt Dareia. In *his* family home. Nick had just assumed that by this point JD would be in prison, or worse.

It was time for Nick to go. He had an early start in the new store, as it was the first Sunday they were open. He said goodbye to his aunts, uncles and cousins who he'd see at the next wedding or funeral, or perhaps his sister's engagement. And this thought made him shudder.

'Thanks for coming.' Melanie reached up and hugged her big brother. 'Look after yourself.'

He wanted to tell her to look after *herself* and leave this ape right away. That she could do better. But as he saw her there in her chair with a new party dress on, lapping up the adulation of her friends and family, with her fiancé's hand resting protectively on her shoulder, he knew he'd never seen her happier and knew that he couldn't. Melanie deserved a little joy. She'd been through so much.

Joshua shook hands with him, firmly. 'So great to finally meet you, Nick.'

'Yeah, nice to see you again, J ... um ... mate.'

Nick turned to go.

'Hey, Nick,' Joshua said. Nick turned. 'You got a little something under your nose.'

Joshua reached over and wiped Nick's top lip gently. His finger displayed a blob of hot barbecue sauce, which must have come from the spare ribs. Nick's family smiled at the gesture.

'Thanks,' Nick said, slightly embarrassed, wiping away the rest on his sleeve and departing.

Maybe people deserved a second chance two decades on, thought Nick, as he unlocked his car door. People grow up, even people like JD.

But as he got into the driver's seat, he thought he could smell that unmistakable odour of shit, the kinda shit he could never forget, right there on his top lip, and suddenly he wasn't so sure.

CRAIGIE

Jay was hosing down the tiles of the kids' pool when he saw that old familiar form drag itself out from the change rooms. Long, unkempt grey locks. Pockmarks rising up through his patchy beard like cinder cones in the rough. The tatts. The limp. The keg-on-legs frame. And that smell. He was over on the other side of the pool, yet Jay swore he could catch a whiff of him in those too-tight brown Speedos that were already damp before he even touched the water.

Why they still let him in, Jay didn't know. At least he came when few others did. There was no one there apart from an Asian kid doing laps, and a big guy in his twenties, probably a footy amateur, walking in the water, recuperating from some injury. The spa had a few old men spread out, shooting the shit. And there were the usual gym junkies and bunnies bouncing on treadmills and gyrating on rowing machines in tight Lycra behind the glass like lab rats on meth.

Jay moved along, now blasting the tiles aggressively. He hated this time of night. He watched the old man struggle into the water and lay out on his back like a starfish. Jay used to have a quick dip at the end of the late shift when the crowds had left, when the pump was off. When it was just him and the water. Now he couldn't stomach it since the old man began appearing.

The stock announcement came over the speaker that the swim centre was closing in fifteen minutes. The Asian kid heard it. He came out and dried off, peeling off his red cap as he walked to the change rooms, revealing a pair of those fancy underwater earbuds. The footy bod struggled up the steps, clinging to the railing, and did likewise.

The old guy continued on, deaf or immune to the calls. Just lying there on his back. Jay would have to go over there in ten minutes and yell at him, right near his face, as he always did. Then he'd have to wait while he crawled out and got ready. Did a shit. Sometimes even had a shave. It could be a quarter-past-nine before they got him out and locked up. Jay was unsure why the staff let him in this late. He'd have to text that girl. Not a good look for a second date. He'd miss the start of the movie. Not a good move if he wanted to get her back to his to round the bases.

The man commenced backstroke. This was the first time Jay had seen him do so. He wasn't bad. No Thorpedo, but for a man in his condition, he wasn't terrible. But God, how Jay hated him. Hated this job. Six years he'd been here. Five-and-a-half years too long. Especially when it was only ever meant to be a summer gig.

Jay unfolded the *WET FLOOR* sign. As if he cared if the fat fuck fell and broke his neck. He had to clean the toilets at the end too. If that happened, it would save him a lot of work.

Jay realised he was sweating. He noticed the inch of flab around his belly. He hadn't swam competitively nor trained properly in years. Perhaps he should start. Not since the Commonwealth Trials in 2013, back when the WAIS told him his talents were no longer required. Up till then, he trained every morning, every week, every month since he could remember. It kept mum and dad happy but meant he missed out on parties, friends, girls. An education. He'd sacrificed his teenage years for his country, and they threw him on the heap. Meant the only thing he was qualified to do was be a lifeguard by day or a pool cleaner by night.

Swimming freestyle 1500 metres is such a solitary sport. If he'd been a footballer, he'd have had mates, peo-ple to share the load with. To party, vent, fuck and fight with. Instead of spending all that time alone in his head. And then in the end, not even getting to swim for the green and gold. Getting nothing at all.

Since then, he'd more than made up for it in the partying stakes. He'd hit the booze hard. Dabbled with the harder stuff. Got the sleeve tatts, the big car. Still, he never really knew how to make friends, how to fit in as one of the boys. He knew how to have a go with his fists. It was the *Roma* in him. But he'd had too many second prizes when out of it to consider himself a standout in that area.

Girls were the same. He had the remnants of a swim-mer's body with a strong upper-torso. Enough to get them keen, enough to get them home. After that, he didn't have much of a clue. Meaningful conversation wasn't his forte. He'd spent too much time alone.

Education was another struggle. He'd tried TAFE and failed at everything. And because of that, here he was. Stuck at the scene of the crime, where he'd learned to swim before he could walk.

'Jay! Jay! Fucksake, Jay, come help!' Jay dropped the mop. His boss, Michelle, was in the pool, her teal polo shirt clinging tightly to her breasts. It had been a year or more since he'd seen them this defined. 'Help me!' Her small limbs paddled frantically underneath the deadweight of the man's limp body, trying to haul him onto the tiles.

Jay dived in, not bothering to remove his runners. He grabbed the man's arm and, using all that he had, he dragged him towards the ledge and got him over and out and onto the wet floor. Jay got him onto his side and instinctively stuck two fingers between the black rotting teeth, thumping his back with his other hand to get the excess water out. Jay then rolled him onto his back. The man's heart was still beating, but he wasn't breathing. Jay commenced mouth-to-mouth. He gagged as he tasted the residue of alcohol, tobacco and whatever else the man had ingested since he last looked after himself. Still, Jay pushed on.

After half-a-dozen cycles of breaths, the man spluttered and bolted upright, faster than Jay thought he could ever do anything.

'The ambulance is coming,' Michelle said, wrapping a towel around the man as his eyes slowly came alive.

A small crowd from the gym had gathered, in awe more than concern. The Asian kid had his camera phone out.

The old man's red eyes met Jay's. Jay realised he'd never looked at him properly, never heard him speak. He'd never bothered to look beyond the beard and the limp and the odour which followed him around.

A few of the gym bunnies applauded. A male with a chunky square head and arms bulging out his singlet thumped Jay on the back in recognition of what he'd done, while others told him 'Well done'.

Before Jay had time to collect his own breath, the ambulance was there. The paramedics helped the old man up, replacing the leisure centre towel with a thermal one to stop him shivering.

'He should be fine,' the paramedic told Jay. 'He must have fainted in there. He was nearly a goner. You should be proud. You're a hero.'

They left with the man. Those gathered made their way to the change rooms, now with their phones in their hands, updating their statuses about this outlying occurrence. Jay just stood there. It wasn't until Michelle handed him a fresh towel that he realised he, too, was shaking.

'How come it took you so long to dive in?' she asked.

'I didn't see him.'

'I saw him. And I heard him. And I was two walls and thirty feet away.'

Jay said nothing. He kicked the bucket along the tiles with his soaked Asics and recommenced mopping where the man's body had been.

Michelle moved closer to him, her small, firm body in the polo shirt sticking to those breasts he used to know so well. 'Do you know who that was?' she asked. Jay continued mopping. 'Eric Delaney. Montreal Olympics. Silver medal. Breaststroke.' Jay had heard of the name. Seen it engraved on walls and in trophy cabinets. 'Daughter drops him here. Doctor's orders.'

Jay remembered something else about the man. His son, Ryan, was a couple of years older than Jay. He died in a car accident around twenty years back returning from a swim meet in Bunbury. Everyone knew Ryan Delaney. He was the real deal in every stroke and had been tipped to be the future of the sport. But all it took was one drunk P plater and a rolled Laser to put an end to that.

'I know you don't like coming in here, but ...' Michelle trailed off, wrapping a towel around her, covering herself. 'Listen, leave that. I'll get the morning shift to do it.'

'I'm nearly done.'

Jay continued mopping where the man's outline had been. The floor shone, yet still he mopped. Michelle returned to her office. The main lights were dimmed, and in the semi-darkness, Jay did not stop. He'd miss that movie. He hoped the girl, whatever her name was, would understand.

BULLCREEK

Maggie heard that familiar rumble out front. The rumble she knew so well from the engine her dad could never seem to tune. She put aside the Jamie Oliver hardback she'd been thumbing through and edged herself over to the window on her walker. She reached up to the blinds, pulling them apart. Her mother reversed the LandCruiser, carefully lining up the back of the ocean blue trailer with *PARTON'S POOCH PAMPERING* emblazoned across it into the tight spot. She was never much good at it. Maggie's dad was always the one who drove.

Her mother squeezed out of the driver's door. Her eyelids looked red and heavy from the full day's work, and she was too tired to care about the front-end of the four-wheel drive jutting out and blocking half the footpath. She was just relieved to have avoided the side-wall and be home.

Maggie wheeled over, opening the front door for her mother.

'How was it?' She couldn't wait to ask.

'It was ... it was bloody near impossible work but we got there, just,' the woman said, placing her bag on the bench and collapsing onto the sofa.

'Did you see, Floyd? How is he? How was his hair?' Maggie was so excited and so thirsty for an update that she almost shouted.

'You have no idea. You've never seen fluff like it. I told Mary they could've got another groomer in. We wouldn't have minded.'

'Has Ladybug had her puppies?'

'Four.' She removed her flat shoes and rubbed the tired balls of her feet. 'They are adorable.'

Maggie lowered herself from the walker onto the couch next to her. 'Is Molly doing okay after the op?'

Her mother sighed. 'She didn't make it. She didn't take to the medication. It's so sad.' Maggie looked down, lost for words at the passing of one of her favourites. 'Everyone asked about you, though,' her mother continued. 'Hey, what's with the book?' She was keen to change the subject and cheer up her only child.

'I was thinking, I could have a go at cooking dinner. Basic stuff. Shepherd's pie. Especially since I can't go with you anymore ...' She went quiet for a moment before remembering. 'I made you a sandwich.'

Maggie reached over to the sideboard and presented a white bread sandwich before her mother.

'Things *are* changing,' her mother said, biting into it. She thought it had too much beetroot and not enough cheese. 'Delicious. Thank you, my baby.' She hugged her with her free arm.

'How was the new girl?' Maggie didn't look her mother in the eye and didn't use the girl's name.

Her mother frowned. 'Not great. She's okay with the smaller dogs but scared of the bigger ones.'

'But she's a dog groomer!'

'I don't think it will work out.' Her mother put the sandwich down. 'I missed your dad today.'

'I thought you might.'

'And I missed you too.'

'I know.' Her daughter tried to hold back her tears.

'I'm not sure what to do.'

'I don't know what we can do.'

'I was thinking maybe you could start coming along again.'

Maggie chin's arched up. 'But it's too much work with me there. You can't work as well as lift and lay me.'

'We could get a carer to assist.'

'That's too expensive.'

'Instead of the other groomer. At least you know the pets.'

Maggie couldn't contain her excitement. 'But we'd hardly make any money.'

'Just until the business sells. I'm sure it will soon.' Maggie smiled as the tears came fast, and she cuddled into her mum. 'I can't do this alone.'

Over her daughter's shoulder, she saw the picture of Peter on the mantelpiece and realised how much harder everything was without him here. She held her daughter tight and thought of her cerebral palsy, and how the doctors said she should've been dead by her last birthday.

'We're going to be okay, aren't we, mum?' the girl said.

'I'm not sure, baby. But so long as we've got each other we'll be right.'

'That's true.'

'Each other's all we've got.'

WARWICK

I worked it out on the walk there. I hadn't been in Centre-link in around fifteen years. Not since I started uni and was applying for Youth Allowance. A lot of things had passed since then. I'd graduated as an engineer. Got a job in the city, and met my wife on the morning commute. We elected to stay around Warwick. Dad died when I was in primary, and mum was by herself. She didn't want to give up the place saying it held too many memories. My mates still lived around here too. Toni grew up in Har-vey so she didn't mind. Warwick was like New York City to her.

It's not like we needed the money, but with Toni say-ing she wants a baby, I thought I'd use my RDO and drop in to see what entitlements the government offered. Parental leave and such. I might work in computer soft-ware, but no way could I make sense of the Centre-link website. I felt sorry for those poor bastards who came here from non-English-speaking countries and re-ally needed help.

The building looked more or less as beige and unin-spiring as I remembered. The queue was around thirty deep, mostly men. The ones I could see were between the ages of twenty-five and forty-five, most of them in a uniform consisting of a singlet, boardies and Kmart thongs making me feel uncomfortably suave in my ironed polo shirt, Levi's and Chuck Taylors. There was no music, no air, no anything. Enough to make me wish that I was back at work instead of standing here and imagining the hundred other things I could be doing on my rostered day off.

In the quiet line, quiet but for the guy in front arguing with his mate over money owed, and a woman yelling at her kids who were understandably bored out of their tree, I regretted not bringing my AirPods for tunes or the Audible subscription I'd got for my birthday. Now would have been the perfect time.

An old couple at the front were told to take a seat and wait to see someone higher up the chain. I calculated that at this rate it would be around half-an-hour until that would be me. It could easily be a couple of hours before I got to go to Mochachos and grab lunch, then cram in a few hours of *Call of Duty* on the Xbox before Toni got home.

A girl, a woman rather, was now at the front. Big, thick blonde hair, kinda like a Shetland pony's but in a good way, with a body a little on the skinny side, which I strangely felt I somehow knew. The Centrelink employee typed in her details. Instead of instructing her to take a seat, he held up his hands in apology then pointed to the door. I could hear the girl swearing but couldn't make out what about. It was only when she turned around that I saw her. It was Gemma Taylor.

Gemma Taylor.

The girl at school. The one who, despite being one of the brightest, quit halfway through Year 12 after signing a contract with Ford Models. Thus becoming a minor Perthonality and moving to the States.

Gemma Taylor, who should be on some catwalk or starring in a Hollywood rom-com opposite Ryan Gosling.

Gemma Taylor, the girl I — everyone, even the teachers — fawned over at school. Gemma Taylor was standing in Centrelink.

I'd always wondered what happened to her. Bored at work, more than once I'd punched her name into Google to see if she hadn't married or kept her maiden name and maybe would appear, but she never did.

Why was Gemma Taylor here? There were no winners here. Not that I was a loser. Far from it, given the competition. Perhaps she, too, was planning a child and was examining her options. But no, that didn't sit right with Gemma Taylor. She shouldn't be queuing up for scraps at Centrelink Warwick. Her manager and agent should have all that covered.

I'd had a thing for Gemma since my first day at Warwick High, though I think I might have mentioned that. If I haven't, then I did. With legs up to the stars, that thick blonde mane, and a smile that could light street lamps in a power cut, we all did. All through high school, the guys would pray that they would be in the same sports class as her, especially swimming. A few braver boys, the cooler, tougher, sportier ones asked her out. But all were met with the same polite 'no'.

Gemma was friends with everyone from the cool group to the smart group, right through to the nerds, the bullies and the geeks. She transcended all boundaries. After school and her move to the U.S., she went off the grid. All sorts of crazy rumours spread around Warwick that she was the face of some lingerie range, that she was dating Heath Ledger, that she'd moved to Paris. I never found out. And even when my new life with Toni began, and with school becoming a fading memory, I couldn't help thinking about her from time to time. I think everyone did.

Gemma walked away. The queue edged ahead. I was around ten people from the front. Another twenty or so had filed in behind me. I was glad I'd forgone that extra hour of *COD* in my PJs to come here. I'd never have made it to the front.

When I looked up, Gemma Taylor, *the* IT girl of Warwick SHS class of 2006 and all the years before and probably after, was right there. Gemma Taylor was coming towards me.

Gemma Taylor, with dull eyes which had lost their brilliant blue sheen, instead conveying a tiredness like she hadn't slept in a long while, or had been crying for a long, long time.

Gemma Taylor, who never spoke a word to me at school, not because she was rude or anything. Just because I'd never spoken to her, could never let myself get near her, as I wouldn't know what to say or how to be.

'Ben?' she said, approaching me and suddenly knowing me. I mean, my name was Bern, short for Bernard, but considering we'd never hung out, I was still flattered.

'Gemma, hey, yes.' I tried to keep my voice strong. 'Long time.'

'What are you doing here?'

Were you allowed to ask that in Centrelink? Wasn't this place like the doctor's waiting room and when you spotted someone you knew, you still couldn't ask? She seemed just as surprised that I was in the building.

'Just sorting out some payments. Baby stuff.' Why did I start by saying that? Why that?

'You have a bub?'

'No. Not yet.' I was realising how dumb the whole thing sounded. 'Just planning, y'know.'

'Plan on not using a rubber. I know that works.' Gemma Taylor had actually said *rubber* to me! 'Good luck getting anything sorted here. This lot are such assholes.' She said it loud enough so the front desk would hear and with a slight American twang. 'This is the worst Centrelink by a mile.'

I wanted to know why she was here and why she was visiting other Centrelinks like some social welfare connoisseur, but didn't want to because of the unofficial and unspoken code.

'I thought you were in LA? Modelling and films and stuff. Married to Heath Ledger.'

She scrunched up her button nose. 'Ah, Heath. What a sweetie. I wouldn't exactly say we were together.' No shit, I cursed myself again. He's been dead for over a decade. 'Yeah, I was in Echo Park for a few years. Appeared in a couple of things but . . . ' She shook her head, eyes glazing over as if appearing to lose track of where she was. Then she lurched in close. 'Hey, do you like to party?'

I didn't know what to say. This close I saw through her thick makeup and rehearsed smile and could see the years had not been kind. She was gaunt, haunted even, and had lost too much weight. I mean, we were all getting older, but her skin no longer had its natural sheen, eaten up by pimples and cracks and acne scars. And the stained black Adidas hoodie and snap pants she had on were doing her no favours. And yet she still had that hair.

'I . . . I don't know what you mean.'

I remembered one ugly rumour that the only film she appeared in was a porno, but then heard from my mate Rhian that it had just been a lookalike.

'I'm out,' she said, moving in closer. 'Most people I know are. I know this guy, his gear's good but it's expensive and I don't have that kinda money at the minute.' She forced a smile. Her teeth were faded yellow, yet that smile was much the same. 'Was thinking we could go see him and then head back to yours.' She reached out and touched my hand. My heart melted.

'I . . . I don't really party. Like that. If you know what I mean.' I thought about Toni and our home and our plans. It wasn't perfect, then again, what in life was? Yet, this was my life, our life, the one we'd built. To throw it all away on some afternoon bender. Could I? Would I?

'Brian.' She didn't even know my name. 'They won't give me what they owe me. I got nothing.'

The line moved ahead a metre. I was near the front now.

'Look after yourself, Gemma.'

'Thanks for nothing, Bart.' *Bart*? Who the hell was Bart? There were no Barts in the Class of 2006. 'You're just like the motherfucking rest.' She shot through the doors. The blokes behind who'd heard looked at me like I must be mad to turn down that kind of invite. Everyone in high school would have given both their nuts to get Gemma Taylor back to theirs for an afternoon, getting drunk, high and loose.

I watched her out the window as she stomped to the bus stop, real anger in her steps. The poise she once had was lost somewhere in the States. I should've got a selfie or something so I could at least prove to the guys at the pub on Friday that this happened.

I looked to the front of the queue. If I hadn't been this close to the front. If I didn't have an afternoon of *COD* to look forward to. If it wasn't eleven a.m. on a Tuesday morning. If she knew my name. If things had been very different, I just might've said yes.

KINGSLEY

'I think it's really good you're going,' Jill said at the wheel. 'You used to love the darts.'

Phil glanced out at the familiarity of their white, quiet and predictable neighbourhood as the nicely painted houses and manicured lawns passed by. 'I'm not sure I'm ready.' He fingered the dartboard keyring in his pocket, knowing full well he wasn't.

'The doctor said it's good for you. You'll get to see all those old faces. Get out of the house. Plus, I'll get to watch *Coronation Street* without sending you up the wall.'

She laughed. Phil didn't. It had been nearly a year since his breakdown. Nearly a year since he'd picked up a single dart, since he'd seen anyone apart from his wife and Doctor Amini, who always seemed to have something else on his mind. Phil loved his wife dearly and knew she only wanted the best for him. Still, he knew he wasn't ready.

Jill pulled up outside the Kingsley Tavern. 'Just try to relax, love. I'll pick you up at ten.'

'You don't have to.'

'I want to.' She leaned over and kissed him on the cheek, wiping the corners of his mouth the way a mother might. 'Now get out of my sight.' She playfully pushed him out.

He levelled out his frown and exited. He waved as the car pulled away, even though she wasn't looking back.

Phil stood in the doorway of the pub. He heard laughter from inside. He considered leaving. It was a pleasant spring evening. He could go someplace else. Then he remembered there'd be bugger all else happening in the neighbourhood, there never was. He took a deep breath to steady himself, then pushed open the glass door.

'Great to see you, great to see you,' Benton, the assistant treasurer, marched over, cuddling him. 'How are you? How are you? Wait, wait, no, no, you don't have to answer.' The man with Down's syndrome nervously bounced up and down on his tiptoes, not sure what he was supposed to say.

'It's alright, Benton. I'm okay.'

'Do you want a drink? Oh no, shouldn't have asked that either, oh no.'

'It's fine, Benton, I can drink. Maybe just a middy of mid-strength.'

'Middy please, Fraser,' the little guy called to the barman.

Fraser had a queue of people to serve, yet got to it straight away, placing it before Phil. 'Good to have you back.'

'Cheers, Fraser.' Phil had never heard him mutter anything unrelated to drinks or drink prices before. Fraser waved away Benton's five-dollar note. 'We was crap last year without you.'

'I'm not back,' Phil winced as he took a sip. The doctor said he could drink in moderation, though he hadn't since it all unfolded. 'I'm just here to say hello.'

'Ah, yep, yes, fair dues,' Benton said, gripping his clipboard. 'Don't want to push you even though we need you. But, yep, yep, no, no, fair enough.'

A friendly match was in progress between Kingsley's first and second-string sides. A game to get the players primed for next week's opener against arch-rivals Whitfords. Phil saw the usual sticky high tables peppered around, and an old Premier League game featuring Robbie Fowler playing on one of the big screens, and he relaxed, knowing the place hadn't changed. The familiarity putting him at ease.

Phil positioned himself on a stool near the wall, not wanting to appear distant, yet not wanting to get too close and appear interfering either.

'Alright, Phil.'

'Alright, Conrad,' he replied to the smiling Londoner.

'Heard you went bananas.'

'You're a bit out of order there, Con,' Big Russell said, removing his darts from the board.

'Keep your hair on, Russ,' Conrad told the bald man.

'I'm alright,' Phil said.

'You back working?' Conrad asked.

'Not yet, no. How've you been?'

'Shit. Missus told me her lot are flying over again this Christmas. That'll be five years in a row.'

'That is shit.'

'I remember being back there and thinking "Christmas on the beach, ooh, that sounds rather nice." But honestly, if I have to have another there, I'll be the one going bananas. Sand and flies and sunburnt to fuck? And then her lot here as well? Give me a warm beer and a big woolly jumper and *Only Fools and Horses* on repeat any Christmas Day of the week, thank you very much. Know what I mean?'

'I know what you mean, Conrad.'

'Con, you're up,' Russell called.

Benton returned after collecting more dues for the coming season.

'How'd Royston do at the end up?' Phil asked about the young boy at the oche.

'Finished strongly last season, last season so he did. Couldn't have done any better, so he couldn't.'

The kid noticed Phil watching and gave his old coach a shy thumbs-up which Phil returned. 'Impressed he's stuck at it. Impressed kids still want to play darts.'

'He'll represent Australia by the time he's eighteen if he keeps this up, so he will.'

Phil glanced around at the other guys in the room. A few beards and beer bellies were still on show, the smell of fried chips mixed with beer and tobacco hung thick. 'C'mon, what teenager would want to do that? He'll discover better things to do by the time he's of age.'

Benton was hurt. 'C'mon, Phil, c'mon. I grew up in a darts club and I turned out okay, so I did.'

'Sure you did, Benton. Sure you did.' Phil watched the kid commence his next game. He was good. Could do with straightening up that left-arm on the follow-through, though. He'd mention it to him during the break.

Phil peered above and spotted the Kingsley runner-up banner from 2020. The furthest the club had ever gone. Still, it irked him. He'd been dynamite all year, breaking all sorts of records. Most one-eighties in a season, highest average score, most wins, you name it. And then when it got to the final in Northbridge in front of hundreds of punters, friends and family members, Phil Eastland crumbled. He got all the trebles he wanted, that was never a problem, yet when it came to doubles, he choked. No matter how hard he tried, no matter what he did, he couldn't finish. He blamed it on his eyes, but anyone who observed him closely on the night would've seen it.

The tremors. Or what golfers refer to as the *yips*.

Just occasionally coming through the ranks he'd felt it gripping him suddenly though he'd never consciously acknowledged it. It was like a rubber strap looping round his wrist then up to his neck, tightening as he tried to extend his arm to the point of release. It made it hard to breathe, it made him hesitate, unable to fire, never mind pierce the target. He'd shift his feet, he'd try to inhale and quell the rising sense of panic, while inside he wanted to die.

Everyone at the club said it was okay, that it happened to the best of them and wasn't his fault. How could have it been? Phil was the reason they'd come so far.

After the final, they split up for the break, and he was sure they'd all let it go. It was social league after all, a bit of fun. And when he saw his teammates down at the shops or at the park as they walked their dogs, they all had indeed seemed to have forgotten, talking about holidays to Bali, football and work.

Except Phil couldn't let it go. Whenever he had a shower or a cup of coffee. Whenever his family was around, whenever he was at work. Whenever he shut his eyes, all he could think of were those finishes.

He used the break to practice round-the-clock on the board in his shed-turned-office. His wife thought he was on the computer balancing his books or on the phone drumming up bookings for the gardening business. But he wasn't. He was playing darts. Missing jobs, turning down appointments, avoiding quotes, seeing contracts cancelled because he couldn't drag himself away from the board.

It wasn't his business failing that sent him over the edge like his friends and family all believed. It was the darts.

'Get those cute little buns of yours up to the oche.'

'Hi Annette,' Phil smiled at the woman with the money box. The secretary, the real boss of the Kingsley Darts Club.

'You heard me.'

'I'm still married, y'know.'

'Pity. But I'm not asking for a root.'

'Doctors say I shouldn't,' he lied.

'What, root?'

'Play darts.'

'Get your hand off it. It's not the fucking City to Surf we're running here. Get that perky arse of yours up there.'

Phil shook his head and smiled wider, having been through this same routine with Annette countless times over the years. And just like every other time, he did what they all did when Annette ordered them to do something. He went and did it. She was like a mother to them, baking them treats, tallying scores, organising fixtures, keeping them in line and administering a firm clip round the ear when the time called. She might have had a sailor's mouth, but she worked for Silver Chain as a respite nurse by-day and had the heart of an angel. A heart which was broken when her husband Pete dropped dead from an aneurysm in this very pub seven years before.

It felt good standing there, the darts between his fingers. They weren't Phil's. He hadn't brought his, fearful this would happen. These were cheaper, lighter, felt like twenty-one grams instead of his preferred twenty-four, and had plain black flights instead of his usual Saint George's Cross ones.

Phil heard the noise of the room hush as all eyes fell on him.

'Onya, Phil.'

'Go, Phil.'

'Get 'em, Phil.'

Phil pulled his arm back and instinctively flung the dart. It landed a foot to the left of the board, piercing a pin-hole through the plaster. There was good-natured laughter from behind.

'Better not let Whitfords see you do that,' Conrad shouted.

Phil allowed himself a smile. It was only a bit of fun. He took a breath. Steadied himself. He threw again. A four. He breathed again and threw again and the dart scraped the wire, landing on the right side of twenty to make twenty-four in total.

Twenty-four.

It was rank rotten, and he knew it. Nevertheless, the buzz that he'd missed was back.

On his next turn, he remembered the sage advice that he'd intended to impart to young Royston when he got the chance — follow through, straighten the arm, and relax.

He threw two twenties, followed by a triple. One hundred. He was back in the black.

He lost the first two games against a new guy with a ponytail and a Blackburn Rovers polo whose expression never changed. In the third game, he got closer. So close he needed a double-twelve to win. Phil missed on the first try, the dart landing in no-man's-land. Then he nailed it cleanly on the second. He was never a player who showed emotion, even when he was on fire or when he struggled. Yet here he was, playing in a friendly, punching the air, a grin etched across his face as the bar erupted, so happy they all were to have Phil Eastman back and enjoying himself. Even the two players at the next board paused to congratulate him.

In the next game, after a perfect start of two one-eighties, Phil allowed himself visions of a perfect nine-darter for a moment. This, though, was dashed by a wired treble-one. He shook that off and, still remembering his finishing strategies, was slightly high in twenty with his next throw, then swished the lovely treble he needed to leave fifty-eight for his ensuing visit. With his opponent still in the high hundreds there was little pressure as Phil centred the big eighteen then nabbed the double-top to finish with his twelfth dart still in hand.

Benton consulted his clipboard. 'I'm putting you down for next week, so I am.'

'No, honestly, I'm only here to say hello.'

'Well hello, how are you, nice to fucking see you,' Annette joined in. 'Now ... get his name down.'

Unbeknownst to Phil, he had joined in the scratch match and was representing the reserves. They'd never beaten the first-team in a game, but a few hours later they were on the verge of doing so with the match resting upon Phil's shoulders.

'It's not fair you've got him,' Steve, the captain of the firsts, said.

'Piss off,' Russell told him. 'He hasn't played in a year.'

Phil stayed quiet, winning the first two games of the best-of-five tie out of the park, his opponents nowhere his level. They were all watching now, even those other pub-goers who saw the darts comp as a hindrance to their Thursday night drinking.

Phil was the best player in Kingsley by a long shot. The way he played when he found his groove, fast, yet so very smooth, the darts finishing well within the wire, was something akin to poetry.

It was looking good for the reserves to clinch the upset. Phil was flying, shoulders arched back. He was playing Steve, the man who took his place as captain. He powered through to the third game having won the opening pair and was about to finish on a double-eighteen with all eyes upon him when — BAM — that old rubber band around his wrist and neck suddenly tightened and the dart hit the wire and bounced out, landing at his feet.

Phil dropped his head. There were a few comical cheers from the firsts, and a few frustrated sighs from the seconds.

'Never mind, Phil, it's just a friendly.'

Phil shrugged. Sure it was, as Steve took his opportunity to overtake him, impressively finishing from ninety-six in two darts with a treble-twenty and a double-eighteen to bring it back to 2-1.

The next game Phil ran away with it again, scoring trebles with ease but with constant sweats and trepidation of the double to come. Hope arrived when he was left with a bullseye to finish but he weakly chucked a wayward sixteen instead. This left him needing a double-seventeen which was never his, nor most darts players', easiest finish. Even with that metaphorical elastic snatching at his wrist, the dart landed only millimetres outside the wire. He tried again but could only manage a single.

No biggie, everyone thought. And yet to Phil, it was. He knew what was happening. *It* was happening again. He couldn't finish. It was the thing which had stopped him making that leap to pro when he came through the pub ranks back in Bristol.

Steve got a double-sixteen on his second dart to level the scores.

'Don't worry, Phil, don't worry at all.'

Phil forced a grin and finished his middy. He tried to control his tremors, wishing he'd never come here. Wishing he'd never come back.

After a few solid trebles, the dread of having to end on a double in the decider grew and Phil's game deteriorated down to single-twenties with the occasional four and even a one chucked in. Steve held his nerve and was consistent, if not brilliant. After four attempts he got the double-one he needed to edge the encounter for the firsts.

'Unlucky, Phil,' Steve said, shaking his hand.

'Great effort for your first night back,' added Russell.

'We'll see you against those Whitfords bastards, you crazy fucker,' Conrad told him. It was a light insult, but it cut Phil deeper than Conrad intended.

Phil detected the disappointment in his own side's expressions. The type of disappointment he knew well. It was only a friendly, a precursor to the league opener, but everyone in the room loved their darts and nothing beat the thrill of winning.

Phil, though, didn't love darts. He was obsessed with it. The game consumed his marriage, his family, his life. His soul.

'Conrad's right,' stuttered Benton. 'We'll see you next week at Whitfords, so we will. Next week at Whitfords.'

Phil parked his behind on the bar stool. 'I really don't know.'

'You have to, so you do. Clive's in for his knee op.'

'What the fuck else you got on?' Annette barked. 'You get to have a game, plus you get to see me. I'll talk to that gorgeous wife of yours at book club and spell it out.'

'It's not that.'

'It is something.'

Phil finished the fresh middy which had been poured for him. He turned down numerous rides home and said his hurried goodbyes. Jill was parked out front.

'How was it, love?' she asked as she pulled away. 'They miss you?'

'Life goes on.'

'Did you play?'

'I had a throw.'

'Did you win?'

Phil shook his head.

'That doesn't matter, love. So long as you got a go and got to see the old faces.'

She drove on as Phil watched the same houses drift by, this time lit by the full moon.

'I was thinking,' Jill nibbled her lip. 'Maybe if you're feeling better tomorrow, you could mow our lawn. Was going to call someone else to do it, but it seems silly with all your gear still there.' Phil nodded. 'And then, if that goes well, you could spend some time in the back office. You haven't been in there since, y'know ...' she trailed off. 'You could try to get the business going again. Only if you feel up to it.'

Phil said nothing. He'd grudgingly mow the lawn. Then when he was done, he'd pry open the door to the office. And when she thought he was in there oiling the machinery, going through the accounts, updating the website, choosing what font and colour scheme to use for the new flyers and calling old clients, he'd really be in there pounding that board and hitting all those doubles which he'd be replaying again and again and over and over in his head while he tried to sleep tonight, and every other night of the week.

Phil was back, alright. And Phil was dreading it.

BALLAJURA

Toby couldn't remember the last time he'd been in a TAB. Since they'd looked eighteen and started working and earning money, it had been a tradition for the boys. Saturday arvo was pub time. Dogs, horses, footy, you name it, and as many VB jugs, shots and durries they could shift in a sitting.

Toby didn't know if there'd been quite so many betting machines back then in the pub, or this many screens. He was sure there used to be a teller. Everything was computer operated now. He wouldn't know what to do. Just as well as he wasn't flush at the moment.

Justin returned with two pints. 'Things *have* changed.' Toby couldn't resist commenting on how Justin no longer drank middies or schooners.

'Get fucked,' came the stock reply as Justin put down the drinks and parked his plump arse on the creaky chair. 'Just coz you've been away and are all cultured and shit, don't think we don't move with the times.'

Toby took a sip of the gassy, chemical-fueled piss. Ah, Australian beer. How he hadn't missed it. 'So, yeah, the funeral.'

'Fuck, yes, the funeral.' Justin excitedly swallowed a quarter of his pint in one go.

'He actually did it?'

'Mate, everyone did it.'

Their mate, Smurf, had passed away five months before when Toby was still travelling. He'd always said he'd die young, said he'd never reach twenty-seven, and he didn't, dying at twenty-six. Slipping off a balcony while on ketamine at a party in Northbridge. Police couldn't conclude if it was suicide or foul play, or just him being a stupid cunt. Anyone who had ever come into contact with Smurf knew it was probably the latter. This was the guy who'd ingested everything growing up, ice and heroin being standard fare for him. He stood just five-foot-five but loved to take on the biggest and baddest blokes when shit went down. He had a passion for graffitiing trains, particularly moving ones, and had a real fetish for stealing cars and driving fast whilst high. He was a mad fucker of the highest order. An honest, good, loyal fucker, but a mad fucker nonetheless. He never got a trade or qualifications because he believed he wouldn't be around long enough to make use of them. And he always said he would have it in his will that everyone had to do magic mushrooms at his funeral. And this he did.

'Ah, man, it was horrible,' Justin said. 'I've done my fair share of shit as we all know, but these shrooms were off the rack. Even I was off me tits, sweating like a motherfucker, seeing flashing lights and shit. I still had the sense to semi keep it together and try and enjoy the ride.' Justin took another gulp then continued. 'His mum and dad were *not* comfortable. His dad couldn't look in the coffin, while his old dear wanted in the fucking thing. Was wailing that Toby was calling to be incinerated with her. Wouldn't surprise me. He fucking hated the bitch.'

Toby shook his head. 'Man, that is awful.'

'It's fucking funny now but, yeah, at the time it wasn't. And the nan, fuck I almost forgot, she was about a hundred, and they lost her during the service. She went wandering around the grounds of Pinnaroo and the whole thing was put on hold so we could all go and find her. And no cunt could. It was about four-hundred degrees too. The next stiff's family was queuing down the path, waiting. We had to get the groundsman. Someone even suggested calling the police. The fucking fuzz when a hundred cunts are tripping balls?!'

'Fuck me.' Toby was feeling paranoid just hearing about it.

'Fucking oath. Luckily, one of the young cousins who wasn't on anything found her after about an hour up a tree. She'd never been out of her scooter in ten years and suddenly she's twenty feet off the ground clinging to a branch.'

'What the fuck . . . ?'

'Man, it was too weird. When I die, I don't want nothing stronger than red cordial there.'

'Done.'

They both leaned back, sharing a rare and solemn moment's silence for their fallen friend.

Justin grinned. 'Remember he told us he used to paint his nails before he had a wank so he'd look down and think it was a chick doing it for him?' Toby laughed. 'And remember when he was seventeen, and he had that thirty-two-year-old girlfriend? And her two boys with the ratties called him dad?'

'That was the best.'

'Fucking right, it was.'

They drank their beers and looked up at the screens. The dogs were starting.

'You should've been there.' Justin said it casually enough, but his remark stung Toby. They'd all been mates since footy, since primary. Marriages and deaths, mates should always be there, and Toby wasn't.

'Yeah, I shoulda.'

'Shit happens.' Justin didn't say this with any warmth, nor with any malice. He just said it. '*Meh-hi-co*, wasn't it?'

No one yet had asked Toby how it was or looked him in the eye when talking about his time in Central America. A year Toby had been there, and everyone still insisted on taking the piss about how it was supposedly pronounced.

'It was awesome,' Toby said, watching as a greasy plate of steak and chunky fries were delivered to the table next to theirs. 'The food's spectacular.'

'Yeah, right,' Justin replied, one eye on the screen.

'And people are just, I don't know, different.'

'C'mon, you cunt,' Justin mouthed to his greyhound in the black-and-white check jacket as it shot out the traps. 'What do you mean different?' he said, tuning back in.

'I dunno. More relaxed. They all work, but everyone seems to have something else on the go. They're artists or musicians or craftsmen or whatever.'

'Sounds gay.' Both eyes were back on the screen.

'Nah, it's just ... like you only ever hear about it here in terms of drugs and guns and murders. That shit's more towards the border. Northbridge is dodgier than Mexico City.'

'Fair enough, but I wouldn't go near that fuck-hole. For a month, yeah, but not a year. This country's the best fucking country in the world. Why'd you wanna trade it in for some third-world shit tip? Bali's round the corner if you need to stick your dick in that brand of nasty.'

'You'd have to spend time there to understand.' Toby, though, knew that even if his friend spent a lifetime there, he still wouldn't get it.

'Fucksake.' Justin ripped up one of the slips. 'Fourth.' He took a gulp of beer, then belched. 'What are the women like? Big moustaches and shit, yeah?'

'They're out of this world.'

'You would say that. You always did have a thing for Top Decks with hairy spider legs.'

Toby thought of Marianna back there, a woman with such class and style that none of the girls in Ballajura could touch her. Especially not any of the girls Justin had been near.

Justin was lost in thought between his beer and his betting slips, and the Sky Racing channel and his buffalo wings which had arrived. Toby felt for a moment that things had shifted between them. Then he remembered that Justin had always been like this. If the conversation didn't directly involve him, or pertain to a topic relating to him, he zoned out or took the piss. Especially if it was something he didn't understand and wasn't an expert in.

Toby tried a different tack. 'The festivals are unreal.'

'Yeah? Who'd you see?'

'Tame Impala. Parquet Courts. Slowthai.'

'Sick.' He had dragged one eye from the screen to mutter this as he devoured another one-dollar wing drowned in Jack Daniel's barbecue sauce.

'And there's none of this queuing up for beer tokens, bollocks. They have dudes with kegs of Corona on their backs who walk around while the bands play and refill you for a couple of bucks.'

'No shit?' Justin was all eyes and ears now.

'Yeah, popcorn and ice cream and tacos and all that as well. You don't have to leave the pit.'

'But a man with a keg?' Justin repeated, not quite believing.

'Yeah. While the band's playing.'

'That's genius.'

'Should have it here.'

Justin laughed. 'Nah, man. He'd last two minutes at a festival here. Cunts like Smurf would have Keg Man on his arse via the old hip-and-shoulder routine before the kick-drum started.'

They both laughed at the truth in this. The hot-blooded Latino temperament had nothing on the Aussie loose-as-all-fuck spirit. A Perth audience would be inca-pable of handling that novelty.

'Still good, though,' Toby mumbled when he'd lost Justin again to the dogs and the wings.

'Listen,' Justin said, with his mouth full. 'I can get you some work onsite. I've got a heap of jobs on. Thirty bucks an hour, cash.'

'Sure.' Toby was broke since his return and needed the money. The beers he was buying were on his card.

'Got a load of young lazy cunts on-site. Them and weak-as-piss Indian students who can't lift shit.'

'Cool. Thanks.' Toby had another sip as the reality of working with Justin on a building site again sank in. The casual racism and sexist jokes during the shift. The mandatory piss-up right after. The holiday was definitely over as he contemplated replaying the last decade of his life over again.

'And before I forget,' Justin said, wiping the sauce from his mouth with his sleeve and winking. 'Kitty's having drinks at hers this weekend. Seemed really keen that I tell you.'

'Sounds like a plan.' Toby saw their glasses were empty. 'My round.' He got up. No way could he drink the local beer. Hopefully they had a cerveza lurking in the fridge. Far smoother on the palette and the head the next day.

As Toby waited to be served, he noticed the picture of the pub's cricket team above him. The team which won the social league in 2012, him and Justin and Smurf hamming it up at the back. They had taken dexies before every game that season to quell their hangovers and give them focus. Toby's back teeth still gave him trouble from all that grinding the pills made him do.

The barman laughed when he asked if they had any Mexican beer, so Toby ordered Little Creatures instead, paying four times what he had for quality beer for the past year. While he waited for it to pour, Toby thought of where he was in life. Living back at home. Working for Justin. Hanging out at the old local. Going to his ex-girlfriend's parties.

Before he returned to his oldest friend, sat at the table with empties and screwed up slips and chicken bones piled high, Toby thought of Marianna. The apartment they shared in Condesa full of music, love and light. And situated above their favourite taco joint. Going back seemed crazy. He had no family there. He knew nobody apart from her friends. He had a very basic grasp of Spanish and no qualifications to make him stand out in what was still a developing economy. And yet, he was done here.

Toby lifted the beers and gave a final glance to the cricket photo. He cursed himself when he returned to the table and saw Justin's look, realising he'd got middies instead of pints.

It was crazy going back to Mexico, bonkers even. But in a strange way he thought of Smurf and knew it was exactly what he would've wanted.

DALKEITH

The batteries of the radio died, shutting down the sounds of classic hits. Jack knew this meant Bob would want to talk. Bob never could stomach the sound of silence.

'I hate this place,' Bob said.

'You ever been here?' Jack asked.

'Wouldn't piss in it.'

'Christ, that's a bit much.'

Up three floors with a squeegee in hand, Jack had a good view of Dalkeith. The large rooftops. The long driveways. The Swan River shimmering in the unrepentant sun.

Bob climbed the next ladder and started on the next set of windows. 'Liberal-infested white-trash shithole. Yup, wouldn't piss in it.'

'They're just people like you and me. Well, maybe not you,' Jack joked.

'If you love it so much, why don't you move here?'

'Nice comeback.'

'You could sip your Moët and join a yacht club.'

'Even funnier,' Jack said.

'Have another life, a different family.'

'I nearly did.'

'What?' Bob looked up.

'First girlfriend was from here. Diane. Fuck, I loved Diane.'

'What happened? She get sick of the smell of ya?'

'And she loved me. Her *dad* hated me.'

Jack thought back. He was probably halfway through his life now, a different life, alright. He hadn't thought of Diane and Dalkeith in a long time.

'Every week I would drive down in my VL and he'd be all like "Diane, darling, your little northern terrier is here,'' all insecure like I was about to rob the joint.' Jack smiled and continued wiping. 'One day, he got a new motor for his boat. Couldn't make heads or tails of the thing. Now, my grandad was a boat builder up in Karratha. I grew up on the waves. I got it going, alright. Did he thank me? Did he, fuck.'

Bob laughed so hard and his belly rolled around so much that he had to grip hold of the ledge.

'This other time, winter it was, and I'm round there watching a movie with the family. *Titanic* or some Leo Di Caprio shit. The mansion was colder than the fucking Atlantic Ocean in February. They had this antique fireplace. Turns out he didn't know how to light a fire. So, I goes and does it. Thirty seconds later and we're all nicely toasted. I look over and he's gone. He was that raging, he had to take the Jag for a drive.' Jack finished the window and leaned back, admiring his work. 'The next day Diane called me, saying she wasn't allowed to see me anymore. The mum loved me. Her little brothers too. *She* loved me. I loved her.'

Jack came down the ladder. He loaded a pack of new Eveready batteries into the dead transistor.

'Then what happened?' Bob asked, so entranced by the tale he'd stopped wiping.

'What do you think? I never saw her again. And she never told me why. But I knew.'

'What an up himself prick.'

'Saw in *The West* a few years ago that he drowned in the river.'

'What? What are the chances?' Bob laughed and wobbled again. 'Thought you were gonna say he died in a house fire.'

'Yeah, Buckley's chance of that happening with me not around. He'd have died of frostbite first.'

Jack got John Mellencamp on the radio and started on the last window. He thought of Diane and of maybe driving past the old house on their way home to the eastern suburbs. Seeing if anyone was still there. Then he remembered that his own wife and daughter would be waiting for him.

And no way would Bob be happy hanging around south of the river any longer than he had to.

WANNEROO

When he arrived home, all the lights except for the kitchen one were out. His family was in bed, asleep. The only sound came from the cat purring at his feet, rubbing itself up against the spokes of his wheelchair.

His wife had left him a bowl of meatballs and spaghetti for dinner, which he heated up and ate, washing them down with a glass of Hi-Lo. He rarely drank nowadays and was glad he'd stuck to three beers. His body would thank him in the morning.

He took a handful of different coloured pills from their bottles, the same ones he took every night, then brushed his teeth. He kissed his children goodnight, careful not to ride over any noisy objects as he wheeled seamlessly into their rooms. As they dozed peacefully, he marvelled at the little people they'd become, that he'd helped create and shape. He was so proud of how they were doing. Little Lucy with her horse riding, Ellie with her swimming. Both of them getting A-grades. And how they always helped him out whenever he needed it and Caroline wasn't around, and how they were never embarrassed of him in front of their school friends who had able-bodied dads.

He crept into the master bedroom, removed his *Use Your Illusions II* t-shirt, then his Aerosports, and lowered himself into bed.

'How was it, darl?' his wife muttered.

'Sorry, didn't mean to wake you.'

She turned over and curled up next to him, holding him tight and nuzzling into his neck. 'I was still awake. I wanted to know.'

'It was good,' he told her. 'Real good. Not like Calder Park in '93, but what do people expect? Everyone's older now. They played all the hits.'

'That's good.'

'You should've seen some of the clothes on show in the crowd. There were a few mothballs flying about tonight, let me tell ya.'

'Yeah, right.'

'But the sound was unreal. The band's still got it.''

'How was Stu?'

He paused. 'Not great.'

'I thought not.'

He struggled round onto his back and stared up at the ceiling in the darkness. 'He was late. A half-hour late.'

'Shit.'

'And he was drunk. I could tell he was on the gak, too.'

'How?'

'He offered me some.'

'You didn't, did you?'

'Nah, don't be silly. That would kill me now. He wandered off twice to have a line. I ended up losing him halfway through 'Knockin' on Heaven's Door'.'

'He was supposed to look after you.'

'I was fine,' he said, forcefully.

'I know you were. I'm sorry.'

'At the end I met a bloke and his son in the taxi queue who were heading up Tapping way. You should've seen the traffic coming up Wanneroo Road. Bumper to bumper. I reckon the streets between Warwick and Koondoola would've been deserted during the show.' His wife giggled. 'Would've been an ideal night to do a break-in. The police would've made a fortune if they'd had a booze bus out the front of Big Rock Toyota.'

'That's probably true.'

He paused again. 'Stu backed into this girl during 'Nightrain' and her boyfriend pushed him. It was his fault, but he wouldn't say sorry. They would have went at it if I wasn't there.'

'Oh, geez,' she laughed harder at the hopelessness of it all.

'Wasn't funny. He spilt Cougar and Coke over my new jeans.'

Caroline yawned and went quiet.

'I dunno,' he continued. 'He walked away from that accident. Lee died. I was in hospital for a year. Had to learn to talk again. And still things are so hard for me every single day. But I got on with it and met you, and we've got kids and it's tough. But we get through and make do. Stu though ... I dunno.'

Caroline was almost asleep. 'Don't worry about it, babe. You did a good thing going with him.'

He lay there thinking about Stu and Lee and how they'd been so alike growing up. Three crazy fuckers who lived for playing Gunners' records, getting girls and getting loaded. And how that one fateful night driving back from Serpentine, when Lee veered off the road and hit that tree, changed everything.

'Stu said something to me just before he went AWOL. It sounded like he wished he had legs like me. Wished he wasn't the one who's okay.'

Caroline had drifted to sleep. He wondered what happened to Stu tonight. He knew he wouldn't hear from him again until Metallica or Acca Dacca or someone rolled back into town. He twisted and turned, thinking about what had happened to his friend, wondering where he'd gone, knowing he would probably never know for sure.

PERTH III

It had been a long time since Darryl had been in the Art Gallery of Western Australia. Not since the '80s when his mother's work was on display, before she died. Back when coming here for exhibitions was a regular thing.

It had been so long that he'd forgotten his way around the building. Maybe the layout had changed. The paintings sure had. Or maybe he couldn't remember it so well through time and all the effects that go with it. All that was like another age, when struggling to merely exist hadn't yet ground him down.

He eventually found the room where the Year 12's work was exhibited. It was up the stairs on the floor above. Shit, there were a lot of them. He shuffled from foot-to-foot, working out which way to turn, feeling sweaty and nauseous under the bright lights.

An old security guard in the room eyed him. Darryl hoped the other gallery-goers, students, parents and grandparents didn't notice him. He hadn't showered in God knows how long, brushed his hair or cleaned his teeth. He prayed that nobody from Kasey's school was here and would recognise him. Or worse, if *she* was here. He wasn't allowed to see her. Not until next year, when she could make that choice. Surely being here wasn't against the rules. Surely, he could say he was Bess Fuller's son, and he was here admiring everyone's work, not one piece in particular. Surely that would stand up.

It was at the other end of the room that he spotted it. His sister told him he would but didn't give him any more information, telling him she didn't want to ruin the surprise.

Darryl approached the piece. The pencil sketch was raw, brutal, unforgiving, yet beautiful. The picture was of him, was of Darryl's face. Or rather, it would have been if he had a fresh haircut, new teeth, unweathered skin and innocent eyes. It's how someone who'd only seen him in photographs back in his better days might imagine him. Someone who'd never met him, rather dreamt of him.

Standing there, he could make out his actual reflection through the Perspex. Shaking, shivering now, with his matted hair, a two-week growth, broken teeth. This was the real him. Plain broken. Darryl observed the plaque.

KASEY WORTHING-FULLER
MERCEDES COLLEGE

She'd incorporated his family name into that of her adopted parents. Darryl swallowed hard. This gave him hope that she was proud of her roots and wanted him to be part of her life and would come looking for him. Though it couldn't hurt to have the same last name as one of the state's greatest painters. Not that *that* had done much for him. He was deemed another useless reprobate dragged up by fucked up parents. Useless, no matter how well-respected or how good they were with a brush in their hand.

The old guard moved to Darryl's right-side to get a closer look. Almost willing Darryl to give him something to work with. If the bloke only knew who his mother was, he thought, knew who his mother had been and what she'd done for this gallery and this city back in the day. That would change his tune. It always did.

He thought about Kasey. She was talented, alright. Must have taken after her grandmother in that department. She must have brains too, making it all the way through school. Probably all set for uni now. All the crap in his life must have skipped a generation. He tried to picture her life. He wondered who she was, what she was into, who she looked like. And if he'd get it together within the year so he could meet her. Wondered if she even wanted to. And yet, she must do if she'd made him the focus of her final school art project above all the landscapes and pop stars and comics that the other students had composed. He could only pray that the disappointment of who he really was wouldn't break her.

'Scuse me, sir.' Darryl was lost in the picture, letting it overpower him, letting it purify him. 'There's no drinking in here.'

It was the voice of the guard. Darryl looked down at his trembling left-hand and realised he'd taken out the bottle of shiraz and was sipping from it.

'Sorry, fella. Don't know I'm doing it.' He quickly placed it back inside his pocket.

The guard stood over him. 'Sir, I'm going to have to ask you to leave.' He had an Eastern European accent, and Darryl saw greeny-blue ink in a spider-web pattern creeping over his tightly buttoned collar.

'It's just ...' Darryl felt the lump in his throat growing, unable to take his eyes from the piece. 'It's me daughter. It's me daughter's painting.' The guard pressed a button on his control and whispered numbers, a code Darryl didn't understand. 'Me mum was Bess Fuller. There should still be a few of her works around the joint.' Darryl pointed to a scar just above his eyebrow and then across the floor. 'Fell down the stairs there one time. Practically lived here as a kid.'

'Sir,' he turned on Darryl. 'We won't ask you again.' The guard was joined by another larger guard, this one African. They escorted Darryl out the backdoor. But not before they'd searched him and photographed him and told him he was never, under any circumstances, to visit the gallery again. The gallery which was his only link to his mother's past and his daughter's future.

Darryl went quietly. He forced his legs to carry him over the bridge towards the train station. Maybe if he cleaned himself up like the man in the picture, things would be different. Things would be better.

Still, the bastards could have let him keep the bottle. It was a twelve buck one from Margaret River.

MOUNT LAWLEY

The driver lifted my largest suitcase and placed it in the boot of the car. I was thankful as this was the heaviest, weighed down with my uni books and various Australian souvenirs for my family. T-shirts, hats and beach towels. This despite my village being over a thousand kilometres from the sea.

I asked the driver to take me to the airport. I asked him to hurry as I had only thirty minutes left to check-in. I'd been waiting by the phone for Brad to call. I'd waited until the last possible moment to book an Uber. And then the driver was ten minutes late, blaming the traffic.

As we drove through my suburb, a hint of the city skyline visible between the rooftops, I thought of how much I'd miss this city. The warm weather reminiscent of Northern India. I'd miss the friendly people, the free-dom.

For four years, Perth had been my home. I'd arrived here a mere boy from a small village who'd never spent more than a night away from his family. It had been such a source of pride for my parents when I gained entry to Curtin University, studying engineering. Such a source of pride that I went against my will. I was young, just turned nineteen. I was small for my age, barely five-and-a-half feet tall, and my English was patchy at best, language skills not being my forte. Also, I'd never been without our housekeeper, Kuma. I'd never cooked a meal, made a bed, swept the floor or had a job.

'You going home, brother?' the driver asked. I knew his accent. Brash, loud. Delhi, inner-Delhi, not too far from where I was born.

'Yes, mate.'

'Home for good?'

'Yes.'

'That's too bad. I go home, then come back. It's better here. I love India, but Australia is better.'

The doors locked. It was almost peak hour. As the Commodore passed through the outskirts of the city, the traffic got heavier. I thought of how things had changed during these four years. I cooked a mean vegetarian curry now. How strange it was that I had to leave India to learn to do that. I could drive. I even got a job working at the local petrol station.

I had changed. It was on the graveyard shift that I met Brad. And that's how my life really altered.

Before Brad realised that he'd left his card back at the bar and couldn't pay for his fuel, life for me in Perth had been all studying, working and slowly figuring out how to fend for myself. But after that night, the lid of the jar I'd been imprisoned in unscrewed itself. I discovered electronic music, clubs and bars. Drinking and occasionally drugs. Late-night meals in fancy restaurants. Lazy cafe breakfasts with lots of coffee. Sex. And love.

I'd always felt like an outcast. Raised in a conservative village, I didn't talk right or walk or dress as was expected. At first when I arrived in Perth, in some ways it was just as bad. I had the wrong skin tone and was no longer from the right side of the tracks.

After that night, it all changed. Nothing else mattered. I learned what it was like to be me. What it was like to find someone you cared for so much that you felt your heart could go pop. What it was like to completely and utterly give yourself to someone.

I loved Brad's friends, gay and straight alike. So welcoming, so open, so accepting. I loved his golden hair, whitening slightly at the roots. I loved how he held me, his larger body firm against mine. I loved our trips away. Margaret River, the Great Barrier Reef, Thailand. And how he would never ask for a penny for them, though I always contributed. I loved his family. His younger sister in the hills. Her twin daughters, and her husband who taught me how to barbecue, hold a pool cue and drink beer like a man.

We planned to travel. Europe and the States. Brad wanted to do South America too, a place he'd had a fondness for since he travelled there when he was my age. Then he wanted to return here and open a small bar with me. I wanted to. Engineering was never really my thing. That was the old me.

The door unlocked. The car stopped in traffic as we waited to turn onto the Tonkin. I checked my watch. Fifteen-minutes until check-in closed. The sun was preparing to set over the city. People were hurrying back to their homes, to their families. To their swimming pools, patios, maybe the beach.

'Always traffic now at this time,' said the driver. 'Becoming like India.'

'Almost.'

'I went back to get a wife. You going home to get married?'

'No.'

'You should. Get a nice traditional girl and then come back. Australian girls are good to love for a short time but no good as wife.'

'Right.'

'I hope you had some fine white *phudi* while you were here, yeah?' He winked in the rear-view mirror.

'Sure, I did,' I lied.

'You come back here with a real woman and have lots of kids and raise them to be good Hindus. We need more Indians here.'

All that with Brad was then, and this was now. My course finished. I'd neglected my studies and only got a credit, which made it hard to get a job and save for our plans. However, that didn't matter because I'd overstayed my visa. Even Brad's lawyer friends couldn't help me.

The final nail in the coffin came last month when my father had a stroke. Being the only son, I was ordered back to India by my uncle to take over the factory. Manufacturing roof tiles. What did I know about roof tiles? Brad coming home with me was never an option. He couldn't leave this life. And he wouldn't be welcome in mine, not even for a visit.

We were both sad. We were angry. So angry that we quarrelled for the first time. Quarrelled so hard that he wouldn't drive me to the airport, wouldn't be there to say goodbye.

When we turned onto the highway, we were gridlocked. I saw the driver glance at me again in the mirror. He was mumbling and sweating, swearing at his lot in life. I hated meeting Indians here, had no Indian friends. I didn't see the point in coming all this way to talk about cricket and weddings and petty caste differences.

'Too many homosexuals here now,' he said suddenly, eyeing a heavy cricket bat lying across the passenger seat. 'That's the only bad thing.'

'I see.' I pushed the button on the door to let some air in.

'Usually have to pick them up at night.'

'Okay.'

'Just had one before, right where you're sitting. It's too bad in this country.'

'Right.'

'But they will get theirs in the next life. You'll be okay back home. No one like that back there. We don't stand for that. You be fine.'

The doors locked again. The driver laughed as he touched the bat, refusing to break eye contact. I could feel his disgust. The traffic wasn't moving. I was no longer religious, but I prayed to God it would move soon.

'Look at this traffic. Maybe you miss your flight and have to stay here after all.'

I checked my watch. I had ten minutes to check-in. I thought of Brad and about climbing out of the cab right in the middle of the highway, leaving all my luggage behind and running back home to him.

WEST PERTH

Elliott Bamford had the best job in the world. All his uni friends told him so. A computer programming graduate, he worked in I.T. at Gotzer and Son, a boutique and almost obscure investment firm in West Perth. So obscure that many of those in the know had never heard of it.

Elliott had his own office, his own floor in fact, and never saw anyone, boss or otherwise, from the company during his day-to-day activities.

'All we want is a troubleshooter for when things go wrong,' Gotzer Jnr had said during Elliott's second job interview.

'Not that things ever go wrong at this company,' Gotzer Snr added.

'That's it?' Elliott asked.

'That's it,' said the younger Gotzer.

'I could update your entire computer system. I could spread my wings and give you a social media imprint too.' Elliott was desperate to impress, just like his university advisors had told them to.

'No, no. God above, no.'

Gotzer Jnr put his hand on his father's arm to calm him. 'What my father is trying to say is that we've had problems with this position in the past. It's not the work as such. To be honest, there really hasn't been any work, no work ever, in fact. You're here as a mere precaution. All we ask is that you're present nine-to-five, waiting for our call. We'd be placing an enormous amount of trust upon you, and we ask that you stick to this.'

'Not a problem,' Elliott said.

'I really can't stress this responsibility enough,' said the younger Gotzer.

Elliott nodded a few more times than he needed to. 'I won't let you down Mr Gotzers. I assure you.'

'I hope so, young man,' Gotzer Snr said sternly. 'I ruddy hope so. For all our sakes.'

Elliott Bamford had the best job in the world because Gotzer Jnr was right. Nothing ever did go wrong. Nothing whatsoever. What's more, he never ever saw anyone from the company who, he assumed, worked on the other floors despite never seeing anyone, ever, in the lift. And with no intranet, no website, no phone, no anything for the company he worked for, he couldn't be sure there even was anyone else. He wasn't even sure how they'd get in contact with him should anything actually go wrong.

Elliott's job turned out to be the best in the world due to the amount of free time it gave him. He read graphic novels. He built up the top score in the state for *Candy Crush*. And he compiled dozens of short stories of

Star Wars fan fiction, which were lauded in that community. His secret dream had always been to write a *Star Wars* story that George Lucas himself would select for the next film. It was also the best job in the world for another reason. Across the road, at the opposite building on the adjacent seventh floor, was a hotel room. In it, a couple not quite young, not quite old, she black, him white, would meet between the hours of one and two p.m. every Monday, Wednesday and Friday without fail. With the blinds open, they would shed their business attire and their wedding rings and, wasting no time, would make unabashed love. Always in a different position. Oral, missionary, doggy, cowgirl, reverse cowgirl, anvil, forty-nine, sixty-nine. There was sometimes bondage. One time they attached a swing to the bathroom door frame. As the months progressed, they'd even taken to bringing in various other players — usually hotel staff and Southeast Asian sex workers — to keep things moving.

Elliott Bamford was twenty-one-years-old, yet had never slept with a girl. Via church during his late-teens, he went to a few movies with members of the opposite sex, held a few hands, though had never taken the plunge. He'd never been given the chance. More recently he'd joined a cosplay group to meet girls but had little success so far. Self-conscious due to his ginger hair, blotchy complexion and spectacles, he didn't know what to do. Getting front row seats to this endearing spectacle filled a hole in young Elliott's life, providing him with a wonderful education.

So, this was Elliott Bamford's job, and aside from the interview, he never saw the Gotzers, senior or junior. He never saw anyone from the company which suited Elliott as he had minimal social skills and being around people, not only females, made his palms sweat no matter what the season. He waited and watched the door for the elusive knock when he would be asked to throw himself into action, yet it never came. The only contact he had with the company was when a considerable chunk of his six-figure annual salary was credited to his account each month. A flattering sum for a new graduate still living at home. An even more flattering figure considering he did absolutely nothing to merit it.

Despite this, after a few months, the novelty wore off and Elliott became bored. He stopped wearing his father's ill-fitting blazer to work in the summer months. The tie went next, then the suit pants. Before long he was rocking up in his *Adventure Time* t-shirt, jeans and Cons.

Sure enough, he started coming in late. Ten-past-nine. Then quarter-past. With no one monitoring him, he even stretched it out to a quarter-to-ten. He'd never rebelled before. Not at school, not at uni, and it felt exhilarating. However, he justified this by never taking lunch. He had nobody to spend the hour with, and he didn't want to miss the show in the hotel room over the road.

The year went by. There was still no work to do. The couple across the road continued to experiment, with an American sailor and light torture added to the mix. Elliott used the hours before and after the spectacle to work on his upper-body strength via push-ups and pull-ups, and to sharpen his skills at virtual chess.

One day, Farah, his friend from uni texted. Her friends had bailed, and she wanted to know if he would attend the afternoon showing of the new *Star Wars* film with her. Farah was still at Edith Cowan University, having elected to stay on and complete her Masters.

Elliott had always been infatuated with the Malaysian exchange student, one of the few girls on the course, but she had a long-term boyfriend, some guy from home in the business faculty. Perhaps they'd broken up.

Elliott planned on seeing the film that night with his old pal Reuben, though figured he could go with her first. It's not like he wouldn't see it again and again, anyway. He saw *The Rise of Skywalker* four times at the movies. This instalment, should it live up to expectations, he'd see even more due to the substantial hike in his disposable income.

The movie was showing at 12.55 p.m. at Greater Union Galleria, which obviously clashed with his working day. However, not wanting to appear like he was still a square, he agreed.

He wasn't worried about his job. He worried that he was wearing an *Alien* t-shirt, shorts and thongs. But maybe Farah would be impressed that he could dress so casually at work. His other regret was that, being a Friday, he would miss the couple across the road for the first time, though by this stage he felt he'd seen it all.

The movie turned out to be good, good if not great, and Farah had indeed split up with her boyfriend. Elliott and Farah shared choc-tops during the picture, and at the end went for a quick bubble tea to discuss how relieved they were that the movie didn't suck. Though Farah admitted to seeing the opening twenty minutes via a link she'd copied from Reddit the week before.

When they parted, she kissed him on the cheek, close to the lips, and Elliott's heart leapt for the stars. He was too flushed to turn and wave goodbye as she got in her mint green Fiat 500 bound for her family's home in the western suburbs.

Elliott returned to his office in an Uber around 4.30 p.m. with a bounce in his step. He skipped into the lift of the Gotzer building on Hay Street, missing a heavy shower by seconds and praising the heavens above for his good fortune. Farah had been seriously impressed by his job as he'd boasted about how he was his own boss, how he made a small fortune, could wear what he wanted, and take a four-hour lunch break, no sweat. He didn't tell her about the couple he watched, deeming this, quite rightly, to be a more suitable tale for Reuben and his older brother.

But as he entered the empty lift and made it back to his office, everything was about to change. Waiting for him were the two Mr Gotzers, the first time he'd seen them since that second interview. And if that wasn't awful enough, what was much worse was who they were joined by.

The couple from across the road.

The man paced with a furious look. The woman looked down, mascara running down her cheeks. Also present was an older man with a handlebar moustache, wearing a grey suit featuring a *RICHARDSON HOTEL* badge, and the name *LEVON SCHMELL* on it, with the word *MANAGER* beneath.

'Please sit down,' the younger Gotzer motioned.

Elliott did so in the chair laid out for him in the centre of the room as gracefully as his nerves would allow.

'Is this the pervert?' the hotel manager asked the couple, his accent conveying something French or Swiss.

'Yes, this is him,' the woman said, not looking up.

'That's the pervert alright,' said the man in something akin to German or Russian as he cracked his knuckles, which displayed a gold wedding band.

'Please, if you will,' Gotzer Jnr said, adjusting his wire-rimmed spectacles. 'Let us deal with this from here on in.'

'You'd better deal with it,' said the hotel manager.

'You shall be adequately compensated,' the old man said.

'We'd better be,' the manager said, eyeballing Elliott. He helped the man and the woman to the door, shielding them from Elliott. 'We'll leave. But just you remember, Gotzers,' he suddenly spat, pointing. 'If one of my valued guests has to suffer this beastly abomination ever again, then the gates of hell shall swing open and there shall be blood!'

The door slammed behind them. Elliott felt dizzy. He sucked in some air between his quivering lips and managed to ask a question which he really didn't want to know the answer to. 'What's happened?'

'You don't know?' asked the older Gotzer.

'He says he doesn't know,' said his son.

'I think you do,' said the older man, his back straightening.

The younger Gotzer shuffled his chair to the left, revealing something. On the window behind him, which looked out onto the hotel room, was a large smudge, waist-height, appearing as if it had been made worse by a hasty attempt at cleaning.

'Surely we don't need to paint you a picture,' said the older Gotzer.

'You were there,' the younger one added.

'Sans nether garments they said.'

'That's what they said.'

'Naked as the day you were born.'

'That's what they also said.'

'Pleasuring yourself so you were.'

'Proud and happy they said.'

'Went off like a Tommy gun.'

The younger Gotzer tutted. 'This really is such a pity.'

'That pane of glass shall have to be replaced. We should take it out of your salary.'

'I didn't do that,' said Elliott.

'You didn't?' Gotzer Jnr stared at him, confused.

'No. I saw them. Nearly every day I saw them. But I wouldn't do that. The truth is, I've never done that.'

The father and son glanced at each other.

'Then who was it, boy?' asked the older man. 'I surveyed the crime scene with my own eyes. Such depravity does not occur by itself.'

'It certainly doesn't, I'm afraid,' the younger Gotzer shook his head.

'You know, young Bamford, we pride ourselves on being a good employer. Some might say the best in the game. If you maintain it wasn't you, we'd believe you. We'd back you to the bloody hilt and back.'

'You would?' Elliott relaxed into his chair.

'Of course, we would.'

'And then we'd fire you.'

'You'd fire me?' Eliott repeated, sadly.

'Because it would mean someone else did it and you'd been away from your station. The most vital part of your job.'

Elliott was curious. 'And what if I said it was me?'

The two men laughed like the question was a ridiculous one.

The father cleared his throat. 'Here at Gotzer and Son, we pride ourselves above all on loyalty, and if you say you did it, and that you're sorry for doing it, then we'll stick by you.'

'This isn't the first time this has happened,' said Gotzer Jnr.

'We know what to do,' Gotzer Snr nodded. He leaned forward, putting an arm on young Elliott's shoulder. 'So, which is it?'

'Okay, then,' Elliott mumbled, processing the horror of what he was about to own up to.

'Okay, then, what?' the older man asked.

'Okay then ... I did it.'

'And?' the older man prompted.

'I'm ... sorry?'

'There, that wasn't so hard, was it?' said Gotzer Jnr as the two men sighed with relief.

Elliot, though, was far from relieved. 'So ... what happens now? We continue as normal?'

The two men looked to each other and laughed. 'Oh, no,' said Gotzer Snr. 'Oh, no, no, no, boy.'

'There'll have to be six months of intensive sex therapy run by us. Just to keep our good neighbours at The Richardson happy. And you must give up the office now we know that our trust has been breached. You'll move down to a cubicle in the basement. That's where our 225-strong staff operate from. Of course, they'll all have to be briefed on your indiscretion. In detail at a dedicated EGM. It's only fair.'

'And you won't be allowed to visit the toilet unaccompanied,' the older man added.

'Wouldn't it be safer if he was alone?' his son asked.

'Hmm, I see your point. We'll cordon off the area when nature bellows its siren call for young Bamford.' Elliott's head drooped. The old man reached across, giving him another firm pat on the shoulder. 'Don't worry, Bamford. We won't hang you out to dry. We'll get you there.'

When they left, Elliott packed up the contents of his office. His *Star Wars* figures, his *Short Circuit* block mount. He saw the smudge staring at him, goading him from the window. Across the road, workmen were measuring the hotel window for a new blind. Elliott wondered how long he could keep the news from his parents, his uni friends and Farah that he no longer had the best job in the world. Just an ordinary job, like everyone else.

Well, kinda like everyone else.

EAST PERTH

'I've seen it all out here on the streets but that, that...'
The old man laughed so hard that beads of grey snot
dripped down onto his mangy yellow beard. He laughed
harder than anyone on a park bench had ever laughed
before. '*That* was beautiful.'

His younger friend reddened. It had been a while
since the kid had done anything to be proud of. Even
longer since he was told he was good at something.
'I told ya, works every time. People love dogs.'

'Here's to dogs then.' The old man cheersed him with
the brown paper bag, which cradled his tawny.

They drank greedily and stared out onto the park, lit
only by the full moon because years ago the old man had
drunkenly smashed the floodlights with another young
accomplice. They could just make out the black mutt off
in the distance, urinating against a wattle tree.

The old man began giggling again. 'But the way you
told that Nip kid, the way you told her *my dog will be
put down if I don't get the twenty bucks it needs for its
operation.*' He hiccupped and spilled more of the wine
down the front of his singlet. 'And then you got another

twenty off her, saying you both needed to sleep in a shelter tonight. On a warm night like this. Now that, *that*, was a thing of beauty.'

The younger man swigged from his bottle, then held it aloft. '*This* is a thing of beauty, Ron.'

'You're right there, tacker. And not having it would be an eternity of hell.'

'Here's to dogs,' said the younger man.

'To dogs.'

They cheesed again and drank again and admired the dog running across the park, its muscles arching out majestically from its shaggy mane. Through their foggy vision, they could make out a shirtless figure who had appeared from the trees and approached it. Draped in the moon's glow, this larger man stroked the animal's head. Then behind its ears. And then its neck.

'People love dogs,' said Ron.

The figure in the distance rolled the dog over, slowly stroking its belly. They watched, growing uneasy as he moved his hand lower and began working the animal from down below.

'He's, he's . . .' the old man nearly choked on the port. 'And now he's . . .'

'Reckon we should do something?'

'He's fucking nuts,' said Ron.

'He really loves that dog.'

The old man threw himself off the bench. 'You, you. . .' he yelled. 'You dog-fucking arsehole cunt!' He hurled his bottle at the man and the dog. It went a tenth of the way, smashing on the pole of the disused flood-light.

The shirtless figure released the animal.

'He's coming,' the old man panicked.

'Shit.'

'That thing's pointing right for us.'

'Let's go to the shelter,' said the younger man.

They quickly gathered their bags and scurried off as far and as fast as their drunken legs could carry them.

'What about the dog?' Ron wheezed.

'I'll find another one tomorrow. It was a flea-ridden thing, anyway.'

'I've seen it all out here on the streets,' Ron managed to say. 'But I've never seen anything like that.'

WESTMINSTER

The 389-bus hummed in the bay. Cars zipped along Wanneroo Road as the driver stood on the kerb and fiddled with the wing mirror, trying to coax it into its sweet spot. Quan looked up at the shopping centre on the hill. On the pavement there was an old man driving an electric scooter with a small Australian flag flailing behind. In the car park, pre-teen hoons jumped kerbs and dodged trollies on BMXs, while a toddler pushed a doll in a pink pram, her shoeless mother holding her hand.

Quan couldn't see anyone loitering by the shopping centre's doors. On his seat beside the back door of the stationary vehicle, he rested his head against the tag-scratched window. The cool glass felt good against the bruised right-side of his face, the vibrations from the engine soothing it.

He glanced at his wrist and saw it was 10:27 a.m. He couldn't remember the last time he'd worn his father's Citizen watch with the steel band which pinched the hairs on his wrist. He always used his phone.

Quan expected to see a few of the boys hanging around the shops, marking their turf. Perhaps last night was big for everyone. He certainly felt it. Never much of a drinker, all that Smirnoff Ice was working its way back up from his guts, jabbing him bullseye between the eyes. Quan reached into the backpack by his feet for a strip of Nurofen. He swallowed down three to be sure. He had a long day ahead.

Westminster was eerie with only a few people around. Perhaps it was the rain. He'd been catching the same bus to the city for three years, and he rarely got a seat to himself. Today there were just six people on board. An elderly couple, a girl younger than him wearing a Woolworths blouse, and two older vagrants taking up the backseat, sharing something funky in a paper bag.

Quan looked at his watch again. It was now half-past. The driver climbed back in, bringing a waft of tobacco with him, giving away the real reason for his unscheduled stop. The odour filled the bus, providing a relief from the stench of old piss coming from the back.

As the vehicle pulled out onto the road, Quan exhaled. So much so that his whole upper-body lurched forward. He hadn't noticed he was trembling. The bus passed Hungry Jack's and made it through the intersection at Balcatta Road. Four Sudanese boys around his age were walking the opposite way, their heads bobbing left to right, searching. Quan recognised one of them as Deng's younger cousin. He gripped the seat and thanked God above that the mirror and the driver were okay and they were on their way.

Quan opened his calculus textbook and took out his calculator. This was the time he would usually cram twenty minutes of homework. He needed to study. WACE exams began next week, and calculus was Thursday. He should have asked his uncle for today off, but he was already taking next Saturday and he needed the money for his savings. The money that would move him to whichever city gave him university entry. Any city, any place that was far away from here.

Quan tried, yet his eyes struggled to focus on the equations. He wasn't sure if he'd slept. He'd laid out on the bed, fully clothed, on top of the covers for five hours, but he couldn't remember sleeping. His head was sore, his cheek sorer.

He put the book away. It would have to wait until his uncle or whoever dropped him home after closing. He hoped he wouldn't be too exhausted. He remembered he had a half-packet of No-Doz in his bedside drawer to help. Physics, chem and trig were a dawdle. Calculus was hard. That and English. Usually the way for kids like him, no matter how much he gave it or how smart he thought he was.

He closed his eyes and rested his cheek back on the glass and let the cool seep in, and tried to forget last night. Though he knew he never could.

'You fucking late.'

'Good to see you too, Uncle,' Quan answered, putting his backpack over the peg of the kitchen's fire exit. He'd been woken by the driver at the Busport and ran here. Still, he was only five minutes late. With the amount of unpaid time he'd given the restaurant over the years, he wasn't going to apologise.

'You wanna be great chef?' his uncle asked, all sweat and stubble and grease stains, even at this early hour. 'If you're not half-an-hour early then you're late.'

'I don't wanna be a great chef, Uncle. I don't even want to be a chef.'

'Right answer. You bright boy. Must take after our side of family. You stay at school. Not like that dumb-fuck son I have.' Uncle Huong opened a bottle of Heineken, taking a long swig. 'He no show up last night.'

Quan remembered the sickening sound of Tay's head hitting the kerb outside the rec centre. This was the moment when things went from bad to the fucking worst.

'You know where he been?' His uncle held his look. 'You two hang around all the time like a couple of gay boys. Do everything 'cept hold hands.'

'No, I don't know.' Quan turned away, careful to keep the bruised side of his face from view.

'I call you earlier to get here quicker. Some *mi dang* answer.'

'Fucker,' Quan mumbled, knowing he'd never get his phone back now.

'What you say?'

'Nothing.' Quan wanted to punch the wall. He had no insurance and knew Optus would still make him pay the sixty bucks a month for the new Samsung.

'You have all these dishes to do.' Uncle Huong pointed to the sink where a stack of pots and plates were splayed. 'We have little party last night when we close. Your aunty have another great-niece.' Uncle Houng lit a Marlboro Red, blowing the smoke out of the small, top window. He'd started to light up inside again since the health department gave the place the all-clear. 'Why that kid have your phone?'

'I lost it.' Quan had it before the fight. One of the Africans must have pocketed it from his backpack during the all-in. Or it could've slipped from his pocket while he was running.

'Maybe you not so bright after all? What did you do last night? You sure you no see Tay, no?'

Quan put the plug in the sink and turned on the creaking tap. Uncle Huong had looked after him, his mother and his sister since his dad returned to Vietnam when he was in his last year of primary. His uncle was sharp, knew Quan better than Quan liked to admit. And Quan could never lie to him. He turned away, avoiding his glare. 'No. I didn't see him.'

'You study like good boy, yeah?'

'Yeah.'

Quan put in a generous amount of the no-name bright orange liquid and began scrubbing. He knew that if his uncle hadn't already busted into a six-pack, he'd be more alert. Quan would have been found out. His uncle would have discovered he was there last night, that they were both a part of it. He would've found out what happened.

'Good,' the older man said. 'If you don't be a doctor soon, I kick your ass. My son, he have to come here forever. That's why I keep this crap-heap. He dumb-fuck. Not you though.'

The phone rang. Uncle Huong stubbed out his cigarette on the side of the bin and went to his office to answer it.

Quan's head throbbed again, which set his cheek off. He hated Tay right now for pulling the guilt card that Quan would be leaving Perth soon and making him go to that party when he should have been home studying. Studying to forge a path away from this world and everyone in it.

Quan rinsed each dish carefully, setting them to dry on the bench. This was monkey work, though Quan took a certain pride in it. He was a quick and precise dishwasher. Uncle Huong would never admit it, but the kid was the best he had, and he was sad he could only work two days a week. Quan, too, would never admit it, but he liked the work. The mundanity and repetitiveness of the process allowed his mind to let go and lose itself, if only for a little while. To forget about Year 12, and his mum, and his sister, and their money worries. And the gang, and Westminster, and all that this fucked up life entailed. Just two more weeks, he told himself. And then school would be over and he would be on his way to uni. And not in Perth, where his mum, Uncle Huong, Tay and the Dragon Crew still had their hooks in, but Melbourne or Sydney, or Singapore or the US, should he get a scholarship. That wasn't such a pipe dream. He was a natural pessimist even at such a tender age, yet his marks were good, the best in his year at Mercy College, and all his teachers said he had a good chance. If he could only keep his head down and focus for the next fortnight, he'd be okay. He'd be the smart one who got out.

Within an hour, the dishes were licked. The kitchen had filled with the chef and the prep cooks rushing and yelling, swearing and occasionally cooking. Quan came out of his zone and felt sick again, the sensation heightened by the stench of sizzling beef, chicken and pork. Quan hadn't told any of his family that he'd been trying hard to be a vegetarian for months. A near impossible thing to achieve in a Vietnamese family. The taste of meat appalled him. And seeing up-close the personal hygiene of the kitchen staff, how they spat, scratched, coughed and belched over the food, he made sure he never ate anything from here, meat or otherwise. Quan was sure his uncle had bribed the part-Vietnamese girl from the department who renewed the restaurant licence.

With little to do until the lunch dishes made their way back to the kitchen, Quan took an early break. He grabbed his backpack and snuck across the street for a slice of veggie pizza from the Italian cafe. He drank a can of coke, the full-strength kind, and felt better. So much better that he did something he hadn't done in a long time and purchased a pack of Marlboro Lights. It must have been months since the last time. He couldn't remember paying forty bucks before. He rarely bought cigs but thought they were a necessity today. He was nervous about last night, about what had happened and what the fallout would be.

These arguments, these fights, had been going on since the Sudanese moved in. Before then it was with the Aboriginals, or between the Asians themselves going back a generation or more. Even men now his uncle's age had been involved. And it was getting worse. Though Quan never heard of any battles as big as last night.

On James Street, he lit a tailor and inhaled. He relaxed. He reached into his pocket to text Tay to find out how everything unfolded after he scrammed from the scene, then remembered he had no phone. Ever since his dad left, he'd never been without a phone.

He looked over and saw a phone box. He went in. He hadn't used one before and didn't know what to do. He'd only seen people use these in movies. Those and junkies and dealers around the northern suburbs.

It wanted fifty cents. He fished in his pocket around the cigarettes. He only had two dollars. This old thing had better have change. He did the math and discovered he'd have to work two minutes to pay for the call. Then he thought of the smokes and cursed himself for spending nearly two hour's wages on them.

He dialled his own number to see what would happen. Straight to voicemail. He thought of Tay's number. Did it end in a six or an eight? He tried the eight. Number not connected. He tried the six. It rang, then rang out.

The phone gave him no change. Still, no news was good news, right? Tay would just be sleeping off his hangover and a bit of bruising, same as him. He would probably drop by later and make up the hours from last night. Not that Tay needed to. It was practically his restaurant anyway. It's not like he would be fired no matter how much his father complained.

Quan trekked back through Northbridge. It was a Saturday afternoon and was getting busy. The cafes and bars were filling up. He'd been working here since he was fourteen. Hanging out on weekends before then when his cousin brought him here and his mum was glad to have him out of the house for a few hours.

He passed Pot Black, where they used to play pool and later snooker. He remembered that last time, a year ago, when he hit that half-century break. Fifty-three he thought it might have been. Apparently, that was really something for someone his age. The game came naturally to him. He liked how it was based on angles and pacing, how making a break was all about the process of elimination. He hadn't been in there in so long. It'd been a long while since he'd done anything fun with the boys. Everything now was so serious. So violent. They were hanging out in Balga and surrounds instead of venturing to the city. Staking a claim to that territory. That handful of shitty povo-stricken, soul-sapping streets when he should be home studying.

'Where the fuck have you been?'

His belly did a somersault when he saw her. Tran, the waitress, was leaning against the draining board in her uniform, in that shirt and skirt which were a nice few sizes too small. It was another vision of her which would keep him up at night. Pity she was two years older. Pity she was Tay's girl.

'Just out. Early break.'

'Huong wants you chopping.'

Quan nodded and moved to the fridge where the veg was stored.

'So, what happened last night?' she asked, not moving.

Quan was on the spot. What did she know? What didn't she know? He laid the carrots out on the wooden board. The blade's serrated edge gleamed from the strip light above. Quan's nausea returned.

'Nothing.'

'Bullshit, nothing. Did you get that bruise walking into a wall?'

She pushed herself away from the sink and came closer, making sure no one was listening. There was a TV on the wall at the end of the room. One of the new chefs was watching it. 'Tay has a much bigger bruise. I had to pick him up from the hospital at dawn with his head stapled together.'

Quan started on the bok choy. The vegetable came apart with ease as he ran the knife along it, his hand unsteady.

'You heard the news, right?' Tran continued. 'Sudanese boy's been stabbed.'

Quan dropped the handle. It fell to the floor, the blade just missing his Nikes. The pizza and the Coke, the cigarette and the Nurofen, and all that Smirnoff made a run for it. He dived for the bin and vomited.

The chef at the end looked up from the news. 'Is he okay?' he asked in Vietnamese. He turned back to the screen, not waiting for an answer.

'Are you?' Tran asked Quan.

'Yeah.'

'You're bleeding.' She pointed. Bent over, his t-shirt had ridden up showing blood around the waistband of his jeans. Dried blood. Tran got closer, trying to control her voice. 'What the fuck happened last night. What the fuck happened to you guys?'

She was so close that Quan could smell her peach perfume, topped with the sweet mint from her breath. Normally this made his knees teeter, but now it only compounded his sickness. 'Don't tell Uncle Huong.'

'It's all over the news.'

The door spun open. Quan jumped back, knocking over the bin. But it was only Thanh, one of the older waiters who hadn't been here long and couldn't speak much English. He was carrying two trays of dirty dishes, which he placed next to the sink without looking at the pair.

Quan knew that Tay was still seeing Megan, and he'd spent all night with the girl from Floreat the night before last. No, he couldn't tell poor Tran this, though he wanted to, so bad. He wanted to hold her and tell her that his cousin was a thug, a brainless thug who didn't respect her and no longer loved her. He wanted to tell her the boy who she'd been with since she was fourteen was now a man and not a good one, and was making his younger cousin just the same. He wanted to hold her and whisk her away to Sydney or Melbourne or Singapore or America or wherever, where everything would be put right. Where Tay wouldn't be around. Where'd there'd be no Dragon Crew or *mi dang* or Westminster and none of its hate.

'What do you mean about the news?' Quan asked when no one else was within earshot.

'I mean what they're saying. Big brawl. Sixteen-year-old got stabbed.' She picked up the carrots he'd dropped on the floor and placed them on a plate. 'This is really fucking bad, Quan.'

The door sounded. Again, it was only Thanh with more dishes. Quan moved back to the sink to make a start. He ran the water, put in the plug and more detergent. He picked up the bowls. He was trembling so much now that he dropped the top one, smashing it into thick shards. The chef looked over from the small screen. Quan dropped to his knees and scooped up the pieces.

The door swung open yet again. Once more it was Thanh, though this time he didn't carry a tray. 'Your uncle … he wants to speak,' he said in his best English.

#

Quan crept down the hallway and knocked.

'Enter,' said Uncle Huong.

The office had a labyrinth of power cords and thumb-marked files covering the desk, and stray dishes and beer bottles strewn across nearly every inch of the carpet. It also had a one-way mirror where Huong could look out onto the floor. Quan never went into the dining area. When he started, he was too young to be a waiter. Everyone thought he was crazy to be happy as a dish pig or chopping veg, but he was. He was happy with the peace and anonymity.

His uncle had his back to the door. He was facing the TV. The sports news was on with the sound turned off. The Wildcats had beaten some team from over east.

'You wanted to see me, Uncle?' Quan edged in and stood there, feeling like a small boy again. There wasn't a seat which wasn't covered in shiny new takeaway boxes.

Through the glass, he saw families eating their afternoon meals. Australian families, Asian families, African families too.

Huong didn't turn. He didn't move. His Heineken sat empty. He lit another Marlboro Red. 'Where's that mark on your face from?'

'Which mark?' Quan edged back to his right.

'You think I'm fucking stupid?!' he swivelled around on his chair, his face darkening. 'Don't lie to me you little shit-fuck.'

Quan had never heard him talk like this. He talked to Tay like this all the time, but not to his nephew, his godson. Not Quan, his favourite.

'Tay is all night in hospital nearly brain damaged, and you don't respect me enough to tell me?'

'I'm sorry, Uncle,' Quan lowered his head.

Uncle Huong lobbed the empty bottle into the bin. It hit the others, shattering. He turned off the TV, which was now covering tennis. He pulled himself towards his desk and tried to relax his arms.

'Your grandparents. They risk everything for me and you mother and Uncle Dat to come to Australia and be safe and be happy. To raise our own good families.' He glanced away, trying to keep his emotions in check. 'And you two race around all night fighting. The shame. They turn in grave now.'

'I'm sorry, Uncle.'

Quan wanted to go. But Uncle Huong couldn't let it go. He was drunk. He was always drunk, and still he couldn't let it go.

'And you, you bright boy. God give you brains. And this is how you spend your nights off?'

Quan moved to the door. He couldn't take any more of it. He wanted back to the dishes. To that safety and solitude. He didn't want to think about any of this. He pulled the handle. He stopped when he heard his uncle sob.

'The boy is dead, Quan. The black boy is dead.' Quan's fingers gripped the cold steel of the door. 'I speak to Tay at home. The police are there. I know what happened. *They* know.'

Quan watched his knuckles freeze around the stainless steel. 'May I take the rest of the day off?'

The man said nothing. He was crying so hard, the words wouldn't come.

Quan walked back to the kitchen. He passed Thanh and the chef watching the news. He passed Tran.

'What happened?' She was crying, tugging at his sleeve. 'What the fuck's happened?'

Quan didn't answer. He couldn't. He grabbed his backpack. He shoved aside the pallets covering the fire escape, kicked open the door and left the building.

In the alleyway, he unzipped his bag and took out the switchblade, the one he loved with the red dragon engraved on its handle, dropping it down the side of the bin which stank of old meat and rice scraps.

Quan hit William Street. He lit another Marlboro and inhaled, deeper this time. It tasted better. He headed for Pot Black. He wondered if the tables were busy around this time. If he knew anyone there. If he could top that half-century. He didn't care so long as he got a table and could think about something else for a little while, something not so heavy. Like they did back when they were young.

CRAWLEY

Lloyd beat his fist against the steering wheel.

'MOTHERFUCKING-OVERPRICED-GERMAN-HORSESHIT.' Peak-hour horns blared around him as the rear-end of his Mercedes S-Class blocked the outside lane of Thomas Street departing the city.

Tonight was not the night for this to happen. The trial started tomorrow. All the press would be there. Lloyd was defending the West Australian Symphony Orchestra's piccolo player Mairead Bannister, accused of murdering a new Czech immigrant, and fellow player, who she feared would take her place. She'd also been implicated in the disappearance of a young WAAPA graduate, along with the murder of the original player whom she replaced back in 1998. She was as guilty as all hell and Lloyd needed every minute tonight to go over the case, which had attracted the city's imagination, and try to find a way, any way, he could get her off.

He'd seen the road veer left a tad too late and had climbed the curb, taking out a grass tree and totalling his bumper. Sure, he'd driven this road home a million times, but it was the other driver's fault in the Honda in front for talking to her kids and driving too bloody slow. But the Merc should still go. A hundred and fifty grand's worth and the thing was dead as dirt.

Lloyd dialled roadside assistance. One of their grease monkeys should be out within the hour, the operator told him. A fucking hour. All that money and they couldn't even guarantee someone would be here within sixty bastard minutes.

Lloyd got out into the baking sun. He removed his suit jacket. 'Don't toot,' he yelled at the cars jamming themselves into a single lane to pass the tail of his Merc. 'Fucking help me!'

'Suck a dick, Mercedes wanker,' a young tradie hanging out of a ute shouted as he revved past, his mate next to him laughing. Lloyd gave them the finger. He let down the handbrake and pushed. The big man's veins popped, his forehead unleashed a torrent of sweat, and he found strength he didn't know he still had as he got the rear-wheels up and over.

Where the fuck was that tow truck? Lloyd thought about hailing a cab and leaving the thing. Then he thought better of it. He didn't trust that any parts of the car would be salvageable if he left it overnight, even in this area.

He sat back in the vehicle and, with the air-conditioning dead as well and the windows failing to open, he opened the doors. Look at this thing, he thought. Like a bloody computer. If one thing didn't work, it all packed in. Next time he'd buy a used Holden.

Lloyd tried to sift through his folder of notes for the

trial. The defendant was still swearing her innocence no matter how much Lloyd tried to cajole her into going the other way. His fingers were too sweaty, dampening the corners of the pages. It was hot. Much too hot. He was not feeling good about this at all. He hadn't lost a case in a decade but felt himself skating precariously close to the edge on this one.

A rap on the window woke him. He looked at his watch. The tow truck was early, fifteen minutes shy of the hour. He closed the folder and got back out.

'Motherfucking overpriced German horseshit,' he repeated, though somewhat quieter than before.

'Cool your jets, mate,' said the man in the wraparound sunglasses. 'I don't build them. Don't even work for them. I'm just a humble contractor.'

'Just get it out of my sight,' Lloyd seethed as he got out his phone. 'Black and White cabs,' he told Siri.

'Wow, wow, cowboy. Hang on a sec. I might, I just might be able to get you on the road.' He placed his big oily hands on the fender and pushed with all his weight.

Lloyd watched with concern. 'I hope you're not shafting my warranty.'

'I always wanted to work for Mercedes,' he said.

'Why didn't you, then?' Lloyd propped his bum against the door and lit a cigarette.

'Because I … because I …' The driver let go of the panel and removed his sunnies. He paused, peering closer into Lloyd's face. He saw the deep wrinkles from the years of stress. The hundred buck comb-over, the nicotine-stained teeth. Lloyd, in turn, saw a ragged mullet pushing out the bottom of a trucker cap, the sun-cracked skin and fading tattoos. Yet through the heat and all the noise and the traffic racing past a metre away from them, he could make out who it was. That the man had a face much like his.

'Charles?' Lloyd half-asked.

'Charlie, yeah,' the tow truck driver replied, moving in for a hug. Lloyd groaned as oil and God only knew what else inevitably smeared onto his Paul Smith powder-blue shirt. 'Long time, buddy.'

'It is rather.'

The brothers had not seen each other in over twenty-five years, not since their mother's funeral. Back then Charles was strung out during the mass and couldn't stay for the burial. He was living on the streets. He had always been an embarrassment to the family. Lloyd was convinced he'd be dead by now.

'I see you on the telly all the time.' Charles wiped his brow with a rag. 'Called your office a few times, your secretary always says you're under the pump.'

Lloyd's two assistants were under strict instructions to tell absolutely everyone, including his wife and ex-wives and children that, aside from clients and the very utmost important associates, he was busy. Which he almost always was.

Charles popped the bumper back with the careful touch of someone who'd done this many times. It looked like it had come off the factory floor. He began fiddling under the hood.

'See you're on that big trial tomorrow.' He spotted Lloyd's surprised look. 'I might have been shithouse at school, but I can still read a paper.'

'Right, yes, tomorrow.'

Charles took stock of his older brother's car and suit. 'You've done alright, haven't ya.'

'I've done okay.' Lloyd lit another cigarette.

'Are you happy?'

The question threw Lloyd. The whole proposition was something so blithe he'd never considered it. 'Of course, I'm happy.'

'That's all that matters then.'

'Cigarette?' Lloyd held out the packet of Dunhill Blue.

'Nah, mate. Gave them up years back. Gave everything up.'

'Thought you looked better.' And he did. He'd acquired some much-needed muscle. His eyes were clearer, and his hand steady as he strummed the engine.

Charles stood up straight and shut the hood. 'Start her up.'

Lloyd climbed in and did so. The electronics illuminated and the engine hummed like a dream.

Charles wiped his oily fingers on his trousers. 'I'd still take it into the shop, but she'll get you home. And to court tomorrow.'

'Thank you, Charles.' Lloyd removed a fifty from his wallet. 'Please. A small gesture.'

'Get stuffed. You should see how much I'm billing the Jerries for this.' Charles angled his head, spotting a hip flask down the side of the driver's door. He gave his brother a curious look. 'You sure you're okay to drive? I mean, you don't smell all that great.'

Lloyd popped a Mentos. 'Just needed a sharp one after my last meeting. I'm fine, really.'

'Where you off to now? I'm going to meet Kate and Grania. Remember my girls? Big girls now. Bringing the grandkids. My wife will be there too. You haven't met her. It's only a pub meal, but you'd be more than welcome.'

'Thank you. But I've a busy day tomorrow.'

'That's right. The case. Well, good luck. I'll try your office again when it's all done.'

'Sure, please do.' Lloyd lifted the handbrake. He was suddenly feeling light-headed and needed to move on. Above all, he needed a drink.

'Nice seeing you, Lloyd. Look after yourself.' He squeezed his older brother's shoulder through the door. 'Mum and Dad would be so proud of what you've achieved.'

Lloyd wanted to say the same thing but found the words wouldn't come. He found he couldn't even look his brother in the eye as he pulled into the outside lane and gave a final toot, careful to avoid the curb.

He was happy his brother was okay. He'd always regretted not doing more to help. Charles lost his dad when he was twelve. Lloyd was twenty, he was already out of the house, had already moved on in more ways than one and hadn't relied on the old man in a long time. It was different for Charles. He was at that age.

He'd more or less lost his big brother too. No wonder he went off the rails.

The episode made Lloyd think of how long it had been since he'd sat for a meal with his own family. Lloyd couldn't even remember the last conversation he'd had with his wife as they slept in separate wings of the house. He hadn't heard from either of the kids in months.

He was a few hundred metres along the road when he had to indicate and drive the car back up onto the verge. He did it more carefully this time. There was nothing wrong with the vehicle. It was just that he was sobbing so hard that he could no longer see the road ahead.

BEDFORD

All the dads whose kids attended Jelly Babies Daycare knew Raymond Pines and knew they didn't like him. When they dropped their children off, he was already there with his similarly afro-haired three-year-old twins, a boy named Jackson and a girl named Tegan, playing with all the other little ones in the sandpit or helping the staff setup for the day. Wearing his tight Bonds t-shirt and skinny jeans — the kind most of them had given up hope of ever squeezing into again — and with those lush, well-oiled curls. And then, because he had no job and nothing else to do during the day that anyone was aware of, he'd be the first one there to collect his kids and help the staff pack everything away again.

When the dads got home at night from the office or the building site, all they heard about from their wives and partners — often with tears of admiration in their eyes — was how Raymond had it so tough. A single dad with twins after his wife (allegedly) died in child-birth, he'd quit his job as a director of a not-for-profit and downsized the family home so they could cope.

The dads didn't like him because they were sick of hearing about how great a father he was. How funny he was. How he baked the most delicious carrot cake. And how he was always there for the mothers with a sympathetic ear to listen to about their parenting ordeals, or a welcoming shoulder to cry on. The dads would have to listen to this after they'd worked an eight-hour-plus day and spent another hour or so in traffic and barely saw their kids, just so they could earn the money required for family outgoings such as childcare.

And every day, when they either dropped their children off or picked them up (they couldn't do both, they were too busy working), they saw Raymond there with his afro and his tight t-shirts and jeans, listening to the mothers and hugging them or air kissing them and making them smile.

On the rare occasion two of the other dads crossed paths, they would joke about his jeans so tight you could see the outline of his manhood, and make fun of his nipples poking through his cotton shirt like golf tees in the breeze. And his carrot cake, and that lisp when he talked, and on and on, broing-it-up over how much they loathed him.

They didn't joke when, in the new year, their wives became pregnant around the same time. And definitely not the following year when all the newborns were growing that similar afro. They weren't joking then.

They no longer disliked Raymond Pines. They wanted him dead.

EAST VICTORIA PARK

There was Gomer Pyle in *Full Metal Jacket*. Single rifle shot. Not a problem in America where every man and his pit bull carry a firearm, but slightly trickier Down Under. *Leaving Las Vegas* protagonist Ben Sanderson. Alcohol poisoning. Not being much of a drinker, this held very little appeal for Vic, even in his current state. And then the sisters in *The Virgin Suicides*. Gas oven, hanging, sleeping pills and carbon monoxide poisoning. All achievable, though hardly appealing.

He would have to think of some other way.

What Vic wasn't hung up on was actually doing it. He'd been thinking about it for months, and this week he'd made up his mind. Sure, trade in Vix Pix slowed during the warmer months, but this was over the line. There'd been five customers on Monday between midday and eight p.m., two of whom rented a single weekly each. Four on Tuesday. Four on Wednesday. Two on Thursday. And here he was on Friday night with a half-hour till close, and there hadn't been a single soul.

He always said that when the day arrived that no one came into his shop, that would be it. He'd walk away gracefully. He'd had a good run. Over three-decades in the trade it had supported him, providing him with a good life, though admittedly having no partner or children had made that more attainable. All he ever felt he needed were the movies.

Now, with a stack of bills and multiple court writs for unpaid bills, the pictures were no longer enough. They'd already taken his 1969 Mustang, the one he reconditioned to look exactly like Steve McQueen's in *Bullitt*. Next, they took his house. Not much of a house — a three-bedder around the corner, in much need of TLC. However, it was on a quarter-acre block, ideal for a bulldozer and a new block of units.

Vic looked around the store. The new release section hadn't been updated in a year because he didn't have the capital. The phone line was cut six months back, which meant he couldn't chase up the couple of dozen members who'd forgotten or chosen not to return his prized discs. The A/C was long buggered. The red matted rug and cream shelving had been here since he moved in and took over from the hardware store, and they were, much like him, beyond redemption.

He'd fought off the rise of the big video chains such as Movieland and Blockbuster, dealt with the industry's flirtation with Betamax and LaserDisc, its evolution from VHS to DVD, and the advent of Foxtel and cable TV. But it was the pirates and all that illegal downloading that kicked in a decade back which hit him hardest. He lost nearly all his members under thirty.

Then Netflix arrived, and that was it for every demographic across the board. Unlimited movies and TV for ten bucks a month? He'd hand out two movies for that. Four if they were really old. Yup, it was Netflix, fucking Netflix, which had finally wiped out Vix Pix.

Vic, of course, had considered wiping them out. Finding where Netflix was and working out a way to blow its entire collection to high heaven. Until he discovered their movies were already literally in the high heavens. While their head office was in California, their TV shows and movies were stored in satellites orbiting space, making his plan somewhat difficult.

There was really nothing else for him to do except kill himself, and he was okay with this. Friends or girlfriends were never for him. As for family, the only member he saw was his nephew, and that was only because he was an unemployed stoner and Vic gave him free rentals. No, all Vic had ever had in his life were the movies, and now that people could pick them out of thin air thanks to Netflix, it rendered his once-famous collection, the most niche and respected in Perth back in the day, about as much worth as the dust on his shelves.

And yet he still didn't know how to make himself dust. People probably checked out this kind of thing on the internet, Vic guessed. But Vic didn't have the internet. Probably the reason his business was in such a mess.

He settled on doing it the old-fashioned way. The way his father had before him. Force down a box of pills with a bottle of whisky. The bottle shop at the end of the complex was open all hours. He'd grab one from there.

He opened his front door with no intention of lock-
ing it behind him, when a man walked in. He was im-
possibly tall with Brylcreemed hair, a pencil moustache,
and wearing a purple pinstripe suit. Vic jumped at the
surprise of seeing someone dressed like this, someone
who didn't appear wasted and wasn't in a singlet and
thongs.

'Can I help you?' Vic asked.

The man strode in and looked around the store with
a pungent stench of contempt. 'You are Vic Goodrington?' he asked in an accent which Vic couldn't place,
pitched somewhere between New York and Portsmouth.

'Yes, I am.' Vic had seen countless parties enter the
store of late seeking money owed, but this was different.
This was after normal business hours.

'Vic Goodrington the director?' the man asked, a sudden facial tic causing the left side of his face to sharply
leap out from the jawbone. It occurred every twenty seconds or so, bringing an edge of vulnerability to his otherwise prickly demeanour.

'The director?' Vic repeated. 'I *was* a film director.
A very minor one. And a very, very long time ago.' It was
1983, to be exact. Vic won a scholarship to NYU's School
of the Arts to study film and moved out there. He made
several short art-house films, one of which, *Wild Roses of
May*, a love story about a biker couple from rival gangs,
was lauded by none other than Martin Scorsese himself
at the end-of-year viewing. Vic's lecturers encouraged
him to submit his work to Hollywood producers, but by
the end of the course, he wanted home. His father had

recently ended his life and for Vic, all alone over there, the novelty of New York began to clash with the reality of living in the ole U.S. of A. He returned, cared for his mother, and used an advance on his inheritance to start the business.

'How did you know?' Vic asked.

'I'm a film producer. It's my job to know.' He perused the Robert Corman section with a sneer. 'I have a script, a screenplay, a damn fine one too, which you'd be perfect for.'

Vic almost laughed at the madness of it all. 'I don't know about that. It's been so long.' Vic didn't even know where his camera was.

'Nonsense,' said the man, not looking at him, more looking through him. 'What have you got going on here? This little shack is hardly raising the roof.' He walked on, twitching his way down the horror aisle. 'It'll be set in Perth. You needn't leave your cosy hamlet. You'll be paid industry rates. We'll give you an assistant, crew, the whole shebang. Casting is taken care of, some fine young people from NIDA are waiting for you to mould them like putty.' He turned back to Vic. 'It's time to get back in the game, old man.'

Vic thought it over. Despite the producer looking much the same age as him, he did have a point. 'It's a short, yeah?'

'My God, man,' he threw up his arms, resting both hands on Vic's shoulders, shaking him as his face twitched back and forth. 'It's a feature. It's financed. There's distribution. I'll even give you final cut.'

Vic paused, letting it sink in. 'For the cinema?' Vic's one big regret when he died would be that he'd never made a film that was shown on the big screen. Butterflies awoke in his belly, and his breath shortened at the realisation that this could be it. *This* could actually be the moment he'd been waiting for.

The man let go and shook his head instead. 'Don't be ridiculous. No one goes to the cinema anymore. This will be a Netflix movie, man.'

At the liquor store, Vic splashed out and bought the Black Label instead of the Red, remembering from his college days that it was easier to get down the hatch. He thanked Tim in the shop, who was surprised to see him in there, remarking that he didn't know the man from the video shop was a drinker. Tim appeared even more surprised when the miserable old git told him to keep the seven bucks change.

As Vic returned to his store, he thought about the producer's offer and how it was never going to work. It had zombies in it, for starters. And then the deal breaker — a Netflix movie. No way. Not after what they'd done to him. Because when all's said and done, you've got to have principals and you've gotta stick to them. Your principals are all you have in this industry.

Scorsese told him that.

QUEENS PARK

The two friends sprawled out behind the goals, same as they did every second Sunday afternoon. Same as they'd been doing since they started high school.

'Tell me you've banged her,' Duncan said, lighting another rollie.

'Oh yeah, yeah, fuck yeah,' Joel replied, picking at the grass. 'She's all you thought and more.'

Duncan paused. 'You haven't done anything with her, have you?'

Joel flushed. Duncan had known him too long that feeding him fibs was pointless. Keeping the truth from him, impossible. 'Not as such, no.'

The referee blew the whistle and the second-half began. The local women's side, state league table-toppers Queens Park, were trailing the team one spot beneath them on the ladder, Eastern Redbacks, 4-1. Joel felt his stomach dive and flutter as Queens' winger, Jessie Redondo, gathered the ball and drove at the Redbacks' defence. At seventeen, she was the youngest player in the side, her nimble feet and quick thinking making her one of the best, and her blonde bob offset by her Latino complexion and big dark eyes making her the most popular amongst the majority-male crowd.

'You finally ask out the girl which every cock around the ground wants to be ball-deep in,' Duncan said. 'And then when she finally says yes, you don't know what to do with it.'

'I dunno. I'm trying. I offer to pay for everything. Say all the right stuff. I even wrote her a poem. She just doesn't seem that into me.'

'You're fucking gay.'

'Nah, I'm serious. She's always insisting that Ashleigh comes too. Movies, park, the lot. And every day she's hanging round when I go over.'

'Sounds like you got a nice threesome happening there,' Duncan grinned. 'If Ashleigh wasn't such a pug-faced dyke.'

A cross drifted in from the right. Towering above the melee of players was captain Carli Jones. Big shoulders, big breasts, big everything, heading the ball straight into the top right-hand corner.

Duncan leapt to his feet, punching the air. 'That's my girl. The comeback is on!'

Joel nervously lit a tailor. 'And what's it like being with an older woman?'

'Ah, mate, you have no idea. Let's just say that all the rumours you've heard about Little Miss Jones are true. And then some.'

Joel sighed. Feeling sufficiently satiated and queasy from the hit of tobacco, the cig only serving to remind him of why he quit, he passed it on to Duncan. 'Own money, own car, doesn't live at home. You're smart, alright.'

Duncan nodded. 'Yeah. And it fucks like a beast.'

Queens Park were dominating, pinning the away side deep into their own half. Under pressure, the Redbacks' centre-half sliced the ball into her own net to make it 4-3. Game on.

Straight from kick-off, Queens Park retrieved the ball. Jessie played a neat pass to Carli who, under pressure, lost her footing inside the box, but the referee waved away the penalty claims.

Duncan rolled another and rubbed his week-old growth. 'Can I ask you something? Just between me and you, like?'

'Course mate, always.'

'You know her flatmate? The brickie who drums in that band?'

'Sorta.'

'Every time we do it, we have to wait till he's gone out.'

'Right.'

'She only ever wants to do it on his bed.'

'Hmm.'

'Then the other day, she made me wear his clothes before I saw any action. Check shirt, jeans, steel caps, the lot. I heard him come back in, and I freaked and locked myself in the bathroom. He was livid, saying his bed wasn't made right. Saying he had to practise and his best clothes had gone. He's a fucking wild cunt too. The others had to calm him down. He didn't suspect me, but I left out the window so he might now.'

'That's fucked up, dude.'

'It is, isn't it?'

They stared out. Jessie twisted around her marker. She sidestepped the centre-back and shot. The ball hit the post and bounced to Carli who cracked it first-time, blazing it high and wide over the bar. The final whistle sounded, and the crowd groaned, knowing that Queens Park had surrendered top-spot with only three games to go.

Duncan stood and ashed out. 'Still, it's pretty good us going out with the two best players in the team.'

'That'll show everyone,' Joel agreed.

'We've come a long way, baby.'

The boys watched the girls shake hands with their opponents. Duncan and Joel hoped for a wave or some sort of acknowledgement, but Jessie and Carli slumped off the pitch, not bothering to look over to where the boys were standing away from the crowd.

'Reckon the girls will be in a bad mood tonight?' Joel asked.

'I reckon we're about to find out.'

ROCKINGHAM

George was glad to see Pierre's face. The delivery boy was his favourite of the three drivers, even if calling him a boy seemed a bit strange now. He was a boy when he started, a boy of sixteen, so short his feet couldn't touch the gravel when he sat him on the scooter. But here he was now, ten years on, filled out and taller than George. A man.

George felt blessed to have him and wasn't sure why he still did. Pierre had completed his schooling, securing a place at UWA studying English, and stayed on to complete his masters and then a PhD. And yet here he was, a man of letters, working five nights a week at Leaning Tower of Pizza, and increasing his shifts each year. Never once had a sick day. Never once been late or taken a holiday, and George had never had anything but glowing reports from customers about him. George knew the pizza he made was good, the very best in the area. Though he also knew that many of his customers kept coming back because of the delivery boy's kind nature and bright smile, and how he would always remember not only their names but the names of their children and even their pets. George had offered to train him up, make him a pizza chef, a renown one, but all Pierre really wanted to do was ride.

Pierre knew these streets like the back of his hand and loved navigating them. He'd lived down here his whole life and seen Rockhingham grow from a small coastal holiday town to a city in its own right. While the books he'd read and studied transported him to the mean streets of old London or Paris, and far-flung outposts of China, India, South America and beyond, 'The Rock' was the only real-life setting Pierre had ever known. He loved riding the bike, loved the wind in his hair, and how the job gave him time to think. The one thing a writer needs most.

In the two years since he'd finished his exegesis on 'Interpretations of Serfdom in 19th Century Russian Literature', he'd been offered tutoring and lecturing posts across the nation. But he believed all these positions would clutter his mind and deprive him of the time he needed to think. Pierre wrote poetry and short stories, but what he wanted most was to write a novel and a great novel at that. It had taken him nine years to complete the first draft of his book, a sprawling 314,000-word fantasy covering the fictional first world war between early humans and dinosaurs. And he knew, he just *knew*, that the sale and subsequent auction of the film and/or TV rights would make all the work and sacrifice worthwhile, allowing him to clear his HECS debt and move out of his mother's home. She pleaded with him to send it off as it was and move on to something else, but she worked in a care home, so what did she know? thought Pierre. What she *didn't* know was that Pierre's job allowed him to play out that awkward second-act, the one which wasn't quite clicking, over and over and again and again in his head, trying to unlock the puzzle.

Pierre's first few deliveries on this particular Saturday evening were to young families on the edge of the suburb. His third was to a regular, an old Greek widower in Safety Bay. And his fourth was half-a-dozen jumbo pizzas to an apartment on the Esplanade, obviously some function. On the way there, Pierre tried to figure out a deeper motivation for the young protagonist in his story. He also felt the narrative needed something, another character perhaps, to add to the plot, but he couldn't seem to tie the whole thing together. Once that fell into place he could finish the work, and it would only be a matter of months before he found an agent and optioned the novel and flew out of Rockingham to Hollywood to work on the screenplay.

Pierre pulled up at the imposing block facing the water. He grimaced. As he suspected, a large gathering was in progress. Loud electronic sounds with thumping bass, which Pierre wasn't a fan of as he only ever listened to jazz, boomed from the balcony leading him there.

The revellers couldn't hear the doorbell. He considered calling the number George provided him with, but when he tried the handle and the door opened, he knew from experience it would be fine to let himself calling, 'Pizza! Pizza! Pizza delivery!'

It was a beautiful home. Terracotta tiles with hanging prints. A Kandinsky, a Lichtenstein, a Warhol. Art for people who knew nothing about art, though the polished brass frames didn't look cheap.

He turned the corner to where girls in bikinis and taut, tanned males danced around a spa, drinking, getting off with each other or doing chunky lines of white powder off the glass coffee table. Kinda like the music videos he sometimes saw on the ABC after a late shift. It wasn't out-of-the-ordinary for Pierre to deliver to parties, especially on weekends, but this sort of decadence was unknown in these parts and way beyond the gatherings of the teenage stoners who usually made up George's Saturday night clientele.

'Um, guys. I have pizza here.' They all ignored him. All except for a guy in the spa with a goatee and his arm around a girl who had long blonde curls and smudged eyeliner, his hand cupping her bare breast.

'Pav!' he shouted. 'Pav!'

'Fucking what?' a shirtless guy with a shaved head bounced into the room like a cage fighter. He looked at Pierre and his face broke into a wide smile, like his day, his week, his month, his year had been made. 'Well, if it isn't fucking Bookworm himself. Remember me, Bookworm?'

Pierre could never forget Pavel Palowski. They'd gone to school together. Primary *and* secondary. Never in the same classes, as Pavel was always in the weaker ones. Their mothers had been friends, though this didn't stop the stronger, cockier, infinitely stupider Pavel bully Pierre mercilessly. Hiding his bag, burning his folder of notes with his Harley Davidson Zippo. Waiting for ages just to follow him to the toilet trough so he could turn and urinate down his trouser leg.

'What the fuck is Bookworm doing in my house?!'

Pierre felt a trail of sweat gather under his armpits. Pavel had always been bigger and scarier than him. Now he was positively huge. 'Um ... I'm here to bring you pizza.'

Pavel, his eyes bulging, looked at Pierre, then down at the Leaning Tower of Pizza logo on the blue polo shirt he wore, and finally at the steaming pizza boxes stacked in his arms. And slowly, very slowly, he pieced it all together and slapped the floor, letting out a wicked high-pitched snigger.

'You have got to be fucking kidding me! Hey, Brax,' he called to the guy in the spa who was now holding a cigar. 'Check out this guy. The biggest nerd at school, won awards every year. I never used to hear the end of how much better he was than me when I got home every night. I thought he would grow up to be President of Australia or cure AIDS or some shit. And here he is delivering my fucking dinner.'

The man in the spa sniggered, pressing the button on a barbecue lighter to ignite the cigar, his hand having relinquished the bare breast.

'I ... I ... I have a PhD,' Pierre mumbled in a vague attempt to impress.

'A P-H-what-da-fuck?' Pavel smirked.

'I'm a doctor.'

'Really?' Pavel was suddenly very impressed, coming in closer. 'Could you seriously write me a script for some shit?'

'A doctor of philosophy. In English literature.'

Pavel held his stare to see if he was serious 'A doctor who?' he snatched the food, not understanding and suddenly not really caring. 'Whatever the fuck you are, just grab a beer and sit down.'

'I really can't. It's Saturday. I have deliveries to make.'

'You're actually serious about this pizza shit? C'mon, I have someone you have to meet.'

Pavel pushed him past the kitchen and down the hallway. There were portrait pictures of young children on the wall with Pavel's prominent jaw and intense blue eyes. Blown-up photographs of him at the Brazil World Cup with his arm around Tim Cahill. Another on a racetrack wearing Red Bull overalls and standing shoulder-to-shoulder with Daniel Ricciardo. And in the others, there was Pavel with a girl Pierre recognised from school.

Kelly Stanic.

'Kell, you are not going to believe what's turned up on our doorstep.'

'Better be food, I'm fucking baked,' came a girl's voice, her back-end sticking out the fridge. Her pink g-string was peeking out the top of her tight black leather pants.

'That and something better,' Pavel swung her around.

Pierre had loved Kelly. And here she was, all grown up and even cuter than back then. She looked at Pierre like she'd never seen him in her life, never mind gone to high school with him. 'The delivery guy? Yeah, great, Pav.' The hottest girl at Rockingham High Class of 2011 took a box and tore into its contents like a wild puma.

'It's fucking Bookworm.'

She looked again with her mouth full of meat lovers and her bloodshot eyes. 'Oh my God! What are you doing here?' She noticed his shirt then doubled over in hysterics, spitting beef and bacon over the tiles.

Pierre wanted out of there. 'Just ... y'know, working. I'm writing a novel by day so I need time to do that, and it's got cavemen and dinosaurs in it and ...' he trailed off, feeling more and more ridiculous being there, causing Pavel to laugh harder.

'Sure you do, Bookworm, sure you do.' Pavel handed him a beer. 'You want a line or something? You can say it's research.' The solid marble kitchen top was littered with empty baggies and bowls of weed and various powders.

'No, really, I can't.'

'Yeah, you already sound off your tree with that book idea.' Pavel snorted a large line and screamed out wildly as it hit home. 'Having a bit of a celebration. Sold a patent I designed for the ultimate formula in muscle building powder.' He squeezed Pierre's puny bicep. 'You could do with some. We're heading to L.A. next week. They gave me a Green Card. I'm going to immerse myself in the whole tech thing. Apps and shit.'

'Oh, wow. When I get an agent, that's where I'll be heading.'

'Lots of pizza shops out there, Bookworm.'

'Yeah, um, speaking of which, I should really be on my way.'

'Suit yourself. Bookworm, everybody.' He hoisted Pierre's skinny arm aloft in a mock victory salute. 'Never had his nose out of a book at school. Never missed a class. And I never handed in shit and got kicked out in Year 10. And I'm worth five mill and he's delivering pizzas.' He lit a fat cigar with the Harley lighter. 'I love this country.'

Pierre made it out there, past the drugs and the giant TV and the girls and all the pictures on the wall, and found himself lost for breath, sweating right through the polo shirt. He got on the bike and sped back to the pizza shop. He couldn't think of any ideas for the story or about how it still needed a title. All he could think of was Pavel bloody Palowski.

#

'I quit.' These were his first words upon re-entering the store and removing his helmet. He'd decided on the way he was going to apply for one of those lecturing posts after all and would leave Rockingham.

'But why?' George asked, putting down the dough in his hand and removing his cap. The boy had been so happy two hours ago when he started his shift. Now he looked like he'd been crying. 'Did something happen, my boy?'

'No, no, nothing. I just need a change.'

'I can get you a better bike. Is that it? A newer uniform?' Pierre shook his head. 'How about a raise? Three dollars extra an hour.'

'Thank you for everything. Really. But I'd rather finish these orders and then that can be it.'

George wasn't sure what to say. Only now did he realise how he'd grown to love the boy like his own, and how vital he'd become to Leaning Tower of Pizza.

Pierre read the next order. The Esplanade. Another six pizzas back at the party. Either they had munchies real bad or Pavel was taking the piss. Pierre felt he couldn't say no. The other driver was out on a delivery, and Pierre was a professional and didn't want to give George any more grief on this, his last shift. He would just drop the pizza, take the money, and that would be the end of it.

Pierre headed there as speedily as the little moped would take him. This time, he wasn't sure why, he elected to take the backstreets. Maybe it was to say goodbye. He thought of school, how he'd joined all the dots and given it his all. Same with uni. Said no to all the parties, studied hard, never drank or smoked and still lived with his mother. And then Pavel, a thug, a moron who did nothing, who didn't have a brain in his head, somehow hit the jackpot. And it angered him.

It angered him so much that it blinded him. So much that he didn't see the hatchback reverse out of the driveway until it was too late. He swerved but couldn't turn quick enough and it got him, throwing him thirty metres down the road, flipping him onto his back.

The impact and the fall hurt. He flashed briefly into unconsciousness and then straight back out of it. He managed to move his head and watch the bike land on its wheels and continue on, crashing into a fence. George would need to buy a new one now, for sure.

An old couple got out of the car. The woman held Pierre's head, and the man took his hand as they called out to their neighbours who hurried out their homes to phone for an ambulance for the pizza boy.

Pierre wished they'd all leave him alone. He struggled up, dodging the array of jumbo pizzas strewn along the road. He stretched and cracked his shoulder blades. He walked away from the gathering crowd towards a flickering street light surrounded by fat flying bugs.

And then it came to him. The new character should be someone who gives his all for the tribe, yet ends up with nothing. Then there's another guy, the antagonist in another tribe who does nothing, yet life gives him everything. And he, by sheer fluke, defeats the dinosaurs. These were the characters the novel needed.

Pierre would get a new bike and ask George to order in a new uniform, something a bit less obvious. And he'd give the job another year. Just one more year to finish his masterpiece. What was another year, anyway?

The paramedics arrived and tried to get him on the stretcher, but he was too full of adrenaline to settle. He wouldn't be seeing Pavel and Kelly again until he got an agent and was in L.A. the same as them. On the level with them. Then he'd show them. Things would be very different then.

BASSENDEAN

It had been a few years since Billy watched Swan Districts play. Even longer since he'd been to a game with his grandfather.

'You alright, Pop?' he asked as he helped him up the steps of the grandstand.

'I'm alright,' the old man rasped, refusing his grandson's hand, preferring instead to clasp his bony fingers around the rusty railing and let it guide him up. 'You go and get us some beers and a couple of pies.'

Billy did so with a crumpled twenty-buck note forced into his hand, knowing that it wouldn't be enough. He felt guilty leaving him, but that was his Pop, independent to the last, cancer or not.

When Billy returned, he found the old man had chosen seats close to the toilets. When the players took the field, he roared louder and clapped harder than any of the thousand or so in the ground. The siren sounded and the thirty-six men on the field got stuck in. Billy and his grandfather sipped their beers and ate the lukewarm meat pies. Billy had a big Sunday league soccer game the next day so he really shouldn't have been consuming such fare, however there weren't many opportunities for him to spend time with his grandfather due to his work and study commitments. It didn't look great for the old man, with the doctors giving him six months at best, and being the last game of the season, this could be their last time at the footy.

'The beer alright, Pop?'

'Could be a bit colder, but it's okay.'

'The pie okay?'

'It's alright.' Pop leapt up, suddenly screaming. 'Holding the ball, umpire! Holding-the-ball!'

Billy smiled. He hadn't seen him this animated in years and had missed it.

The Swans lost three quick goals. It wasn't a good start. Billy took out his phone.

'What are you doing?' Pop asked.

'Just putting a bit of a bet on.'

'You're either putting a bet on or you're not.'

'Then I am.'

'What are you betting on?'

'This game.'

'But it's already started.'

'You can still bet.'

'What's your tip?'

'You don't want to know.'

Pop shook his head. 'You young fellas have the attention span of newts. Couldn't pass a game of tiddlywinks without having a punt.'

'It's just a few bucks. A bit of fun.'

'I remember the days when the game was all the fun we needed.'

By half-time the Swans had fought back to within a point.

'How's your bet looking now?'

'Not so good.'

'Ain't that a shame,' the old man grinned.

They used the break to stretch their legs and go to the toilet and make another visit to the bar.

'Two beers,' Pop told the young girl.

'I'll just have a light, thanks,' Billy told her.

'You pregnant or something?' Pop said.

'Nah, I've got a game tomorrow, remember?'

'Soccer's not a real game.'

Billy laughed having heard this all before. Pop winked at the girl. 'I feel like I've failed the nation knowing you play it. It took a certain kind of so-called bloke to play soccer back in my day, if you get what I mean.'

'It's different now. Bigger than footy.'

The old man shook his head wearily as they lifted their plastic cups and made their way back to the stand for the second-half. 'What a world.'

In the third-quarter, the Swans hit the front. Pop brightened, giggling and kicking his legs like a schoolboy. Sitting there with him looking out on Bassendean Oval brought back memories for Billy. Since he could remember, his parents worked in the butcher's shop every weekend, and every week in the cooler months his grandfather would take him to see his beloved Swan Districts home and away. This changed in his teenage years when Billy began working Saturdays, yet he always cherished those memories as a special time. *Their* time.

'This is what it's all about, Billy Boy,' Pop said, squeezing his grandson's knee when the Swans kicked a goal from fifty. 'Real grassroots footy. Your AFL can't beat it.'

The wind howled, the rain working its way through the gaps of the creaking grandstand.

'Another beer?' Pop asked.

Billy still hadn't finished the one in his hand and didn't think he'd manage it. 'Better not. I've got to go out for dinner tonight too. Ling's parents are in town.'

'From China?'

'Singapore.'

'You met them before?'

'Tonight's the night.'

'That's nice.' The old man peered up at the sky, which was fast losing its colour. 'You've gotta take love where you can find love.'

Billy had been dating Ling for almost a year and often mentioned her to Pop. His response was never overly warm, but was far more evenly measured than his other grandfather, who tutted and said he hoped Billy wouldn't marry her as he didn't want to have great-grandkids with 'funny eyes'.

Right on the full-time siren, the Swan's full-forward rose highest amongst the pack to take a mark. Trailing by three points, and thirty metres out from goal and a little to the right, the pressure was on him to win or lose the game. With the wind against him, he stepped up and kicked. His shoulders relaxed when the ball darted upwards, landing dead centre between the posts.

'Woohoo!' the old man punched the air, the goal taking years off him.

'What a finish,' Billy agreed, applauding. He took a final sip of the light beer and lifted his keys. 'C'mon, let's beat the traffic.'

The old man didn't move. When the cheering subsided, he sat back down, his moist eyes soaking it all in as the players did their end-of-season lap of honour despite finishing outside the finals. 'Give me a minute. Just a minute, son.'

As he took a seat, Billy felt this could also be his last game. He loved his soccer. When he wasn't watching that, he'd gotten used to the AFL. The speed and the athleticism on the ground, and all the glitz, glamour and drama off it that the semi-pro game lacked. Pop was what made the WAFL for him.

He helped the old man down the slippery steps. He was tired and wheezed more than before, and Billy had to catch him when he stumbled.

In the car, Billy let the engine run a moment to warm it up.

Pop cleared his throat, then spoke gently. 'You know I'm not your real grandad.' Billy's mother had mentioned this a few years before. 'Your nan's first husband was shot in Vietnam.' The old man's frown then broke into a wide, false-toothed smile. 'Makes sense when you think of it, hey? He was English and loved that big girl's game same as you do.'

'I know,' Billy said, looking into the old man's watery blue eyes. The old man who had cared for him every weekend. Taking him to watch either the Swans or cricket every Saturday of the year, and then fishing, always fishing, on Sundays. The old man who helped make him the man he was. 'It doesn't matter.'

The old man clasped Billy's neck. 'Never mattered to me neither.'

The car hit Guildford Road leading back to the care home. As the oval behind got smaller and smaller in the wing-mirror, Billy noticed Pop watch it all the way as it faded into nothing.

WELSHPOOL

'We have Cheryl on the line from Welshpool. Hi, Cheryl.'

'Hi, Gavin.'

'What's going on today?'

'I'm at work.'

'And where exactly is work?'

'I really shouldn't say,' Cheryl lowered her voice. 'The boss might be listening.'

The DJ laughed. 'We wouldn't want that now, Cheryl, would we?'

She giggled. 'No, I'd rather not.'

'Here's something that might make it worthwhile. You are caller number nine. You know what that means?'

'I hope I do.'

'It means you've scored two tickets to John Farnham's 'For The Very, Very, Last, Last, Last Time Tour'. How's that sound?'

'Pretty damn good, Gavin.'

'You look after yourself, Cheryl. Thanks for listening to 96FM, and say hi to your boss for me.'

Cheryl giggled harder. 'I won't.'

'Didn't think you would. News time is almost upon us. To take us there, here's Maroon 5.'

Cheryl put the phone down, enjoying the giddy high that winning competitions always gave her as she hummed along to 'Moves Like Jagger'. Each day this week she'd won something either on the radio or online. Evelyn at the desk across gave her a quick, withering glance. Cheryl stuck out her tongue, not letting the old killjoy burst her bubble.

This promotion was working out well. Since moving from the hectic shop floor to head office, she'd added $12,000 to her annual salary and had more spare time than she knew what to do with. Competitions filled the hours. In six months, she'd won a holiday to Fiji, a new Hyundai Accent, $1,500 in cash, a year's supply of Margaret River cheese, dinner for two at The Vines and a new mountain bike. So many prizes, she couldn't keep track.

Cheryl didn't feel bad. Everyone in the office had something else going on. Facebook, footy tipping, crochet. Jash by the wall was even creating his own app where your phone could work as a nail varnish dryer. The only one who didn't was Evelyn, and that, Cheryl decided, was Evelyn's problem.

Teresa from HR visited her desk. 'Cheryl. Mr Mercer would like a word with you.'

She followed Teresa, wondering if they were going to offer her another raise. On the way there, she made a brief estimate. Since she'd changed roles, she'd won $32,000 in cash and prizes. She couldn't believe she'd initially turned down the promotion when it was first offered.

Cheryl was feeling good about everything until Teresa led her into the manager's office, where Mr Mercer sat. He was flanked by the guy from legal with the wine-stain birthmark down the left side of his face whose name she couldn't remember, and a member of security, a Polynesian giant she'd never seen before.

Five minutes later, she was walking back to her desk with the security guard who carried an empty cardboard box for her to collect her belongings. They knew it all. The car, the trip, the cash, the prizes. They had it on their phone and internet records.

She may have made $32,000 in six months, but she'd just lost a $65,000 per year job, so it was true that crime doesn't pay. She could have sworn she saw Evelyn smile as she placed all the magazines she'd bought — the ones with the competitions — into the box even though she'd read them and all the prizes were claimed, many by her. She didn't want that sour cow getting her mitts on them. Plus, she had to take something, otherwise it would look like she really had been doing nothing over the past six months.

They knew about the last thing she'd won as well. A life-sized toy donkey from Toys R Us. Mr Mercer and the other two in the room laughed about that one during the meeting. He said she'd acted like a complete ass as that was the item which brought about her downfall, sending tongues wagging about all the work she wasn't doing when the misshaped package was delivered to the office.

Cheryl didn't get Mr Mercer's joke at the time, but when the guard frogmarched her towards her car, she sure got it. Still, she didn't think it was funny. She had no children or grandchildren. What the hell did she want with a stuffed life-sized donkey?

MADDINGTON

'Time to ride.'

Kenny heard the words and stretched open his eyes. The heat in the tent was already stifling from the late-November sun. Each and every bone in his body jangled when he breathed, his head taking the brunt of it. He'd had a heavy night on the Jacks, must have slammed down a bottle of the stuff. This was backed by a big week on the Dexies. His throbbing carcass felt ragged and life-less inside the heavy leather jacket which had seemed so comforting during the cool night before.

His right hand reached down and found his soft penis hanging out of his Wranglers. He reached out further and found a bare arse. Lying next to him was the naked figure of Jaydyn, the young nominee.

'Fucking move it, Kenny,' came Kim's voice again from outside the tent. 'The funeral ain't waiting for no cunt.'

'Yeah, yeah,' Kenny said, hoisting his upper-half up and, massaging his temples, he tried to fire his brain into action. 'I'm a bit fingered this morn, Kim. Just ... just give us a minute.'

The familiar sound of laughter and Harleys thundered from the carpark. Jaydyn still didn't move. This was the first trip away for the new recruit, and the last few days of carnage on the ride across had taken their toll on his raw constitution. Fuck, it took its toll on Kenny's. Twenty years in the Southern Serpents and he was feeling every one of them. He never used to need an alarm, was always the first one up regardless of the night he'd had before. He must've passed out after he'd smuggled Jaydyn in. He knew they'd fucked. His penis was dry and sore. He couldn't tell if he'd come or crashed halfway through. Wouldn't know until he gave it a pull when he had the chance.

Seeing Jaydyn's tight, hard body, a body not yet showing the ill-effects of drug and alcohol abuse and deep-fried processed everything which it eventually and inevitably would, Kenny felt himself harden. Now, though, was not the time.

He heard the tent next to his unzip. 'Where's Jaydyn?' asked Bilby, the other nominee.

'He's your fucking mate,' Kim told him.

'Must have set off early for brekkie or something.'

'Just pack his shit up,' Kim ordered. 'We shoulda been off these grounds and on the road ten minutes ago.' A boot came through the canvas towards Kenny, which he had to duck to avoid. 'Hurry up, Ken, before I skull drag you the fuck outta there.'

Jaydyn muttered something softly and rolled onto his side to continue his slumber. A sheath of sweat formed over Kenny's thick eyebrows. Being found like this would mean he'd be out of the club, or worse.

A lot worse.

He was a loyal soldier, a respected soldier too, but they'd already let it slide that his mother was an Islander. This gay shit wouldn't stick, no way. He couldn't handle the ridicule and shame anyway, particularly from their rivals.

He took a quick slug from the remnants of the bottle. His nerves settled, and he began to think differently. He was the resident cook for the chapter. He'd never had a partner or fathered kids like the others. He never chased pussy, content with his shelf bourbon, pills and occasional piece of arse on the fly. After all this time, maybe Kim and the others knew. Maybe it didn't matter. He'd broken the mould with his dark features. Perhaps this would be viewed in a similar light.

Kenny was now fully hard and looking down at the tender, hairless form that was Jaydyn's rear-end. The bikes nearby were in full-throttle, the devil's hum filling the balmy campsite air.

'You got two minutes,' Kim called.

'You go without me,' Kenny yelled back.

'We got together or not at all.'

Who was he kidding? This gang and these men were the only life he'd known. Not having a missus and procreating was one thing. Fucking a bloke, fucking a gang member on a tour-of-duty while your brothers slept a few metres away, was off the scale. Kenny cursed himself for being so careless and for being the one who sponsored him when the others thought he was too soft, too good-natured to make it. When he knew deep down that the kid with the baby blue eyes and drainpipe jeans would be his downfall.

'I'll be out in five.'

'Fuck ya, ya useless old cunt,' Kim shouted above the din. 'Get us there, then.'

The swarm of Harleys roared away.

Jaydyn's eyelashes twitched and then fluttered as Kenny spat and entered him from behind. Then they widened in cold terror when Kenny produced a blade and placed his chubby fingers over his mouth. Jaydyn struggled, lashing and kicking and biting as the much larger man fucked him, simultaneously plunging the dagger deep into the back of his neck, severing the spinal cord. Kenny would have to be quick. He knew what to do. He'd use the knife to slice open the ground sheet, grab a shovel, and dig the grave away from prying eyes.

As Kenny shot his load, and the youthful body beneath him grew limp, Kenny knew he'd miss Jaydyn, that he was the best yet. He hoped the others wouldn't remember him. This would be the fourth new member who'd gone missing over the past decade. With any luck the others would forget and Kenny could handpick another fresh young recruit in the years or months or weeks ahead.

WINTHROP

Lauren was delighted when Rob's parents invited her to stay at their home with their son while they went on a three-month caravan holiday up the north coast of Western Australia. Their place was spacious and homely, and had a pool, a kitten and two King Charles spaniels, Kath and Kim, whom she adored. Lauren had dated Rob since high school, but as the McNamaras were proud Catholics (despite never going to church), she always had to stay in the spare room when she slept over on weekends. So, them saying she could move in and not specify where she was to sleep was the symbol of acceptance she'd been pining for.

Like Rob, she hadn't yet moved out of home, and, same as him, she was completing her masters in molecular science, so money was tight. Her own mother and stepfather were fine about Rob sleeping over as she gave them $50 a week for board from her waitressing job. Still, she preferred Rob's place. His parents, Jeff and Elaine, were good people. Jeff was a quiet man who lived for his sport and his game shows. Elaine loved her knitting and keeping up with neighbourhood and family affairs.

These three months would be good for Lauren and Rob. It was uni holidays. Lauren had fixed her old Sony turntable and purchased records of the bands they used to dance to at Amplifier when they were young. LCD Soundsystem, The Black Keys, MGMT. The McNamara's also had Netflix, and she wanted to re-watch *Juno* and finally see that *Stranger Things* series everyone talked about.

She ordered some new lingerie and a rabbit vibrator which her workmate Chan sold her on. She and Rob didn't get to sleep together much. Due to their schedules and sheer logistics, their sex life had dwindled to around once a month. Changed days from a decade ago when any place — cars, parks, the beach, club toilets — would suffice to satiate their burgeoning appetites. These three months would put things right.

On their first Friday night, Lauren cooked her signature chorizo, calamari and risoni salad. After Elaine texted to say they'd made it to Cervantes, Lauren opened a bottle of sparkling and she and Rob sat down to eat.

'Not for me,' Rob gestured as she went to pour it. 'I'll stick to water.'

She'd feared she'd overdone it with the chilli. She placed the stopper in the wine and put Empire of the Sun's 'Walking on a Dream' on the record player. As they ate, she noticed Rob's hairline had crept higher since they'd last sat across from each other and showed flecks of grey. They talked about what they would do over the next few months. In amongst the music and the movies and the time spent together, there'd be swimming and trips into Freo. And they both vowed to have their old school friends around for a long-overdue barbecue.

They also discussed practical things, such as work commitments, car repayments, and how their savings for their own home were faring. They discussed her family and their plans to take her young nephew to Adventure World for his birthday, and how next summer it might be nice to borrow Jeff and Elaine's Hymer to travel the west coast themselves.

Dinner was finished. Rob hadn't seemed to mind about the chilli as he'd had seconds, then thirds. When Lauren cleared the plates, she realised she wasn't in the mood for bubbles either. She brewed a pot of tea instead. Neither had work the next day, but they had to walk the dogs early and it seemed a little late for coffee, though not late enough for bed.

Lauren followed Rob into the front room. 'Do you wanna smoke some weed?' she asked, sitting down and absently picking up the two knitting needles and yarn of wool resting on the arm of the chair.

'You have some?'

'From Chan. I thought it might be fun. Like old times.'

Rob yawned. 'Maybe tomorrow.'

The credits for *Better Homes and Gardens* were rolling. Rob switched the channel to cricket. The Scorchers game was on.

'Mind if I watch this?' he asked, flexing his stiff left shoulder, an injury which ended his indoor cricket days last year.

'Sure.' She wanted to watch a movie or that TV show everyone was talking about, but that could wait. 'Are you sure you don't want a drink? I got some whisky in for you.' Jameson. It had always been his favourite.

'Really?' he said, his eyes not leaving the screen.

'Yeah.'

'It is a bit late.'

'How about another tea?'

'Sounds grand.'

Grand? Where had she heard that before, she thought, as she tiptoed over the sleeping kitten and boiled the kettle.

Grand.

She brought the hot mugs through to Rob, who was reclined on his father's chair, and placed his in the drinks holder.

'Grand,' Rob said again. That was it. It was Jeff who always said it. Jeff loved his tea and his cricket.

Lauren sat back down. Feeling a slight chill from the cooling, she pulled a burgundy dressing gown draped over the back of the chair onto her shoulders. It had a rose motif and smelled distinctly of the Estee Lauder Rob's mother wore.

The cricket ended. The Scorchers had narrowly lost to the team from Brisbane. Rob stared at the post-match interviews. Neither of them spoke as they sipped their tea. Lauren reminded herself this was a good thing. They didn't need to. They'd been together long enough to know each other well and not natter incessantly about nothing in particular.

Lauren glanced down at her lap, admiring her handiwork. She was making good progress. She'd always been creative. She wished she'd done something useful with her talents before she got railroaded into science. The scarf would be a good one, thick and even, something she would wear.

She could really do something with this knitting lark in the time she was here if she dedicated herself to it. But then she remembered the champagne she had to drink, the weed they had to smoke, the friends who were coming over, and the nights of passion she and Rob were supposed to have.

She thought of how good she could become at knitting if she had the next three months to dedicate to it. Or the next thirty years.

QUINNS ROCKS

He scanned the channels, hoping there'd be something he'd missed. He'd seen all the comedy flicks and every *Arrested Development*, *Family Guy* and *Parks and Recreation* episode they had. The only stuff he hadn't watched was *House of Cards* and *Downton Abbey*, boomer shit which he couldn't stand. He should have packed his iPad. He had a drive full of *Seinfeld* and some old show about a guy who ran a hotel in England that his manager had given him, telling him they don't make them like they used to.

Calvin leaned back and pressed the buzzer. He ordered another rum and cola. He'd had a few now. He'd feel it later. Times like these, he wished he was a book guy, but he'd never had the concentration for that, even when the book was about comedy or sports. Even surfing mags were a drag nowadays. He wasn't the best reader, truth be told. It took him months to get through an autobiography. *Scar Tissue* might have been the last a few years back, and he gave up near the end. The cost of not enough time spent in the classroom and too much of it wasted out on the water.

The air hostess returned with his drink. She was red-haired, tall and pink-cheeked in an unremarkable way, with a slight accent. Welsh or something. He smiled, and she forced one in return. He knew she was put off by his feet stretched out on the chair in front and was weighing up saying something. He hadn't worn shoes all flight. He never wore shoes, and his soles were leathery and black, his toenails cracked and jammed with dirt. She didn't look like a beach girl, not with that complexion. She was probably thrown by how someone who looked like him could get a first-class ticket. Calvin couldn't even remember what year it was when he last washed his hair. The sea took care of it. The sea took care of everything. Then there was the beard. He would have to take care of it before the unforgiving West Australian sun struck it. He remembered any growth he used to have itched like fuck when the heat got into it, way worse than anything California could ever throw up.

He tried to work out how many planes he'd been on over the past year. Fifty? An incredible sum for someone afraid of flying. He took a sip of the drink. Felt the bubbles tingle the back of his throat, the alcohol rising to his head. He wanted a cigarette but knew that would be pushing the boundaries of his ten grand ticket and the patience of the Welsh-or-whatever girl. He knew because he'd tried all this shit before.

He looked at the fat man snoring next to him after his umpteenth meal and all that single malt. Happier than a pig in shit. Calvin envied him. Envied the million-dollars he claimed each year for boozing, schmoozing and whoring. Not having to train, perform or worry about his body or deal with who he had to. He decided he might give advertising a go in his next life.

Calvin reclined his chair as far as it would go without being in the bed position. He put on his headphones and cranked Tame Impala loud and thought about going home for the first time in four years. Tried to stop all that forgetting and tried for once to remember.

Calvin lay on the bed watching *The Simpsons* in that queer state of jetlag meets hangover, not knowing if you're asleep or awake. It was an old one where Homer gets his dream job in a bowling alley, then has to quit when Marge falls pregnant with Maggie.

The hotel phone rang. Calvin peeled his stiff upper-body off the still-made sheets but didn't answer it. He knew who it was, who it always was. He opened the fridge. He'd finished all the miniatures. He opened the bottle of pear cider instead. He recoiled at its sweetness. He was more of a spirits drinker, though after a few gulps he was finding it oddly refreshing.

The digital clock read 11:11. Had to be a.m., there was still light. He thought for a moment where he was. A plush, generic hotel. Clean and tidy with little character. He couldn't remember how he got here. He remembered being helped off the plane. They wanted to take him to hospital. He got them to take him to a hotel, saying he needed to sleep.

Calvin opened the curtains an inch to see out, know-ing, just knowing, it wasn't Margaret River. And know-ing, knowing, that if it wasn't just how much trouble he'd be in. His view was a myriad of high-rise towers with very little greenery and no blue sky. St George's Terrace. He hated the city, always hated coming here as a kid. Calvin had a sudden urge to smell the sea air. To feel the sand between his toes. He even felt the need to be out on the waves, and he never felt that anymore. His body had an ache for it. His joints, his heart, his soul told him he was close to him, close to where it all began. Still, he didn't want to be in that comp. Not today.

The phone rang again. He let it. Calvin could smell the stench of his own skin and hair. His feet still black, he got in the shower. The first he'd had in days. The soap and water mixed together feeling heavenly on his skin, his head under the shower helping it clear. It started to feel okay being back here. Not good yet, but okay.

Over the sound of the water, he heard a knock at the door. He couldn't remember ordering room service.

'Sir, sir? Are you there? Are you okay?'

'I'm okay.'

'We tried to call you,' said the hotel girl. 'There's somebody who wants to speak to you.'

Calvin turned the shower off. Dried himself. 'I'll pick up now.'

The phone rang. Calvin answered.

'Where are you?' said the voice. Calvin said noth-ing. 'You missed the flight. Then we got you another, but you're still not here. And now you're in some fucking hotel — sorry, I promised myself I wouldn't curse — when the heats start in one *fucking* hour.'

Calvin gazed out the window and sat by the bed. 'Y'know, this was my hometown. *Is* my hometown.'

'I know, kid,' said the voice, only softer. 'I know it must be hard. But listen, let's do what we gotta do and get the fuck outta here. If you blow this, this is it. The sponsors said so. All these people have bought tickets.'

'I know. I'm sorry.'

'I can delay them. I've got you a helicopter. Forget everything, just get here. A car is coming for you in ten.'

'I'll be out front.'

'Good. Let's do this.'

Calvin returned the receiver. There was no way he was going to Margaret River. He knew he couldn't. No matter what Vaughan or the sponsors or the people who bought tickets or anyone else thought of him.

He reached for the fridge and grabbed the last cider, opened it and drank deep. He moved to the window, clouds rolling in. He saw an Australia flag jerking back and forth on the building next door. He looked below at the people moving about like tiny ants, and the cars like the Matchbox kind he and his brother played with as kids. He touched the window frames. They were sealed. No wonder with this bleak view.

He switched on the box again. *The Simpsons* was still on. It was now the episode where Bart sells his soul to Millhouse. Calvin smiled despite having seen it a hundred times.

He hit the channel changer. AFL. Eagles playing St Kilda. A night game, so it must be a replay. He hadn't watched a match in years. It was hard to get overseas. He'd been good at the sport, all through primary and into high school. Coaches said if he'd stuck at it, he would be a shoo-in for the draft. A good ruckman, tall, strong, mobile with quick hands and an eye for a pass, that was how his last coach at West Perth had described him. But he didn't have the heart for it. Didn't like the training, didn't like all that scrapping and machismo. Was more at one with the world out on the waves. Felt he could touch God out there.

He picked out number seven on the field. Chris somebody. Thought he might have known him from back when he played. He saw him get tackled. He didn't look anything special. And yet there he stood in front of 50,000 punters. Calvin pictured how his life would be if he stuck at it. It probably wouldn't be so lonely. Would have had twenty-odd other blokes to share the load. Not just himself and these shoulders.

He felt for the remote and switched through the channels. Playing footy was okay, but fucked if he could be bothered watching it. Sport was not his thing, not to sit and watch. Why people would pay to gawk at some stranger booting a ball or riding a wave, he didn't know.

There was nothing else on apart from cooking shows and the news. He wasn't hungry and didn't want to know what was happening in the world. He wanted to know what he was going to do in five minutes' time when Vaughan would be informed he wasn't in the lobby and off would start their little game again. Maybe the big Hawaiian would have the door broken down this time.

Calvin didn't hate his manager. He was part of the machine, only doing his job, only wanting his cut. But he knew Vaughan didn't give a shit about his well-being. Neither did the sponsors or the organisers. He'd told them for years he didn't want to compete at Margaret River. They didn't listen, so why should he give a fuck about them? One of the good things about surfing was there were no real fans like in footy. They were fickle, leant towards who was hot, in vogue. He answered to no one but himself. No one except his own stupid, fucked up self.

Calvin landed on a radio channel. A Tame Impala track. The first song from their first album. This band was all he'd listened to over the past decade since he'd left Australia. Reminded him of the sun, the beach, and Jarrad and life around here back when all he ever had to worry about was the swell and getting high and none of the bullshit which surrounded being on the tour.

Fuck this, he thought. Fuck this. He called the front desk. 'Can you hire me a scooter?'

'That should be no problem,' said the girl from before.

Calvin looked at the clock. 'I need it right away. I need it out the fire escape and ready to go.'

She paused. 'Is this really Calvin Albright?'

'I'll pay whatever you want.'

'I think I can manage that.'

Calvin experienced a short, sharp blast of drunken euphoria. He finished the stubby. He flung on his old boardies and found a new Rip Curl singlet in a sealed bag. He looked at his feet, still black. That fat fuck and his stalking had made him forget to scrub them. No time now. He kicked on his thongs. He cranked the song louder. Wished he had a blunt to sing along to it and knew he had to put this right.

The door knocked. 'Calvin?' It was the girl.

Calvin checked himself in the mirror, and could barely recognise himself. He left his phone on the table — fuck being contactable — and answered the door.

#

Calvin got out of the city as fast as the bottle-green Vespa would carry him. He headed up the West Coast Highway. He longed to be near the ocean. He also wanted — no, he needed — a smoke. Vaughan couldn't touch him. Vaughan and all the rest couldn't stop him now.

He pulled over at the old Observation City. Workmen and roadworks, it looked like the main strip had been bombed. A few high-end bars and cafés replaced the beer barn, which had been there before that. The one he'd got his jaw broken in as an underager after that Panics show. The one where his brother saved him and his smart mouth from getting worse.

Calvin now wished he had brought his phone. He hadn't bought weed here in so long, yet he still remembered who to call. He'd get some lined up before he got to where he was going. It was the only number he'd ever memorised, even ahead of ex-girlfriends.

The first two phone boxes were busted. The third one worked, but he didn't have any coins. He didn't even have his wallet. He had to ask for some. There he was, a multi-millionaire, or so Vaughan often told him, begging for change like a bum. The locals he asked crossed the street, a few others politely told him to get fucked. A Belgian backpacking couple eventually helped him out with a buck, his limited French skills getting the smiling local over the line.

Calvin made the call. 'Steven Elmar speaking.'

'Elmo. It's Calvin.'

'Fuck off it is.'

'Yeah, I know.'

Elmo called out, 'Fuck me, it's Calvin on the phone.' He heard a cheer from the room. 'I got a bunch of fellas here to watch you on the big screen.'

'Right you are.' Calvin was paranoid of social media, always wanting as few people as possible to know what he was up to. Now more than ever.

'What the fuck ya doing? How come you never answer any of my texts, ya cunt.'

'I'm in town for the Pro.'

'Yeah, only apparently no cunt can find ya.'

'You still smoke weed?'

'Do Kiwis love their sheep?'

'Dealing?'

'Nah brother, those days are over.'

'Was thinking we could grab the boards and have a smoke.'

'Shit, those days are definitely over. Sold the board. Haven't surfed in years.'

'Right.'

'But I can help you out with a stick.'

'Legend. You still at Beverly Crescent? I'm heading up now.'

'Mate, you *have* dropped off the radar. I'm in Scabs.'

'No shit? I'm outside The Lookout.'

'I'm in one of those new apartments to the left of it.'

Calvin saw them above the strip, all angular and modern, looking out over the beach. 'How'd ya manage to buy one of them?'

'Cheeky fuck. I'm in real estate now.'

Steve Elmar, Calvin thought. The Weed Lord of Quinns. And not a bad surfer, either. Given it all up for a suit and a tie and a swank Scarborough pad.

'Come up and meet my boys. Have a beer.'

This was the last thing Calvin wanted. Not the beer bit, but meeting a bunch of blokes who worked in real estate with smartphones ready to give the game away.

'Actually, you wouldn't mind giving it to us on the street, would ya?'

'Huh?'

'It's just, y'know, now you mention it, I should be getting down to Margs for the comp.'

'It's like that then, is it?'

'Nah, don't be stupid.'

Elmo dropped his voice. 'No one's gonna believe me that it's you.'

'I'll come round after the event. Check out your place.'

'Sure, mate.' But he sensed in Elmo's sigh that his old friend knew this wouldn't happen. 'I'll pop down with it. Just let me put my thongs on. The lift's out of order.'

A crowd of teen surfer girls and guys had spotted Calvin in the phone box and were waiting outside. Calvin felt naked and vulnerable. He didn't want the press knowing. Didn't want any trouble.

'Hey Calvin, can we have a pic?' a Maori kid asked.

Calvin opened the door and put his helmet on to keep the Perth cops off his tail. 'You got the wrong guy.'

He got on the bike and revved it. The Italian-made engine hummed nicely. He'd ridden one in Bali years ago and remembered the smoothness of it. He zipped off towards the apartment. One of the bleach-blonde girls flashed her tits. The Maori kid gave Calvin the finger, shouting something he couldn't hear.

Calvin reminisced about growing up next to the ocean. He thought of Jarrad, his brother. He was a better surfer. Everyone knew it. He would have made it. He was the smarter one too. Jarrad would have handled all the hype that came with being decent at something a lot better than Calvin could. Calvin felt bad for his mum for the first time in a long time. The poor, stupid woman.

He hit Marmion Ave. He didn't know Perth's sub-urbs anymore. It used to be bushland after Hillarys. Now there was an endless stream of housing developments, all offering marginally cheaper house and land pack-ages the further he went. And all with a shopping cen-tre, servo and the obligatory McDonald's. Hang yourself 'burbs, is what they called them in the States. Fuck, is this all he'd been missing?

Elmo's smoke was good, soaking right through him. Made him think he was weightless. The sea to his left was how it existed in his dreams. Deep blue, pure as night. On the right all was very different, but the vacuum it camouflaged wasn't changing.

Calvin made it to the family home in just over half-an-hour. He could have been quicker, could have beat the traffic and taken the freeway, but didn't want to risk it with the alcohol and leaf through his system.

The old place hadn't changed, though the lawn had been mown and the tree branches trimmed. She must have been using some of the money he wired back each month on a gardener. He offered her a new place wher-ever she wanted. Even Scarborough. Calvin wasn't sure why his mum stayed here. Why she stayed here with those memories of that day when her oldest son went for a surf and never came back. But it was like the house, the area, had become an extension of the Albrights. Both the good and bad bits. For Calvin, mostly bad. All the memo-ries of all those abusive men she'd shacked up with over and over, a new one every few years until the same thing happened again and again.

Calvin knocked. No answer. He heard flip-flopping footsteps from behind. 'Looking for Nora?'

'Yeah,' Calvin turned.

'Hello, love.' Mrs Doukas, their neighbour since Calvin could walk, stood before him. 'Didn't recognise you through all that hair.' Calvin hadn't seen the old woman since the memorial, and she was talking to him like it was yesterday. He realised that aside from everything sterile and stale and shitty and horrible in this city — in *his* city — he longed for this kind of familiarity. 'Aren't you supposed to be at the tournament?'

'So they say.'

'Your face is all over the paper.'

'Do you know where Mum is?'

'Went down to surprise you in Margs.' She removed the glossy junk mail from the letterbox. 'She's with a new bloke now. Wanted you to meet him. Don't ask me his name, I lose track of them.'

Calvin was glad he wasn't down there. Missing out on a meeting with his mother and her latest wall-puncher of a partner.

'No worries, Mrs Doukas.' He moved to the side window. He had never needed a key growing up, as this lock had been busted since the day they moved in.

'She'll be sorry she missed you.'

'So am I,' he lied as he jimmied the lock.

'But you'll be back.'

Calvin got one leg in the house. 'I don't think so.'

He climbed in. Nora had done up the joint. New terracotta tiles. Sky-blue leather sofas to replace the ripped futon. Ocean prints. The place looked European. A tray of cat litter lay in the hallway, with no smell of old Labrador. Timmy mustn't be around anymore. Nora should have told him. He'd been a loyal dog to them. That dog had seen it all.

Calvin's room was much the same. The bed still stripped. The boxes of old clothes, trophies and surfing magazines stacked up against the wardrobe door. Calvin had told her to get rid of them, telling her to turn his room into a sewing room or something. But she always said she never would. Said her boys needed a place to fall back on. He knew Jarrad's room would be the same, only his stuff wouldn't be boxed, and he was never coming back.

Calvin found the whale's tooth chain stuffed down the side of a banana box with all his old surfing VHSs. He pocketed the pouch. On his way out, he grabbed a box of Coles-brand Pringles from the kitchen cupboard and left via the front door. There was no reason to hang around.

He heard the snip, snip, snipping of Mrs Doukas's shears and saw the hedge over her side of the fence wobble. He got on the bike and noticed a *FOR SALE* sign on the lawn of his family home. Things between his mum and this new bloke must be serious. The sight gladdened him. The thought that Jarrad's room would have to be cleared. That there would be another family in there making memories. Better ones.

Calvin zipped a few streets over. The day was turning out okay. Calvin thought about his manager and how he'd be tearing his hair plugs out right about now. Poor Vaughan. It wasn't his fault, all this. Maybe it wasn't anyone's.

Calvin passed Elmo's old place. The old party house. It had a sign out front that said *LEASED*. One smart cat, that one. Calvin always knew it.

He made it to Zania's shack. She would be in. No way she would've moved on. On the overgrown lawn lay dog shit and a busted-up kid's cop car. Calvin heard loud music, Aussie hip-hop from beyond the busted fly screen door.

'Hello,' he shouted. He heard some movement as the music was turned down.

'Thought I'd see you.' Zania's waif-like outline appeared through the mesh.

'Wanted to stop by.'

'What for? Ain't you got better ways to spend your time here?'

'I wanted to see Ned.'

'How come?'

'You know why.'

She opened the door but wouldn't look at him. 'He's with ... he's with his dad.' Calvin's head suddenly became unbearably heavy. 'I always told ya I wasn't sure.'

'Don't talk shit.'

'I said it could be yours, but I wasn't sure.'

'You were sure enough when you were collecting child support and all those gifts.' Calvin hated going through this again. Hated the dank smell of tobacco and 2 Minute Noodles coming from her house. Hated how any child should have to be brought up in a hole like this with a mother who was worse.

'Thought you was just being nice.'

'And I thought he was my son.'

'Well, you ain't exactly been around, have ya?'

'I've been a bit busy, as you know. On the tour and all.'

'The tour comes to WA every year, and you haven't been here in four years.'

'Been injured.'

'Now who's talking shit.'

'It's a bit fucking hard to come back with everything's that's went on, isn't it?' Calvin didn't want to lose his temper, something he hated doing with her, especially right now in front of her. But it shut her up. She knew this wasn't about her.

He heard a can crush from inside the house and a male cough and curse. Straining his ears, Calvin could make out that the Margaret River Pro heats were on the TV. 'Just give him this when he's older.' He opened the screen door and handed her the pouch. 'It was my grandfather's. Ned might as well have it.'

Calvin felt something else, something smoky and acrid, akin to paint thinner, attack his senses. Zania looked truly awful in the light, like her cheekbones were caving in. She was nothing like the girl he'd spent his teenage years with. Or was she? He was glad Ned was out of the place. He hoped who she said was his father was really his father. Hoped he was a good man. A better man than him. It was like a massive weight had lifted. It made everything easier.

'Don't sell it.'

'What the fuck's that meant to mean?' She snatched the pouch and slammed the fly screen door. 'Good luck at the comp. If you haven't thrown it all away.'

Calvin walked on, relieved that he would never have to come back here. Glad he'd laid the whole thing to rest. It wasn't until he started the scooter's engine that he kicked himself. Ned would never see that chain with the tooth set in antique pearl and gold. He looked back as Zania stood in her doorway and removed it from its pouch, her eyes greedily expanding like murky puddles in a downpour. That thing would be in Cashies in Joondalup first thing tomorrow. The chain which had been passed down to his grandfather from his grandfather before him, a pearl diver in Broome. That Calvin wanted to give to his own son. The boy who was no longer his son. Who had never been his son.

Calvin parked the bike at the beach where it had all begun. The place where he learnt to surf. The one thing that gave him an escape, helped him float above it all. Gave him so much joy and, lately, so much despair. The beach that had swallowed both him and his brother up and never even bothered to spit them back out.

He saw the plaque with Jarrad Albright's name etched into the rock. He kissed his fingers and placed them on it as he always did. A group of kids played kick-to-kick with their dad on the white sand. A dog barked in the distance, chasing a bigger one that was off its leash. But there were no surfers or swimmers today.

Calvin sat and lit another joint. It was good stuff, always was from Elmo. Some things never changed. He let that weightlessness wash over him again. Felt himself rise up and out from his body.

He removed his singlet. He lay it on top of his thongs on the sand, put the joint out and walked into the water. He waded out. The water was cool against his skin. It had been so long since he'd entered the ocean without a wetsuit. The swell was low, and for a moment he wished he had his board. Then he realised those days were gone. The comp. The career. Zania, Ned, his mum, Vaughan. And Jarrad. Gone as all things must go.

A voice inside told him to keep swimming until he found his brother. Until the whole of Quinns Rocks, the west coast, the world behind didn't matter anymore. Until it lapsed into memory.

ALSO FROM PAUL J. LAVERTY

Chronic masturbators, mass adulterers, punk rock cler-gymen, giant incontinent lobsters, sex workers, terror-ists, murderers, child-killers, drunken sailors and a ship which is on the brink of going down with its 3,000 guests completely unawares. A lot of strange things happen on cruises that you dont hear about in the brochures, but in *Man Overbored*, buoy oh buoy are you about to.

Welcome aboard the QE3 (Queen Elizabeth III), the worlds most luxurious of luxury cruise liners. Setting-sail from Portsmouth to New York, it looks to be another wild acid-ride much like any other, only on this trip a mysterious force is boring a hole through the ships core and threatening to tip them all into the unforgiving sea.

Inspired by the stylings of John Kennedy Toole, Irvine Welsh and Hunter S. Thompson, *Man Overbored* is a novella of strange interlinking stories and even stranger characters bound together by the fact that black, white, gay, straight, rich, poor, smart or dumb, weird or even weirder theyre all in the same boat, and theyre all about to die.

NOVELLA OUT NOW VIA ROADHOUSE MEDIA AND AVAILABLE WHEREVER BOOKS ARE SOLD

ALSO FROM PAUL J. LAVERTY

Welcome to Cider Country home to the apple orchards of Australias Central Victorian region. Not only do they produce the nations favourite fruit, its also the main ingredient in one of our favourite summer drinks.

But behind the apples is a myriad of twisted tales and an infinite number of colourful characters including racist supervisors, fugitive journalists, sexually promiscuous Muslims, concert promoters, Thai Princes, rabid dogs, aspiring models, failed writers, French musos, ex-cons, former triads, self-harmers, Jazz man Ryuichi Sakamoto and fucking Angus and Julie Stone (sic).

Theres also a mole whos about to blow the whole industry apart, along with a new blend of cider which might just save the world.

This collection of comedically dark and interlinked tales will have you thinking about apples, cider and life itself in a whole different light.

NOVELLA OUT NOW VIA ROADHOUSE MEDIA AND AVAILABLE WHEREVER BOOKS ARE SOLD